PAUL HEATLEY
SLEEPER RUN

AETHON THRILLS

aethonbooks.com

SLEEPER RUN
©2024 PAUL HEATLEY

This book is protected under the copyright laws of the United States of America. No part of this publication may be reproduced, stored in a retrieval system, or transmitted, in any form or by any means, without the prior permission in writing of the publisher, nor be otherwise circulated in any form of binding or cover other than that in which it is published and without a similar condition including this condition being imposed on the subsequent purchaser. Any reproduction or unauthorized use of the material or artwork contained herein is prohibited without the express written permission of the authors.

Aethon Books supports the right to free expression and the value of copyright. The purpose of copyright is to encourage writers and artists to produce the creative works that enrich our culture.

The scanning, uploading, and distribution of this book without permission is a theft of the author's intellectual property. If you would like to use material from the book (other than for review purposes), please contact editor@aethonbooks.com. Thank you for your support of the author's rights.

Aethon Books
www.aethonbooks.com

Typography, Print and eBook formatting by Josh Hayes. Artwork provided by Christian Bentulan.

Published by Aethon Books LLC.

Aethon Books is not responsible for websites (or their content) that are not owned by the publisher.

This book is a work of fiction. Names, characters, places, and incidents are the product of the author's imagination or are used fictitiously. Any resemblance to actual events, locales, or persons, living or dead is coincidental.

All rights reserved.

ALSO BY PAUL HEATLEY

The First Sleeper

Sleeper Cell

Sleeper Run

Check out the entire series here! (Tap or scan)

For Aidan

PROLOGUE

"She's supposed to be dead," Elizabeth Hoffs says on the phone.

She can't see Darrin Rankine, but she can imagine how he looks. By this point, she knows him well enough. She's accustomed to his face and his reactions. His quirks and his tics. He'll be chewing his bottom lip, his eyes looking around like he's expecting someone to creep up on him, regardless of where he is right now.

It takes him a long time to answer. "She didn't look hurt."

Elizabeth rolls her eyes. She's in her car, pulled to the side of the road. It's dark outside, and the road is quiet. "Nothing major. Cuts and bruises. Superficial. But she's *supposed* to be dead. Did you hear that part, Darrin?"

"I know she's supposed to be dead."

"How do you feel that she's not?"

There's a pause, then he says, "What's that supposed to mean?"

"I'm just curious."

There's a longer pause, then Darrin says, "I'm…I'm conflicted. The mission was not a failure, but now…"

"Now she's gone." He'd developed a soft-spot for the girl, and that was a problem. He was starting to see her as a child, and not as an asset. He was starting to see her, potentially, as a daughter.

"Who are the men who have her?" he asks.

"How should I know that, Darrin? I know as much as you do." Elizabeth sighs hard, down the line, right into his ear. "This was supposed to be the end for me. I was supposed to move on. She should have been incinerated in that explosion."

Darrin does not say anything to this. Elizabeth imagines him wincing.

"Instead, I'm still stuck playing babysitter."

"That's not entirely accurate," Darrin says. "You're nowhere near her."

"Do you think they're going to allow me to move on to anything new while this mess is still running?" Elizabeth can feel her temper flaring and she takes a moment, inhaling deeply. She's had to work with Darrin for too long. *Too* long. At first, she didn't mind. He was a good agent. But over time, something happened to him. He became almost a liability. He didn't do anything *wrong*, per se, but he became naïve and questioning. Everything needed to be spelled out to him. He started spending too much time down in the basement. It appeared to Elizabeth that he started to *care*, and that was a problem. A big problem.

He hasn't said anything since her brief outburst. Elizabeth wonders where he is—if he has reached his hideout or if he's in his car, too, still driving to it. She'll know soon enough. *They* know where he is, just like *they* know where she is. Elizabeth knows she'll see Darrin again soon, though he won't necessarily see her.

"Do you know how she survived?" Elizabeth says once she's feeling calmer.

"No," Darrin says.

"It seems like she wandered away."

Darrin is silent.

"She wasn't programmed to wander away."

"No," Darrin says.

"It's unlikely that there was a problem with her programming," Elizabeth says. "She *is* the Prime, after all, and none of the others have experienced any issues."

"I don't know," Darrin says, but there's a pause before he says it and Elizabeth doesn't like it. She already has her suspicions. "Maybe...maybe she was stronger-willed than we realized. They have to be strong to be the Prime."

"It's happened before," Elizabeth says. "But not since the first sleeper. Even then, hers was only truly broken because of her handler. We haven't had an issue like that since."

Darrin clears his throat. He changes the subject. "Where are you going to go?"

"Into hiding, same as you," Elizabeth says, though she doubts she'll be in it for long. Things are happening.

One missing sleeper doesn't change that. They're going to be very busy very soon. Unfortunately, because of their runaway, she'll likely be tasked with clean-up, which will take her away from where she truly wants to be. She wants to be in the thick of things. The death of the president is because of *her* hard work, *her* sacrifices. *Her* charge. She should be rewarded for that.

She bites her lip. She needs to calm. To be patient. All in time. These good things will come to her. She has earned them.

They sit in silence, listening to each other breathe.

Darrin surprises her by being the first to break the silence. "It's been a long time, Elizabeth," he says. "It'll be strange not to see your face every day."

It's Elizabeth's turn not to speak.

"But I suppose this is what we were working for, wasn't it?" Darrin says. "And here it is, and the world is going to crumble around us."

3

Elizabeth has no time for sentimentality. "You spent the most time with her. Did you see faults in her programming?"

He sighs. "You're not going to let it go, are you?"

"Of course I'm not."

"It's a mystery that doesn't have an answer. I don't know, Elizabeth. *You* don't know. None of us do, or ever will. Whatever happened, happened. There's no explaining it."

Elizabeth isn't so sure about this.

Another long pause is broken when Darrin says, "I need to go, Elizabeth. Good luck with whatever you do next. I don't know if we'll ever see each other again."

We will, Elizabeth thinks. "Goodbye, Darrin," she says and hangs up.

She stares at the phone. She has her suspicions. Her niggling doubts. She bites her lip. She can't let these go. She won't.

Darrin grew weak. He grew pathetic. He grew to be a problem. And now he needs to be watched.

Elizabeth dials another number and shares her concerns. When she's done, she throws her phone from the window, then turns her car around.

1

Keith Wright drives. Kayla Morrow sits beside him in the front, flipping through radio stations. She frowns, jumping from song to song.

Charlie Carter is in the back. His leg is raised across the backseat, resting. He twisted his ankle over a week ago. Keith thinks it's better now, especially after they took a few days in a motel to lie low, but Charlie claims it's still nagging him. Keith thinks he says this to get out of driving.

"Are you gonna settle on a song, pet, or what?" Charlie says.

"Sorry." Kayla leaves it playing something none of them recognize.

They've been on the road for a week now, since they left Washington DC. They've been traveling east to west, cross country. They have not followed a simple route. They did not stick to a straight line. Their journey has been stop-start. They're fugitives. They mixed it up, keeping off main roads as much as they could, avoiding built up areas and their security cameras.

They're going to Death Valley. They don't know what or who they're going to find there or how to get in touch with them. A stranger repeated a series of coordinates over the phone to Keith.

The stranger said a lot of other things, too. A series of words that Keith did not write down, but he hasn't been able to forget—West. Clementine. Buds. Harvest. Red. Run. Ghost. Keith watches Kayla out of the corner of his eye while he thinks of the words. He's never said them, not out loud and not in sequence. He thinks of the coordinates instead. Death Valley. Dom—Dominic Freeman—found out where the coordinates led to.

Dominic Freeman was a friend of Keith's. Dominic Freeman is dead. Killed by a crooked NSA agent. In turn, Keith killed the agent. Destroyed him with an automatic rifle.

Keith grits his teeth and swallows. He tries not to think about these things. About what he did. If he must think of Dom, he chooses to remember him living. Chooses to remember their friendship.

While they were laying low in a cheap roadside motel, hiding out in the kind of place where no one asks any questions of the kind of people who would use such an establishment, Keith did research. He mapped routes, conferring with Charlie as he did so. From DC to Death Valley via the most direct route would ordinarily take around thirty-eight hours. They knew they were going to draw it out. Make it take as long as possible. Stay low and off the grid. They stole a car from the motel they were staying at, drove it until the gas ran out, and then swapped it for another, a Ford, parked up at a strip mall. They're still in the Ford, but they've swapped the plates state to state. When they've had to get gas, they've paid cash and kept their heads lowered while inside the station. They wear caps to cover their faces. They pull up the collars of their jackets. Kayla stays in the car and ducks low, using her hair to conceal her face.

They're getting closer to Death Valley now. They've passed through Las Vegas. It's hot in the car. They have the windows down and the A/C cranked up. Keith feels a trickle of sweat run down the side of his face, from his left temple to his jaw. Beside him, Kayla is staring at the stereo, looking like she wants to change the station again.

"You don't like the song you've picked?" Keith says.

Kayla doesn't answer straight away. She's still listening to it play. "I...I don't know. I don't think I've ever heard it before."

"It's not one I'm familiar with," Keith says. "How about you, Charlie?"

"It sounds shite," Charlie says.

Keith laughs at his bluntness.

"Whenever we've had the radio on," Kayla says, "I always feel like I'm hearing everything for the first time. But there's one song I have in the back of my head that I...I just *know*, but I can never find it. And I...I *know* it, but I *don't* know it. Does that make sense?"

"You know it subconsciously," Keith says.

"I guess so," Kayla says hesitantly. "I guess that's right."

"How does it go?" Charlie says, sitting forward. "Do you have the tune or the words? I'm usually pretty good at guessing these things."

It's clear from the look on her face that Kayla is thinking hard. "I—I can hear the word *darling*...and *child*... But that's it." She hums a little bit of a tune, but it's too short to make anything out.

"Is that all you've got?" Charlie says.

"It's all I can think of," Kayla says.

"It's not much to go off," Keith says. "I'm sure the rest will come back to you in time. Songs like that, earworms, they always do. One day you'll just be walking along, and,"—he raises his right hand from the steering wheel and clicks his fingers—"*bam*, there it is. You suddenly know it all, from beginning to end. *Or*, who knows, maybe it'll show up on the radio."

"Sounded a bit folksy for the radio," Charlie says.

"Folksy?" Keith says, raising an eyebrow. "You got folksy from that briefest of snippets?"

"I told you I'm good at guessing these things."

Keith laughs. "Practically otherworldly."

"I'd be more impressed if you knew what it was," Kayla says.

"Give me a little more to work with and you might have your answer."

They drive on. Kayla starts flicking through the channels again.

"Pet, that's driving me mad," Charlie says.

"Maybe we should go without music for a little while," Keith says, turning the stereo off.

"Sorry," Kayla says.

"Don't worry about it."

"I liked some of those songs," Kayla says. "But none of them were the one I'm thinking of. Any time I hear music, parts of it come to me, but not the whole thing."

"Forget about it," Keith says. "Don't think about it. It'll come to you when it comes, I promise."

The road they're on is quiet. Desolate. There is desert on either side of them. They've only seen a couple of other vehicles on the road, both of them heading in the other direction. Kayla turns in her seat so she can see Charlie. "How's your ankle?"

"Better," Charlie says. "As good as it used to be. I can put my weight on it."

"Maybe it's good enough for you to take a shift at the wheel," Keith says.

"I wouldn't go that far, mate," Charlie says. "Let's not get ahead of ourselves."

Keith chuckles and shakes his head.

"What happens when we reach Death Valley?" Kayla says. "We're not far from it now, right?"

"Not far, no," Keith says.

"I know you and Charlie have talked about it, but if there's a plan, I should probably know what it is."

Charlie snorts. "If there *was* a plan, we'd have told you a lot sooner."

"Truth is," Keith says, "we don't know what we're doing when we get there. We just don't have many options open to us right now. The guy I spoke to on the phone seemed to know a lot about you and about our situation. Maybe he has answers about everything else, too."

"But how are we going to find him?" Kayla says.

"Hopefully he'll find us," Charlie says.

"Death Valley is a big place," Keith says. "If he doesn't find us, we don't have any hope of finding him."

"How big is it?" Kayla says.

"140 miles long, and between five and fifteen miles wide," Keith says. "And I only know that because of recent research."

Kayla whistles.

"It's lot of ground to cover," Charlie says.

"What about the coordinates?" Kayla asks. "Do they pinpoint a specific area? Would they lead directly to him?"

"I mean, they *might*," Keith says. "But I don't think he'd give his specific position away over the phone. He was so vague about everything else, I get the impression he'd be especially careful about that."

"Are we going to go to those specific coordinates?"

Keith taps the phone in his pocket. He bought it cheap from a gas station when they passed through Kansas. "That's why I bought this. When we reach Death Valley, I'll set them up and we'll see where they take us."

"Does anyone live in Death Valley?" Kayla says.

"Again, this is recent research, but apparently up to a thousand people live."

"So he could be with other people?"

Keith shrugs. "He could be. We're not going to know anything until we find him."

"*If* we find him," Charlie says. "So long as this isn't a wild fucking goose chase."

They're silent, considering this possibility. It isn't the first time they've wondered this. And of course, the alternative is that it could be a trap. An elaborate one, but a trap nonetheless. They don't know what they're heading into. When they get there, they'll be careful. It's all they *can* do.

Kayla turns back to Charlie. "Have you been able to get in touch with your wife?"

"No," Charlie says. "It's probably not safe to try, either. All I can hope is that she's still in England and hasn't tried to come to America. She's smart, though. She'll have worked out something's going on. She knows I wouldn't come over here to blow some shit up."

Charlie hasn't talked much about his wife while they've been driving, but Keith knows he must miss her. He's seen the look on Charlie's face sometimes, staring out the window into the distance, clearly troubled. Keith has noticed, too, how sometimes he'll glance at his phone, checking the screen for messages, before remembering it's a burner, it's not his phone, it's not the phone he came to this country with, and his wife doesn't have the number.

"What's her name again?" Kayla says.

"Niamh," Charlie says. "But she's Irish, and it has the Irish spelling."

"What's the Irish spelling?"

Charlie tells her.

"How did you meet?"

"Well, she'd moved over to Newcastle from Dublin for work."

"What does she do?"

"She's a teacher."

"Did you meet her at her job?"

"At her job?" Charlie laughs. "I had no reason to be at the

school. No, we were set up. A couple of mutual friends put us together on a blind date. They both thought we were each too busy with work to meet anyone, so they took it upon themselves to match us."

"And you stayed together and ended up getting married?" Kayla says.

"Pretty much. We had our ups and downs, but we always got through them. You do when you're in love."

"How'd she feel about you having been in the British Army?" Keith says.

"I mean, it wasn't ideal," Charlie says. "But I was never stationed in Northern Ireland, so that helped. I was in Germany. Her family don't know. We told them I'm a consultant. Which isn't too far-off, but we didn't tell them what I consult on."

"Why would it be a problem?" Kayla says.

"I'll explain that to you another time," Charlie says. "It's a long story."

"Why'd you join the army?"

Charlie laughs, but it's without humor. "Same reason I think a lot of people join the army," he says. "I didn't have much else in the way of prospects, and I needed a job when I left school."

Keiths snorts. "I hear that."

"It's funny, cos I was never particularly patriotic," Charlie says. "And I'm still not. But I was good at being a soldier, and I still am."

"I'm not even sure if I was good at *that*," Keith says.

"You were a Seal though, weren't you? That doesn't happen by accident."

"Yeah, and look what it did to me. I have a panic attack if a car backfires."

"From what I've seen, you know what you're doing, mate," Charlie says. He reaches over and squeezes Keith's shoulder. "If we have to be caught up in this shitshow, there's no one I'd rather be stuck in it with."

"Ha, I appreciate that, man."

"*Wow*," Kayla says. "I feel very left out of this love-fest."

"Well, I'm sure I speak for myself *and* Keith when I say there's not a potentially dangerous teenaged ticking timebomb that I'd rather be stuck in a car with while on this long drive and beyond."

"That's very flattering," Kayla says.

"Niamh always says I can be *very* charming when I want to be."

2

Niamh Carter is struggling to sleep. She's struggled to sleep since Charlie appeared on the news, a wanted man in America. He's still over there, and she's still here, in half a world away in Newcastle, feeling trapped in their home. She hasn't been able to go to work, either. Everywhere she goes, it feels like there are journalists waiting for her, assaulting her with a barrage of questions. Cameras and microphones shoved in her face. She called the school and told them what was happening. They were understanding. They don't want the kids exposed, of course, but Niamh picked up on the tone when she spoke to Lily, the headmistress. She picked up on the judgment. Judging her for what her husband is believed to have done. Niamh won't be surprised if she receives her termination soon, though she thinks they'll wait until things are resolved in America, and the full story has come out.

Niamh doesn't go out anymore. She hasn't been out for over a week now. She couldn't take the intrusions anymore. They were driving her crazy. Instead, she spends her days nervously pacing the house and occasionally watching the news, waiting for whatever comes next. She fears the worst. Fears that the next thing she might hear about Charlie is that he's dead. Killed in the attempt to capture him. If the Americans catch up to him, she doubts they're going to take him alive.

It's hard to understand what has happened. It's like a bad dream she can't wake up from. She sits on the sofa or the edge of the bed with her head in her hands, ignoring phone calls and the sound of the doorbell. She's had to rely on friends to do her food shopping. She hates being this helpless. When her friends come with the bags of shopping, they don't look at her with judgment—she sees pity on their faces instead. The pity almost feels worse.

"He didn't do it," she tells them. "I don't know what's happened over there, but I know he didn't have any part in it."

And they nod understandingly, but she doesn't think they really hear her.

She supposes she doesn't blame them. If the roles were reversed, if she were in their position, it would be hard to believe. Would she be prepared to jump down a conspiracy rabbit hole and believe that their husband had been set up as a fall guy? Probably not, but Niamh knows Charlie did not plant any bombs. And he didn't know the other two, the Americans. The girl and the man. Kayla Morrow and Keith Wright. Niamh has heard their names so many times and repeated them back to herself so many times. Kayla's name is a more recent revelation. It was only released yesterday. Keith's name has been known from the get-go. Niamh had never heard of him. Charlie didn't know him—he didn't know either of them. She's been through his computer upstairs in the office, checked his correspondence, and neither of their names come up.

Charlie has always been open with her. He's never kept any secrets from her. Niamh does not believe that has changed now. She has faith in him, even if no one else does.

For now, she stares at the ceiling and struggles to sleep. She can't remember the last time she had a full night's rest.

Except, that's not true. She knows exactly when it was. It was a couple of weeks ago, the night before the Washington bombing, and the death of the Vice-President. The night before everything turned to shit.

Sighing, she gets out of bed and goes to the window. It sounds quiet outside. She looks down into the street. She can't see anyone. Can't see any journalists, but she thinks they're out there, in hiding, always waiting and always ready. Or maybe not—if she's lucky, they might have moved on by now. They might have finally decided they weren't going to get anything out of her and they've left her alone, but she doubts this.

She's tired. She's never been so tired, and yet completely incapable of sleeping. She goes into the en-suite and gets herself a drink of water from the tap. While she's drinking it, she hears a noise. It freezes her. She puts the glass down and listens, stepping lightly back through to the bedroom on bare feet. The noise came from outside, but close. From the back garden, she's sure. But closer. Right up against the house.

There's another noise, and this time, she's sure—it came from the back door. It's opening.

She feels her throat tighten, an invisible hand wrapping around her neck. She feels her eyes go wide. Her heart pounds and for a moment it's overwhelming—it's all she can hear.

She goes to the closed bedroom door and opens it just a crack. The house is in darkness. She can hear movement downstairs, at the back, in the kitchen. She senses it getting closer. Holding her breath, she stays where she is and watches the stairs. Her eyes are already adjusted to the dark. She can see approaching shadows thrown up against the wall. There's something long and thin held out in front of the person coming up in the lead. She realizes it's a rifle. She can see it come into view through the slats in the banister. Then she spots the man's masked head. There are more men behind him.

Niamh closes the door and, without hesitation, drags the bedside table across the carpeted floor, pressing it tight up to the frame. She's as quiet as she can, but they can probably hear her movements. There's no time to care. Turning, she hurries to the window and throws it open as wide as it will go. There's no time to call the police. No time to get dressed. Whoever these armed men are, she needs to get clear of them.

She pulls the mattress from the bed and forces it out of the window, pushing it onto the grass of the front garden directly below. She's wearing yoga pants and a loose top. Her dark hair is loose, but she has a bobble on her wrist, and she quickly ties it back. No bra, no shoes, but this will have to do. It's enough for her to get away and call the police from a neighbor's house—it can't be a close neighbor, though. Neither of the houses either side of her own. It's late and she'll have to knock long and loud enough to wake people and to bring them down to investigate. Instead, she'll clear the immediate street, get around the corner. Going directly next door or opposite will give the men in her house time enough to catch up to her.

If she's lucky, the journalists *will* be hiding somewhere on the street, and they'll see what is happening. So far, since she's thrown open the window and pushed the mattress out, no one has appeared. This should have got their attention, surely?

Niamh starts to climb, taking a deep breath and preparing herself to drop from the window, when she hears the men working at the door behind her, pushing on it, battling to force the bedside table out of the way. They've realized she's aware of them now, and they're not trying to be so quiet anymore. They throw their weight into the door and the bedside table topples.

Niamh steps out of the window and falls to the mattress below. She can hear voices from the men in the room, watching her go, but they're not talking to her. It sounded like they were on a radio. She forgets about that for now and goes limp, hitting the mattress. She scrambles straight to her feet, ready to run, but a weight tackles her from behind and drives her down onto the grass. She's pinned and a hand is pressed over her mouth to keep her from crying out.

Niamh struggles, fighting back, but another man appears beside the one pinning her. They're dressed the same as the men inside the house—all black and masked. She assumes these two were positioned outside, in case she was able to get through. She kicks herself. She should have thought about this. At the moment, everything was happening so fast that her only thoughts were on escape.

The second man holds a needle and syringe. He plunges it into her arm. The two men look around, checking the street and the surrounding houses. The man pinning her asks the other, "How long?"

"Any second now," the second says.

Niamh feels her head clouding. Her eyelids feel weighted, and she can't keep them open.

The second man speaks into his radio, keeping his voice low. "We have her. Grab some of her clothes and let's go."

The last thing Niamh thinks about before she passes out is the sound of their voices. Their accents.

They're American.

3

Georgia stands on the porch and breathes deep, enjoying the Washington air. It's been raining, and the smell of it is thick on the trees and in the dirt.

Jack steps out onto the porch behind her. He's moving stiffly like he's just woken up. He twists, popping his spine, then rolling his neck. He turns his head and spits to the side, off into the bushes. "You're supposed to be keeping an eye out," he says. "Not taking in the air."

"I can do both," Georgia says.

Jack grunts. He takes a seat on the bench behind her, close to the door. Jack made the bench himself. It creaks when he sits, but it remains sturdy. "It wasn't clean enough for you up in Alaska?"

"It was plenty clean," Georgia says. "And usually cold."

"Uh-huh. And how is it here?"

"Muggy," Georgia says. "It feels thick. Why'd you choose here to hide out, Jack?"

He shrugs. "Why not? Why Alaska?"

"It's a big place. I didn't expect anybody to be able to find me there."

"Sounds like I'm doing a better job hiding out than you are."

Georgia looks through the trees. "How *did* they find me?"

"How am I supposed to know? But things are happening. That's clear to see. They could have known where you were for a long time, waiting for their moment to strike."

"I was careful. I kept my area clear. I made sure I wasn't being followed, right up until I was."

"They've got resources we can't begin to comprehend. *Neither* of us." Jack looks through the trees, too. "Have you kept *this* area clear?"

"You know I have, Jack. I've been here long enough now, you know I'm thorough."

"I know *I'm* thorough."

"Did you come out for a reason, or just to bust my balls?"

Jack breathes deep through his nose. "I came out to take the air."

Georgia turns back to him and shakes her head. "You asshole."

He grins. "I'm getting hungry. How about you?"

"I could eat."

"Then let's go inside."

Jack built the cabin. He's kept it sparse. The main room is through the front door. The living room and the kitchen. In the living area is a wooden slat sofa covered in cushions and a rocking chair next to it. There's a rug spread on the ground in front of them. There is no television, but there are a couple of bookcases overflowing, pressed up against the back wall, next to the door that leads through to the room where Georgia is staying. There is also a radio. Jack has electricity, powered by a generator, but he keeps its use to a minimum. The radio is battery-powered, and at night, he usually uses oil lamps to light the rooms. The electricity is to power the computers in his bedroom. It's to get him online. To keep him up to date on world events. For him to monitor situations that might be of importance to him, such as recent events that have brought Georgia to his door.

There are a couple of space heaters spread throughout the cabin for during the winter. Right now, heading into spring, it's warm enough to not need them. It's *too* warm for them.

There are two rooms running off the main area—Jack's bedroom, and a room that was used for storage. Storage consisted mostly of guns, and some weights and dumbbells. Now, it is Georgia's room. There is no mattress in there, so she sleeps on the floor atop a pile of blankets and cushions. Jack offered her the bed, but Georgia declined.

"You're older," she said, chiding him, "you need that comfort more than I do."

Georgia has been waking up stiff, though, and sometimes she regrets not taking Jack up on his offer. But stretching after she wakes has been part of her routine for a long time. Staying in shape. Staying sharp. It's part of her life. It's an important part. Here in the woods of Washington state, she wakes, stretches, and then goes for a run through the trees, armed with a Beretta while she goes, checking the area for signs of life that shouldn't be here.

In the kitchen, there is a cellar door. Jack pulls it open and reaches inside. It's a shallow cellar. He pulls out a couple of tins of soup and some bread. He warms them on the gas-powered stove. There is a round table in the middle of the kitchen. Georgia sits at it.

"Cut the bread," Jack says, passing her the loaf.

"I've been meaning to ask," Georgia says, cutting the loaf into chunky slices. "When did you find the time to build this place?"

"How old are you now, twenty-eight?" Jack says without turning, stirring the soup. "I was working on it before you were born. I've added to it over the years."

"You always knew you were going to have to hide out?"

"I always knew it was better to be safe than sorry."

"And when'd you take the carpentry courses?"

"It's what I did," Jack says, ladling the soup into bowls and joining her at the table.

"What do you mean?"

"When I left school, that was my job. I was a carpenter."

"Oh really? How come you've never told me that before?"

"You never asked."

"So before you took up government work and got involved in shadowy conspiracies, you were building tables and chairs?"

Jack grunts, spooning up soup. "Pretty much."

"You're full of surprises."

"I know it."

They eat in silence for a while. Every so often, Jack's eyes wander toward the window or the door, though he has cameras and alerts set up throughout the nearby area, and an alarm will sound from his computer if anyone is trying to get the drop on them. He stays paranoid. Georgia knows the feeling. It's the paranoia that prompts him to goad her into keeping a vigilant eye on the vicinity despite all his hidden cameras and sensors.

Georgia waits until they're both nearly finished with the soup before she asks, "What was your end plan here?"

"What do you mean?" Jack says.

"Were you just going to hide out forever, all alone? It's not much of a plan. It's not much of a life."

Jack shrugs, then doesn't say anything for a while until he's finished eating. He mops up the remnants of his bowl with a piece of bread and then sits back while he chews. Again, his eyes flicker toward the windows and the door. It's a tic for him now. He's vigilant, but he probably doesn't realize how often he makes these checks. It's not like he's had much else to do here, save for reading and re-reading his books, and tuning the radio.

Jack sucks his teeth, then says, "Have you ever read Walden?"

"No, but I'm familiar with it."

21

"I think Thoreau would disagree with your notion that it's not much of a life."

"We're a long way from Massachusetts."

"You *are* familiar with it."

"I worked in a library," Georgia says. "I flicked through nearly all of the books, even the ones I wasn't that interested in."

Jack grins. "Well, be that as it may, I didn't come out here to live forever, but I wasn't going to stay where I was and face certain death. I've been waiting. Waiting to see when and if they'd finally make their move, and when they did I needed to know what it *was*. Couldn't make any kind of a plan until I knew which way the wind was blowing."

"Did you expect this?"

"Blowing up the vice-president? I didn't expect them to go so big. I expected something a little more subtle, like how they poisoned the president and made it look like a heart attack. *That's* the kind of thing I was expecting."

"Well, it's come to pass." Georgia has finished eating. She pushes the bowl away and leans on the table. "So what's your plan?"

"Since you turned up, I still haven't given it much thought. Because now, it becomes *our* plan. Now seems like as good a time as any for us to formulate it."

Georgia sits back. It's her turn to look toward the window and the door. "I can't say I've been thinking about it either. Well, no, that's not true. I've done nothing *but* think about it. That doesn't mean I'm any further forward. The two of us can't fight this war, Jack."

"There's more than two."

"Not many more, and we don't even know who all our enemies are."

"We got a good idea. That new president, Zeke Turner, is one of them; I'd bet anything on that. They'll need a puppet. They won't show their own faces. They're more than happy to pull the strings from the shadows. They always have been. I assume you've been thinking about the new Kayla Morrow?"

"Of course."

"Did you think they might've retired that name after you?"

"I never gave it any thought. Why would I expect them to reuse it?"

"You know why."

Georgia falls silent at this. She looks down at the table.

"Are you going to go after her?" Jack asks.

Georgia raises her eyes to his. "That's what I'm wrestling with. She's in a lot of trouble, and her face is known."

"They're struggling to find her, though. The fact that they just released her name, that says to me that they're having problems and they don't like it."

"At this stage, they won't need to use the Kayla Morrow name again. It's served its purpose. It's too well known now." Georgia sighs. "Can I gain anything from going after her? Can I help her? She seems to be evading them well enough."

"For now," Jack says. "But those two guys she's with—ex-SAS and ex-Navy Seal? I mean, that's no joke. They could be good allies to have."

"They could be dead by the time we find them."

"That's true, but our options are few."

Georgia stares down into the bottom of her bowl. "I think about what could happen if I was able to catch up to her. Maybe I could give her some answers—maybe she could give some to *me*. And I wonder if that would just be a waste of time. Would it help at all? Maybe I should just look to strike back at them alone."

"You're not alone."

"You know what I mean. But sometimes, sometimes I ask myself…what if I just do *nothing*? Just stay out of it all. Go into hiding. I've done it before, I could do it again." She pauses. "But

I know this isn't an option. Not really. They already found me once. And if they want me back, all they have to do is say seven little words."

"Time is running short, but you don't have to make a decision right now," Jack says.

Georgia nods. "But the sooner the better, right?"

He doesn't say anything to this.

Georgia gets to her feet. "I'm going to take a walk. I'll go beyond the cameras, check our blind spots."

"Okay," Jack says. He doesn't push her. He knows she has a lot on her mind. She has a lot to think about. She has some big decisions to make.

They both do.

4

Ezekiel 'Zeke' Turner was the Speaker of the House. Now he's the President of the United States of America.

The former president, Frank Stewart, died of a heart attack. Zeke was the only person with him when it happened. After the death of Vice-President Jake O'Connelly in the terrorist bombing of Washington, DC, Frank was never the same. Jake's death got to him. Trying to capture the people responsible, and failing at every turn, put him under a great deal of strain. He wasn't an exceptionally old man—he was sixty-two—but the pressure, coupled with the death of his close friend, became too much for him. His heart gave out.

At least, this is the official story.

The truth is, Zeke Turner injected him with a cocktail of chemicals that caused his heart attack, and then he ran from the Oval Office screaming for help. To anyone who inspected the former President's body, it would look like he'd undergone cardiac arrest, and nothing more.

The Oval Office is now the office of President Ezekiel Turner. He's currently between meetings, and he sits with his back to the Resolute Desk, enjoying the view. He's seen it before, many times, but it hits differently seeing it as the president. He smiles, watching. Takes it all in. It's the position that every career politician dreams of, and now it's his, and all he had to do was join a secret organization and kill the former president. His ascension feels Ancient Roman.

The truth is—and Zeke is under no illusions about this—he's not the true president. Not a single vote has been cast for him. He ran on no ballot. He led no party. He was *placed* here. He's a puppet. His strings are being pulled, and he repeats what he's told to say. He has a boss, and it isn't the American people. He answers to the Quinquevirate. It is a group of men he has not yet met, but knows the time is coming soon when he'll have to step before them and thank them for their belief in him. Their messages, their orders, always come to him through encrypted messages, either on his phone or his email or via trusted mouthpieces. He is the public face of the Quinquevirate. Their spokesperson. And no one else knows that they exist.

He's not alone in the Oval Office. There are two other men here, behind him, sitting silently and waiting for the next meeting.

Zeke was sworn into office almost immediately after Frank's death was made public. Things have been non-stop since then. Zeke has barely slept, and yet he doesn't feel at all tired. If anything, he's never felt so energized. He's been busy getting acquainted with his new cabinet. Some of the cabinet are members of the same cabal he is, but not all. He knows this will change soon. There won't be a single member of government who has not joined The Order, who work for the Quinquevirate, and those who refuse—

Well. They'll be dealt with.

His new vice-president has been sworn in, too. Anthony Tomasson, former Secretary of State. He and Zeke already ran in the same circles. Anthony Tomasson knows about the Quinquevirate. At their behest, he was granted his new position. He too has never met them.

Anthony is in the Oval Office. He sits on a chair and runs through paperwork, unbothered that Zeke's back is to the room. They've had their daily briefing from Robert Fielding, the Chief of Staff. It ended an hour ago. Anthony hung around. So too has Matt Bunker. Matt is Secret Service. He was helping out the NSA recently, after all the chaos, but he returned to the fold soon after Zeke was installed as president. Zeke has been told good things about Matt Bunker.

"He's one of ours," Zeke was informed. "He's a good soldier. Place him in charge of your security. You're going to want to keep him close."

Everyone else from the cabinet who was present for the earlier briefing has left. It's just been the three of them for a while now. Matt stands by the door. He checks the time. "They're due in five minutes," he says.

Zeke turns back from the window and slides his legs under the desk. "I don't suppose there have been any promising updates in the last hour?" he says, looking between Matt and Anthony.

Anthony puts his paperwork down and shakes his head. "I don't think people would be quiet about it if there were."

"No," Matt says. "I haven't heard anything."

"Shame," Zeke says. He sits back and laces his fingers.

Five minutes later, almost on the dot, certain members of his cabinet return. Some of them were here earlier for the daily briefing, but they left when Robert Fielding did and have made themselves look busy in the meantime. Matt opens the door for them, checking each of them over as they enter. Secretary of the Treasury, Jill Cummins. Secretary of Defence, Kevin Donaldson. Secretary of the Interior, Hilary Largo, and Secretary of Commerce, Amy Gibson. They're all part of The Order. They all know what Zeke's true role is, and how he came to inherit it. They take seats around the room.

Zeke motions to Matt, who will lead the meeting. "You all know Matt Bunker," he says. "He's not head of the Secret Service just yet, but I'm sure it's only a matter of time. Matt has been taking point on the clean-up of our current issues. Matt, bring us up to date with where things currently stand."

Matt steps forward where everyone can see him. He clears his throat. He stands tall, his hands clasped behind him. "As you all know, we recently decided to release the name of Kayla Morrow. We held off at first in the hope we could recapture her and potentially put her to further use, but it's since been decided that she can now be considered an acceptable loss."

"Do we know where she is?" says Kevin Donaldson.

"We do not," Matt says. "The tracker chip that was in her foot was removed, and placed inside a dog. By the time we caught up to it, the tracker had been...passed. I'll leave the rest of that to your imagination." There are a couple of grimaces at the thought. "But if you save any further questions until the end, you'll find I'm likely to cover all bases over the course of this briefing."

Zeke notices how Matt's tone is firm. He controls the room. To an outside observer, Matt may be lower down on the totem than the rest of the people present, but the truth is that he's higher ranking in their true organization than the rest of them, despite being the youngest present.

"As it stands, we don't know where Kayla Morrow is, nor her two benefactors—Charlie Carter and Keith Wright. We are, however, monitoring various people of interest around the country. Our assumption is that the three of them are feeling very lost and very isolated, and they'll go to the first person who will offer them help. With all three of their names now being public record, and their faces regularly flashed on the news, we don't think it will take long for someone to approach them. If we're lucky, it will be someone we're already watching. If and when that happens, we'll be ready to move in and capture everyone concerned.

"Of course, we remain vigilant in all ways. We're not just working off theories, we're remaining practical. Online chatter is being monitored, and alerts are set up should their faces appear on any security footage. They've done well to evade us so far. They're clearly very careful, but their luck *will* run out, I have no doubt of that. We're already in the process of prompting them to make mistakes. We recently captured Charlie Carter's wife. She's on her way to us now. When we make the news of her captivity public, we're anticipating some kind of response.

"Moving on to potential allies for the group—some of you will be aware of the original Kayla Morrow. She's now going by the name of Georgia Caruso. We came close to apprehending her in Alaska, but she was able to get away from us there—however, some good news. We've been monitoring some woodland in Washington state, which we believe is concealing a person of interest. We think Georgia may have gone there to hide out."

"Who's the person?" Hilary Largo says, not waiting until the end to ask her question.

If Matt is annoyed by this, he doesn't let it show. "Jack Athey," he says. "Some of you may know that name, others won't. If not, I suggest you look into him in your own time. All that is pertinent right now is that he is someone Georgia may trust, and would turn to for aid."

"How long has he been monitored?" Hilary says. It appears to Zeke that she knows who Jack Athey is. Perhaps not on a personal level, but she's certainly aware of him and his story.

"A couple of years," Matt says. "He's been very careful, and we've had to be more so."

"Why sit on that information? He's a traitor. He should have been dealt with as soon as he was found."

Matt looks at Hilary in silence for a moment before he answers. "What benefit is he to us either dead or in captivity? Give him the illusion of freedom, and something good may come of it. And it potentially has."

"We had time," Zeke says, drawing Hilary's attention. "Regardless of whether Georgia went to him or not, we knew where he was, and we could deal with him at our leisure. Things are in motion now, we're emerging from the shadows, and we would have dealt with him sooner rather than later anyway."

Matt nods at this. "That brings us to our final runaway for today. Shira Mizrahi. Ex-Mossad. At this point, I'm sure you're as sick of hearing this as I am saying it—we don't know where she is. *Yet*."

"You know Shira, correct?" Kevin Donaldson says.

"That's correct, yes."

"He killed her boyfriend," Amy Gibson says with a grin.

Zeke notices Matt trying to hide a wince. "We all do what we do in service to a greater good," Zeke says. Amy Gibson's grin disappears.

"Does *she* know about that?" Jill Cummins says.

"She was present," Matt says, looking like he has a bad taste in his mouth.

"Let her come to you," Amy says. "Spring a trap, capture her that way."

"We're not going to resort to using Matt as bait," Anthony says. "We have every confidence that our people will find her."

"*Ex*-Mossad?" Kevin says.

"Officially," Matt says, though the expression on his face makes it clear that he believes this may not be the case.

"Should we be concerned about Mossad?" Kevin says. "Or Israel in general?"

"That's a good question," Matt says. "Thus far, we see no indicators that they're aware of what's happening here, but we keep the situation monitored. When I knew Shira, she never talked of her time in Mossad, not even to James, her partner. James always assumed something bad had happened."

"Have we tried asking *them*?" Anthony says.

"We asked recently, when we put the blame for James's death on her. Mossad are being tight-lipped, which was to be expected. Their official line is that she chose to retire."

"Isn't she young?"

"They blamed work-related stresses—she couldn't cope, basically. Beyond that, they'll say nothing."

"So, with regards to our runaways, we're in much the same position as we were when this all began," Jill says.

"It hasn't been very long," Matt says. "They're stumbling blocks as we find our feet, that's all. And I'm confident we'll have them all soon."

"Couldn't we activate the other sleepers?" Hilary says.

Matt blinks. "To what end?"

"To track the runaways."

"They don't work like that. They know as much as we do—less, in fact. We can't send them to find a person. We need to point them directly to a person, and instruct them what happens next."

"I'm just saying—many hands make light work."

Matt stares at her, then glances toward Zeke and Anthony, like he's not sure he can believe what he's hearing.

"This is why you're not in charge of the sleepers, Hilary," Zeke says, which garners a laugh from the gathering. "And I believe we already have many hands at work already, isn't that right, Matt?"

"Are we talking about the Nazis?" Amy asks and shudders.

"We are," Matt says. "But again, they need to know where to go, too, and we're working on that." Matt clears his throat and glances at Hilary, clearly perturbed by her lack of understanding of how the sleepers operate. "I think that's everything," he says.

Zeke nods. "Are there any further questions? Everyone up to speed?"

There are nods and mumbles of acknowledgment.

"Good," Zeke says, standing and motioning toward the door. "In that case we'll reconvene back here when there are updates worth discussing. Everyone knows what they need to be doing, I'll leave you to it."

The people get up and file from the room and go their separate ways, including Anthony Tomasson. Matt Bunker holds back until everyone else has gone, turning to Zeke. "It's concerning that Hilary would posit such a thing," he says.

Zeke nods, understanding. "I know, I know. Perhaps you could take it upon yourself to educate her further?"

"I'll do that," Matt says.

Matt leaves and Zeke is alone. He remains standing and takes a deep breath, looking the office over. Once again, he reminds himself, he's the president. The Commander-In-Chief. What does it matter that he's a puppet? In the meeting, the people deferred to him. When the ordinary American looks at him, they see a man of power. They see a leader.

He smiles, then returns to the window and the view.

5

Just over an hour out from Death Valley, they stop the car in the town of Pahrump. It's late evening. Keith estimates that it will be getting dark shortly after they finally reach the coordinates.

"Liquids are the most important thing," Keith says after parking the car up close behind a building off the main road, out of sight of any cameras that could be nearby. "It's going to be cool through the night, but we don't know how long we're going to be out there. If we're still there tomorrow, then we're going to need a *lot* of water. It's going to be *hot*. I won't sugarcoat this—if we don't have enough fluids, we're going to die."

Charlie stays with the car in case they need to make a quick getaway. He finally agreed to partake in the driving. "I think my ankle's up to it," he said, winking.

Keith and Kayla leave the car wearing baseball caps. Kayla's hair is loose, and she obscures the sides of her face with it. Keith looks up and down the road before they cross it, checking the vehicles and the people he can see. He and Kayla cross to the supermarket opposite and go inside.

"I'll get the liquids," Keith says, grabbing a shopping cart.

"You pick the snacks. Avoid things that are too salty. Get energy bars, jerky—things that are high in protein."

Kayla nods and they separate. He doesn't like not sticking together, but they need to get in and out. Separately, they can move faster and cover more ground. As they go their separate ways, however, Keith looks back over his shoulder, watching Kayla go for as long as he can keep her in sight. No one tries to talk to her. No one follows her. She does as she's been taught—she keeps her face low, the peak of the cap covering her features. They don't search out the store's security cameras. Don't raise their faces to them, exposing themselves, no doubt setting off alarms somewhere in DC, which are then relayed across the country.

Keith turns, the front of the cart almost bumping into a stand of nachos. He course corrects and goes to the liquids aisle. There aren't many other people in the store. Most of them are hidden down the various aisles, and everyone is minding their own business. Keith reaches the bottled water and lifts two cases—six two-liter bottles apiece—into the cart. He turns and goes in search of Kayla. On his way, he grabs a torch and some batteries, too, just in case it's needed.

It doesn't take long to find Kayla. She has an armful of snacks which she drops into the cart when he reaches her. Keith is pleased to see that she's been quick. He scans his eyes over the snacks. Multi-packs of chocolate and cereal bars. Some protein bars and bananas, and copious amounts of jerky.

"I just grabbed stuff that I thought would be good," Kayla says.

"This'll do," Keith says.

They go to the tills to pay. They use cash, never card. On the road, they stopped off in a small town and Keith went into a bank to extract everything he had. It was a tense moment, not knowing if his account would already be frozen. Luckily, it wasn't. He knew the withdrawal would attract attention from their pursuers. Once he had the money, they quickly set out, away from the town, taking a zig-zag route across highways and side roads, through small towns that wouldn't appear on any map. Making a random route, something nigh impossible to follow.

Despite emptying his life savings, their funds are starting to run short.

Behind the row of tills, the front of the building is mostly one big window, showing the street outside. As Keith starts unloading the contents of their cart, he feels Kayla stiffen beside him. She tugs on his sleeve. She's subtle about it. She doesn't want to draw any attention. Keith looks at her and she nods toward the window.

Outside, a police cruiser has come into view. It's moving slowly. The driver is looking into the store, through the window, and Keith can see the passenger leaning over, too. The cruiser stops, parking directly outside.

Keith doesn't stare, and he motions for Kayla to do the same. He grits his teeth and concentrates on keeping his breathing level. He watches the cruiser out the corner of his eye. It doesn't leave.

The cashier runs their contents through the till. Keith bags them up, then pays. He hands the paper bag to Kayla, then picks up the two cases of water, carrying them under his arms. As he turns to leave, he sees that one of the cops—the driver—has gotten out of the cruiser, and is coming toward the entrance. The other stays with the vehicle, but he's outside of it, leaning against the back of it, still peering through the store window. Keith doesn't look directly at them long enough to see if they're looking right back at him.

"What do we do?" Kayla whispers as they head toward the door, and an inevitable collision with the driver. Kayla sticks close to his side, clutching the bag so tight in front of her the paper is creasing and threatening to tear.

"Just stay cool," Keith says, but he swallows as he says it.

The cop gets to the door before they do. He pulls it open. He sees them coming. Keith can't avoid looking right back at him.

Then, the cop smiles. He holds the door wide for them, and tips his hat as they pass through. "Evening," he says, and then steps into the supermarket.

Keith's heart is pounding. He looks back through the closing door. One of the store's shelf stackers sees the cop and hurries over to him, running into his arms. They embrace.

Kayla sighs with relief beside him.

"Not so fast," Keith says. "Stay alert. Don't get lax for a second."

The other cop isn't looking their way. He's still looking through the window. He sees his partner and the store employee embracing and he smiles to himself then looks away, kicking stones at his feet.

Keith and Kayla don't hurry. They keep a casual pace as they cross the road and return to Charlie. They dump their supplies into the trunk and then get back inside the car.

"Nice and smooth?" Charlie says. He looks at them both, sees the looks on their faces, and frowns. "Something happen?"

"Just a slight scare," Keith says. "Nothing serious."

"Just a cop visiting his girlfriend," Kayla says. "But I swear, I thought he was coming right for us."

"Two of you need a minute?" Charlie says.

Keith shakes his head. "Let's just go while they're preoccupied. Their car is still out there, so take it easy."

"Good thing you said that, cos otherwise I was just gonna go tear-arsing it around that corner."

Keith gives Charlie a look.

Charlie chuckles to himself. "I keep myself amused."

"So long as you amuse *someone*," Kayla says from the back, and the comment catches both Keith and Charlie off-guard and they burst out laughing.

They leave Pahrump and continue on to Death Valley. Keith rests his phone on his thigh in preparation for the alarm to let them know they've reached the coordinates they were given.

The sun is going down and the sky is orange. Shadows stretch across the land. The closer they get to their destination, the fewer other vehicles they see on the road, until the point comes they don't see any at all.

"We got lucky back there," Keith says. He hasn't been able to stop thinking about the supermarket, and the cops. The cop that looked directly into his face and smiled and held the door for them both. For he and Kayla. An adult Black man and a teenaged white girl.

"What do you mean?" Charlie says.

"Back in Pahrump," Keith says. "If that had been a different kind of cop..."

Kayla doesn't say anything, but she's listening. Keith glances back over his shoulder and sees how she watches.

Charlie grunts. "He could've started asking questions."

Keith nods grimly. "That would have been bad for us."

"Aye. Maybe he thought the two of you weren't together."

"We were walking too close for that. He probably saw us paying together through the window, too."

"Might've thought you were her stepfather. Or, y'know, her friend."

"Whatever he thought, we're just lucky he didn't choose to make any kind of assumption. Or else he was too distracted coming to see his girlfriend."

"You know what it also means?" Charlie says. "It also means he hasn't been paying as much attention to the national news as he should be, because our handsome mugs are plastered *all* over it. So if we're lucky, that might be the same everywhere else."

"I wouldn't count on that kind of luck."

"No, but it would be nice."

It gets dark and Charlie has to put the headlights on. They pass a sign that announces their entrance into the Valley. "Is this it, then?" he says, looking around.

"The outer reaches of it, yeah," Keith says. "Keep going until we reach the coordinates."

Charlie does. They're all in silence now. They look around, but it's too dark out to see anything. The dark stretches as far as they can see, threatening to swallow the illumination from the headlights and leave them stranded.

The alarm goes off on Keith's phone to let them know they've reached their destination. Charlie pulls to the side of the road. He keeps the engine running.

"What now?" Kayla says.

Keith doesn't answer straight away. He's looking out the window, but there's nothing to see. Further ahead of them there is a small valley, rock formations rising high on either side of the road. A perfect spot for an ambush. If the coordinators had led them to that spot, they would not have stopped.

"I'm gonna have a look around," Charlie says. He turns off the engine but leaves the lights on. Keith and Kayla get out with him.

Outside of the car, their eyes adjust to the darkness. Keith has the torch with him, but he doesn't turn it on. The landscape stretches outward for miles around them. There is some residual warmth in the air and emanating from the ground, but already the desert is cold, and getting colder. Keith notices how Kayla wraps her arms around herself.

Keith listens. There's nothing to hear. It's deathly quiet. He watches the horizon, hoping to see someone step into view, approach them, and explain everything. No one does.

"It's too dark to see anything," Charlie says. "And even if it wasn't, I'm not convinced there'd be much to see anyway. We're not gonna get very far tonight."

"What about the people that live here?" Kayla says. "Why don't we try to find a community, see if the person we're looking for is there."

"We don't *know* who we're looking for, pet," Charlie says.

"I suggest we get the car off the road," Keith says, "and hunker down for the night. Maybe behind those rocks up ahead." He points.

Charlie nods. "We'll have to sweep the area first."

"Of course. And then we wake up early and explore the area, before it gets too hot. And it's going to get hot."

"It's a lot of area to cover," Charlie says.

"This is where they told us to come," Keith says, holding out his hands. "Maybe they'll come to us, I don't know."

Charlie looks around the desert. "Aye," he says. "Howay then. Sooner we make sure it's clear, sooner we can get back in the car."

6

Charlie is first to hear the buzzing.

It's early morning, before sunrise, and he's about to wake Keith and Kayla when he first notices the noise. It's getting closer. Growing louder. Charlie pulls the Glock from the back of his waistband and raises it, scanning the area.

He and Keith slept in shifts last night after they'd swept the area using the torch Keith picked up at the supermarket and made sure the rock formations, in particular, were clear. They were. The only living things to be found were some small rodents that quickly scurried at their approach. "Probably rats," Keith said. "But watch your step—there might be snakes." Luckily, there were no snakes.

Kayla stayed at the car while they checked the area. They parked it away from the road, out of sight. They made a small fire and ate, then promptly turned in. Kayla slept on the backseat, curled on her side with her face toward the back of the car. Charlie slept upright in the passenger seat until Keith woke him after a few hours. It was quiet on watch, and Charlie spent most of that time working a kink out of his neck. He was vigilant, of course. There was just nothing to be vigilant about. He heard a

40

few more of the rats go scurrying by, but they never got very close.

It was easy to stay awake in the night while on watch. It was too cold to drift back to sleep. He pulled on his jacket and zipped it up tight, and kept warm by pacing the ground. The last couple of hours, though, he's already felt it getting warmer, and he's no longer wearing the jacket.

Now, searching out the source of the sound, he bangs his fist on the roof of the car without turning. The buzzing is close enough now to work out where it's coming from. Turning that direction, Charlie spots something coming toward them. It's moving fast. A drone. He raises the Glock, but he doesn't shoot yet.

"What is that?" Kayla says. She's at his shoulder.

Charlie tells her.

"Shoot it down," Keith says.

"I'm waiting for it to get closer," Charlie says. "I shoot too soon, that's gonna spook it and it'll just stay out of range, watching us."

"Watching us?" Kayla says.

"It's too far away to see, but there's a camera on it."

"How are you sure?"

"Do you see the person controlling it? It can't fly out this far without being able to see where it's going. And what would be the point in flying it out here if not to see something?"

The drone stops.

"It sees us," Kayla says.

"It's been able to see us for a while," Charlie says. "It came straight for us."

"You got a bead?" Keith says.

Charlie nods.

"Take it down and let's get out of here," Keith says.

"Wait," Kayla says before Charlie can squeeze the trigger.

"What am I waiting for?" Charlie says.

"What if it's the people we're here to see?" Kayla says. "What if this is them coming to meet us?"

"Then we shoot it down and they come find us in person," Keith says. "Like they should have done in the first place."

Charlie considers. "It's been brazen," he says, glancing back at Keith. "It's not like it's tried to sneak up on us."

Keith comes around the car, stands with them. All three of them are watching the drone.

"I'm gonna lower the gun," Charlie says. "See if it'll come in any closer."

He does so, and the drone comes toward them. It stops about twenty feet away. The buzz of its wings is loud.

"I'd say it's non-threatening," Charlie says.

"I can see the camera now," Kayla says.

"Doesn't look like it has a speaker," Keith says.

The drone tilts slightly, as if nodding its head, then rises higher into the air and turns. It doesn't leave. It hovers there for a moment and then turns back to them.

"I think it wants us to follow," Charlie says.

Keith is hesitant. "This could be what we were hoping for. At the same time, it could be a trap." Charlie looks at him, sees him deliberating. "Let's follow," he says finally, lips pursed. "But I'll drive, and you keep that Glock out."

"Oh, it's not going anywhere," Charlie says.

They get into the car. The drone watches them. It waits. Keith starts the engine and turns the car so it's facing the drone. The drone turns its back to them, and it moves off. They follow.

7

Shira Mizrahi is in mourning. She's in mourning but tries not to think about it. She ignores her feelings. Swallows down her sorrow. Keeps herself busy. There is a lot she needs to do.

Noam Katz is with her. He's come from Israel. He spends most of his time on his laptop, his eyes rarely leaving the screen, his fingers never leaving the keys. He monitors online chatter. He breaks into databases. He has alerts set up on security cameras and radio signals. While he works, Shira keeps guard. They're hiding out in an upstairs apartment in the Petworth neighborhood in DC. They keep the curtains closed day and night, and the door is locked and chained.

Noam has installed a camera outside in the hall to monitor everyone who comes and goes and to warn them if anyone they need to be worried about is approaching. Shira regularly goes to the windows, opening the curtains just inches, and inspects the ground below. They're four stories up. She keeps a written log of the vehicles that park on the street below, and makes sure none of them are hanging around for too long. She makes sure no one is sitting in them. Makes sure that no one is watching them, either below or in the surrounding buildings.

Being on watch and searching for people who may be searching for them keeps her preoccupied. Keeps her mind busy. It gives her something to think about. Something important.

If Shira thinks about her mourning at all, she thinks about how she is going to avenge James Trevor. She thinks about how she is going to kill the man who killed him. Matt Bunker. He was supposed to be his friend, and yet he shot him dead. No hesitation. No remorse. He would have killed Shira, too, if he'd had the chance.

They can't trust anyone.

Well, no one in power, at least. No one in authority. There are some people they need to try and find, and they might be able to trust *them*.

Noam is hunting them down. Trying to find where they might have gone. Any kind of hint of where they could be.

Kayla Morrow, Keith Wright, and Charlie Carter.

The three of them are out of their depth. They're caught up in things above and beyond them and hopelessly outnumbered. But if Shira and Noam can find them, they may be able to help each other out. The three runaways could aid their investigation. Hell, they might even have some answers. They could be invaluable in proving what is happening in America.

As for Shira and Noam, they're just as isolated and alone out here. They're flying solo. The Americans don't know that Noam is here, but they're all too aware of Shira.

Noam sits back from the computer and rubs his eyes. He pops his spine.

Shira is nearby at the living room window. It's early morning and there isn't much activity below. She lets the curtains fall back into place and turns to him. "Do you have anything?"

"Just eye strain," Noam says, still rubbing. He turns away

from the computer, blinking hard. He had last watch overnight. He's been awake longer than Shira has, and has spent that time on his laptop.

"Seeing stars?"

"Black holes," Noam says, then grins. "I'm going to take a rest before I get a migraine. I have alerts set up—if anything worth looking into comes up, we'll get a ding."

"Do you want to lie down?" Shira says.

"I might," he says. "In a minute." He doesn't leave his chair yet.

The apartment was partly furnished when they moved in. They were able to get it fast and cheap as the previous tenant had committed suicide in the bathroom, and the owner was struggling to find anyone to take over the lease. The property had sat empty for eight months before they arrived. They didn't bring anything with them, save for their clothes and Noam's computer. There's a sofa, which Shira sits on the edge of, and a small desk pressed up against the wall next to the kitchen, used for Noam's work. The desk came with a swivel chair, which has one wheel that doesn't turn.

The kitchen and living room are open-plan. The kitchen is small and basic. It has all they need, which isn't much. It came with a refrigerator at least, which means that Shira does not have to venture out to get groceries too often.

It's a one-bedroom, but they sleep in shifts. It's important to be most alert at night. If someone were to come for them, they'd likely wait for darkness. The mattress did not come with any bedding, but after a long day of online searches and window vigilance, they're usually both too tired to care.

There is no sign of the suicide that occurred in the bathroom. The landlord did not say what their method was, but Noam looked into it out of curiosity and found that the previous tenant had cut his wrists in the bath. Shira has seen no signs of spilled blood in there, neither in the bath nor between the tiles. It has been thoroughly cleaned.

"The Americans have been in touch with Mossad," Noam says.

"Is this chatter, or did you hear this from our people?" Shira says.

"Chatter."

"So they've reached out again?"

He nods. "Again and again, it seems like."

"Has Mossad issued any kind of response?"

"Just the expected shock that you would be part of something so awful, and that you retired from the agency years ago and we have not maintained contact. Beyond that, they won't give the Americans anything else."

"Have they asked for files?"

"Probably," Noam says. "They don't specify what they've asked for in what I've been able to see. But Mossad won't let them in. I'm sure they don't want to take any chances."

"If they were let in, the Americans will dig as deep as they can go," Shira says. "If they're given an inch, they'll take a mile. Mossad won't run the risk of them finding something they themselves might have missed."

Noam nods. "Exactly. But they'll have to be careful about how resistant they are. It's a fine line between standard practice and making themselves appear suspicious. The very last thing any of us need is for the Americans to find out that Israel sent you here."

Shira nods, breathing deep. "If your name gets out, you'll be disowned too."

"I'm fully expecting it," Noam says. He looks back over his shoulder toward the kitchen, like he's trying to decide if he's hungry or not. He pats his stomach. "I'm going to go and lie down now," he says, wincing as he gets up, his body no doubt aching. "Just a few hours."

"Take as long as you need," Shira says. "If the laptop starts making noises, I'll come and wake you."

Noam goes through to the bedroom, closing the door behind him.

Shira sits alone on the sofa. The apartment feels so quiet without anyone nearby. Without anyone to talk to.

It's smaller than where she lived with James, but somehow it reminds her of there. Of the life they were living together. She never intended to get involved with him. She was in America to work. To look into Mossad's concerns. To find out what was happening within the American government. But then she met James. She fell in love with James.

She grits her teeth and shakes her head. She's letting the grief in. She can't do that. Not yet. It will be a long time before she can allow her grief to fully inhabit her.

She gets to her feet and goes to the window, and resumes her vigil of the streets below.

8

Harlan Thompson has been a free man for seven days. After Matt Bunker came to see him and they came to their arrangement, Harlan was returned to his isolated cell under the Red Onion State Prison supermax. He only had to wait a few more days in what had been his home for over a decade. Something strange happened to Harlan, though. All his time in isolation, kept away from everyone else, time had passed at an even pace with his knowledge that he was never getting out. That he was going to die in his cell. But suddenly, with the knowledge that he was soon to be freed, the days slowed. They crawled by.

Harlan found himself growing agitated and fidgety. He paced the cell, willing the minutes and hours to pass. No longer could he just sit in his meditative silences, with only the occasional book for company. He needed to be proactive, feeling like he might explode with the sudden burst of expectation and excitement that had taken hold of him. He'd run on the spot. He'd do push-ups, sit-ups, squats. He did these already, every day, but now he went at his calisthenics with a new intensity, wearing himself out. After, he'd lie sweating, breathing hard on the floor, exhausted.

But, like a child wishing for Christmas, the day he was waiting for *did* eventually come.

Or, rather, the night.

Harlan was sleeping when they came for him. Masked men dressed all in black, pulling him from his bed and clamping a hand over his mouth to keep him quiet until he understood what was happening. It was his extraction. It was finally time to leave.

Another group of men carried a body bag into the cell. Harlan watched as they unzipped it and laid it on the bed, in the warmth where he had previously been. It was hard to see in the dark, but Harlan thought they'd done a good enough job of getting the corpse to look like him.

The men took him by the arm and led him out, avoiding the other cells of the supermax where some of the inmates may have still been awake. COs he recognized had to unlock bars to let them through. Harlan noticed how the guards wouldn't look at him or the men with him. They turned a blind eye to his escape. The prison knew he was getting out, and there was nothing they could do about it.

The couple of days after that were a blur. They hid him in a safe house, still in Virginia. He was given his choice of new clothes to wear. Harlan chose black jeans and a denim shirt. They gave him sunglasses, too, knowing that his eyes are not adjusted to natural light, and likely never will be again.

They fed him food he hadn't eaten in years. They gave him drinks he hadn't tasted in just as long. They brought him fresh fruit. They gave him anything he asked for.

"Get me a woman," Harlan said to see how far they were willing to go.

Within two hours, they brought him a woman. A hooker. A *Black* hooker. He figured it was their idea of a joke, but he didn't care. It had been too long, and Harlan didn't care what color she was. He used her up and sent her away, knowing there'd be plenty of white pussy for him when he got back to Texas.

They gave him a phone and put him in touch with his men. He told them what was happening. Told them not to believe reports of his death—a lookalike had been found. He was out and he was coming home to explain everything, but first, they'd need to come and get him. It would take them a day to drive up. Once again, Harlan found himself with time to kill. This time, at least, he had company, even if the four men assigned to guard him were not the most conversational.

Matt Bunker came to see him. They sat opposite each other in the living room. There was a television, but Harlan didn't watch it much during the day. He stood by the windows instead, looking out at the world, taking it all in.

Matt tilted his head toward the TV. "Did you catch the news report on your death?"

"I did," Harlan said. "It wasn't long enough." He grinned.

"I thought they used a lot of adjectives you might like," Matt said. "Savage. Vicious. Dangerous. Feared."

"Oh yes, that pleased me just fine. What can I do for you, Matt Bunker? You just come out here to see me out the chains?"

"Pretty much," Matt said. "I came to check in. To make some things clear going forward."

"I'm all ears."

"You and I will stay in regular contact. I'll provide you with a number where you can reach me. Until you've fulfilled the obligations for your freedom, we expect you to devote all of your time and your energies, and that of the men who answer to you, in the pursuit of the names we've provided you. If you deviate from what is expected of you, we'll come down on you, Harlan. We'll come down on all of the Vanguard Whites."

Harlan smirked. "And what would that look like? Can't

exactly send me back to the supermax. We're all in this equally as deep."

"I never said you'd be locked back up."

"Uh-huh. What you're saying is, a dead man can die twice. That right?"

Matt said nothing.

Harlan understood clear enough. "I'm devoted to your cause," he said.

"Glad to hear it. After that, you can do whatever you please."

"Let me ask you something, Matt Bunker," Harlan said, leaning forward and clasping his hands. "I saw something else while I watched the news. It came on right after the report of my death. It was our President, delivering some kind of address or other. I don't know, I didn't pay too much attention to what he was saying—I was too busy looking at someone I noticed in the background. *You.* And you were with the rest of the Secret Service."

"What's your point?"

"You told me you were NSA. Are you Secret Service?"

"I'm Secret Service. When I told you I was NSA wasn't a complete lie. I'd been drafted in to help out due to everything going on. But I used my time there productively, wouldn't you say?"

"I didn't know the NSA had a say in freeing prisoners."

"Neither does the Secret Service," Matt said. "And you're not free. You're dead, and don't forget that."

Harlan laughed.

His men arrived to collect him late at night. It was too late to leave, so Harlan told them they were spending the night. The safe house had a spare room. They set off early the next morning, leaving the four guards behind and beginning the long drive back to Texas. Harlan sat in the back, looking out the window as they went. He was finally going home.

And he's been home for the last three days, awaiting instructions from Matt Bunker. None have come through yet, and so these three days have been a party. A celebration of his return. All the local boys have been called in, though the Vanguard Whites are nationwide, and not everyone can make the trip. They've all been informed that the news of Harlan's death is false. That Harlan is free now, and something big is coming. They've all been told to keep their heads down but to be on high alert.

The Vanguard White headquarters is a club house on the outskirts of Midland, Texas. Harlan founded the Vanguard Whites thirty years ago. He was twenty-five, and already a hardened criminal, and at that time serving a short prison sentence for assault. Whilst locked up, he laid the foundations of what would grow to become his empire. Now, thirty years later, there is a faction of the Vanguard Whites in practically every state. They are everywhere. They're an army.

The inside of the club house is built like a compound. If the shit goes down, if anyone comes after them, it's ready to hold out. It's full of weapons, and it's full of food. Thus far, in the entirety of its existence, that has yet to happen. When Harlan was arrested, they took him from his home. If he'd been in the club house, things would have gone down very differently.

There is a large common room in the center of the compound. There is a kitchen directly leading off from it, and beneath the kitchen is where they keep extra supplies in preparation for a siege. Their armory is opposite, also connected to the common room and within easy reach. Down the corridor are rooms, all of them equipped with beds in case any members need to spend the night. Their numbers are many, and spread far and wide, but Harlan is selective on who they choose, and he's made sure all of his lieutenants are, too.

One of his lieutenants comes to see him. His most loyal. His right-hand man. The man who has been running operations while

Harlan has been locked away. The man who was primed to take his place when it seemed like Harlan was all set to die in that cell. The first man Harlan called when he was out, and informed him of what was happening. Earl Borden.

"Have you heard anything yet?" Earl says, entering the room and taking a seat in the chair by the window.

Harlan props himself up on the bed. "Nothing," he says. "But I'm sure it's coming soon." He takes off his sunglasses and polishes them but keeps his eyes closed while he does so.

Earl stares out the window.

"Something on your mind?" Harlan says.

"I'm...I'm just not sure how I feel about all of this."

"Aren't you happy to see me back, Earl?"

"You know I am. Hell, the last few days with all the women and the booze, I think I've more than proven that. You know that's not what I was talking about."

"I'm just busting your balls, man. What's got you concerned?"

"The government," Earl says, leaning forward and raising his eyebrows. "Can we really trust them? This whole thing stinks like a set up to me."

"A set up? What could they hope to gain? They've released me. They've covered for that—they provided a corpse and told the world I was dead. And you've got to remember, this isn't the government we're working with. It goes deeper than that. These are people whose values align more closely with our own."

"You're sure about that?"

"I've spoken with their representative at length. I wouldn't say they're *exactly* in line, but they're close enough. Certainly close enough for us to work with, and to exert our own influence on. This country is changing, Earl. It's already changed and people don't realize it. Soon, the whole world will be a new place.

We just have to be patient. I have a feeling we won't be left waiting long."

"So you trust them?"

Harlan chuckles. "I never said *that*. But what's important is that they trust *us*. And that will be *their* downfall."

Earl nods, understanding. He smiles now. "All right, I get it."

"For now, we play nice. Helping them is benefiting us. And besides, they got a Jew and a Black boy they want us to go after, so it ain't like there's any harm in it."

"We just have fun with it."

"*Exactly*," Harlan says, cocking a finger. "We just have fun with it." Harlan checks the time. "Now, while we're waiting, we may as well continue to have fun of a different kind. We still got some girls up in here?"

"There's a couple sleeping in the common room."

"Well all right. Go wake them up and send them through to me."

"Both of them?" Earl asks with a gleam in his eye.

"That's what I said, ain't it?" Harlan slides down on the bed, lacing his fingers behind his head. "They know where to find me. I'll be right here waiting for them."

9

Charlie, Keith, and Kayla follow the drone in the car. It leads them across the desert, away from the road and toward the distant mountains. The drone is ahead of them, but it's not going as fast as it could. It always remains in view.

Keith drives. He has the A/C turned up high. "This terrain ain't good for the car," he says, as the uneven surface bounces and jostles them. Keith turns his head to the side to try and keep it from hitting the roof.

Charlie keeps the Glock out ready. It's in his lap, gripped tight, the barrel pointing toward the ground for now, out of sight. Ready to be used if necessary. Keith and Charlie watch the drone, but they keep their heads on a swivel, scanning the area, wary of a trap.

"What should I be looking for?" Kayla says, leaning forward.

"Anything that looks out of place," Charlie says.

"Like what?" Kayla says.

"Like a person for a start. They'd be very out of place out here. Or more than one person. Especially if they're armed."

"Got it," Kayla says. She looks around too, scanning the area. It's a wide open space. Too much for even three pairs of eyes.

The drone leads them closer and closer to the mountains. Ahead, on the flat, there is nothing to be seen.

"Where the hell's it leading us?" Charlie says.

Keith doesn't say anything. He's focused. He doesn't like this. He's uncomfortable with the whole situation. It feels too much like a trap.

The car begins to slow. "What's happening?" Charlie says.

Keith stops the car. "If it *feels* like a trap," he says, "and if it *looks* like a trap…"

He doesn't need to finish. Charlie understands. He nods.

"What do you mean?" Kayla says. "It feels too much like a trap?"

"They've brought us far enough," Keith says. "They want us to go any further, they're gonna have to come to us. They're gonna have to show themselves. I'm sick of all this secretive bullshit."

The drone has continued on, not noticing that they've stopped. It reaches the base of the mountains, stops, and turns. It realizes that they're not following. It comes back to them, flying over the ground at full speed. It doesn't take long to reach them. It hovers, swaying irritably from side to side.

"I'll deal with it," Charlie says, getting out of the car. He keeps the Glock low by his side, but he doesn't put it away. He points toward his mouth, indicating for whoever is watching to read his lips. He keeps it short and to the point. "Show yourself!" He waves his arm to dismiss the drone.

The drone stopped swaying and held still to watch. Keith watches it. It doesn't move. He thinks it's hesitating. Considering what Charlie has said. Keith looks beyond the drone, toward the mountains. Checks for movement. He can't see any. It's a lot of area to cover.

The drone resumes movement. It turns and returns to the base of the mountains. It pauses there, hovering. Charlie gets back into the car.

"See anyone?" Charlie says.

"No," Keith says. "You?"

Charlie shakes his head.

"I see someone," Kayla says. She points up the mountain.

Keith and Charlie follow her finger. Keith spots the movement she's seen. It's in the mountains. Not too high—about a hundred feet up.

Charlie sees it too. "Just one guy," he says.

"But he's armed," Keith says.

The man makes his way down the mountain. He has a rifle on his back, and in his hands, he's carrying what looks like a controller. Keith imagines that when he gets closer, they'll be able to see that it's the drone's controller.

"Stay frosty," Keith says. "Eyes wide. There could still be a trap coming. Just because he looks alone doesn't mean he is."

"Should we get out of the car?" Kayla says.

"Wait until he's closer," Charlie says. "We might still need to split."

They watch as the man comes down the mountain. He takes his time. He's still working the controls on his way, keeping the drone in the air. When he finally reaches the base of the mountain, he lands the drone and turns it off. He reaches down and picks it up and comes toward the parked car. The rifle remains on his back.

"Come on," Keith says, opening the door. "Kayla, stay behind me and stick close."

It's hot outside of the car. The sun hasn't long risen, and it promises to get higher, threatening to get hotter and hotter. Already, Keith feels sweat trickle down his spine.

The man gets closer. They can make him out now. Late twenties. His hair is shorn short. He's unshaven, but he doesn't have a full beard. He looks pale, and the skin is dark around his eyes, like he's not getting as much sleep as he should be.

He stops, looking at the three of them in turn. His eyes linger on Kayla, peering over Keith's shoulder.

"Kayla Morrow," the stranger says. "We've been expecting you. We've been expecting all of you. You took your time getting here."

Keith thinks about the man he spoke to on the phone. The man who gave him the coordinates that led them here to Death Valley. This man's voice is not familiar. He's not the person Keith spoke to. He's too young.

"Who are you?" Keith says.

The man doesn't answer. He grins. "You must be Keith Wright," he says.

"Anyone with a TV or an internet connection knows who we are, mate," Charlie says. "But you're not popping up on the nightly news, so how about you tell us who *you* are."

"Doesn't matter who I am right now," the man says. "What matters is you need to come with me." He starts to turn, but Keith stops him.

"It matters who you are," he says, "and it matters where you're planning on taking us. We aren't going anywhere until you start giving us answers."

The man snorts. "You come all this way, and you're *not* gonna follow me? Sure." He starts to turn again.

Charlie raises the Glock and points it at him. "Answers."

"You really gonna use that?" the man says.

"Mate, I'm stressed, and I'm tired, and I'm getting *really* fucking hot out here. You don't want to keep pushing me."

The man looks at Charlie for a while. "I don't think you'll shoot," he says, but he sounds uncertain. "You've come here. You want answers."

"We'll get answers," Charlie says. "I never said I intended to kill you, but I can hurt you really bad." Charlie lowers the gun, but it's still pointing at the man. It's pointing at his right knee.

The man sucks his teeth.

Charlie raises his eyebrows. "Do you need a countdown?"

"All right," the man says, sighing. It's clear he believes Charlie will shoot him. "What's it going to take?"

"You haven't given us any reason to trust you," Keith says. "You haven't done or said a single thing to make us think you're *not* leading us into a trap."

The man scrapes his teeth over his bottom lip. He looks up the mountain. "My name's Ryan Fallon," he says. "And I don't want to be here any more than you do, but you're not here to see me. You're here to see my father. He's the one you spoke to on the phone, and he's the one that led you here." Ryan points up the mountain. "He's up there, in a cave, waiting for us. Waiting for all of you. Waiting for *you* in particular." He nods at Kayla. "As far as I'm aware, there's no one else around here. Just me and him, and now the three of you."

"If he invited us here, why didn't he come down to greet us himself?" Keith says.

"He's not a young man," Ryan says. "He doesn't want to have to come down the mountain just to head back up it soon after."

"Why'd he want us here?" Charlie says. He's lowered the gun now, satisfied with Ryan's answers, but he doesn't put it away.

"It's better that you hear it from him," Ryan says.

"Why?"

Ryan looks at Kayla and he grins. "Because if I tell you I don't think you'll believe me. You've gotta hear it straight from the horse's mouth."

"We're gonna discuss amongst ourselves," Charlie says, motioning for Keith and Kayla to come closer to him. "You just stay where you are, Ryan."

The three huddle close, Keith and Charlie not turning their backs on Ryan. They keep him within sight. Ryan doesn't watch them. He looks down at his drone, turns it over in his hands, and checks its condition after being out in the desert for a while.

"Do we go with him?" Charlie says.

Keith takes a deep breath before he answers. "He hasn't tried to disarm us."

"I think we should go to the cave," Kayla says.

"I know you do, pet," Charlie says. "But we can't just rush in."

"I know we can't," Kayla says. "The two of you are always telling me that, and I'm *not* rushing in. We've listened to him talk. We got answers. Like Keith said, he didn't try to disarm us. He pointed out where the cave was. He's never once pointed the rifle at us. He led us here. There's no one else around. I'm not rushing —I've been careful. I've checked and I've thought about things, and I *really* think we should go up to the cave and try to get some damn answers."

Keith watches Kayla. He feels Charlie watching him. They're both looking back at him, like they expect him to make the ultimate decision.

"All right," he says. "It's not like we have many choices. Just keep that gun ready."

"Always intended to," Charlie says.

They turn back to Ryan. "We're coming up," Keith says. "You're gonna lead the way, and we're gonna take it nice and slow."

"Sure," Ryan says.

"What are you like for supplies up in that cave?" Charlie says.

"We've got things," Ryan says. "Did you come prepared? If you did, you should bring them."

Keith leans toward Charlie. "Kayla and I will carry stuff; you'll keep him covered."

Charlie nods.

"Hide the car first," Ryan says. He points off to the side, at the base of the mountain where an outcropping of rock provides a shaded shelter. "Put it over there."

10

The way up the mountainside is steep and causes their thighs and calves to burn. Charlie has kept himself fighting fit since he left the armed forces, and Ryan is clearly used to the journey. Keith and Kayla keep up, but they lag behind a little way, laden down with the supplies they brought into the desert. Charlie glances back and sees Kayla taking a long drink from a bottle of water. The sun is high. Charlie wipes sweat from his brow and turns back to Ryan. Ryan continues his march, looking straight ahead, his drone dangling by his side.

Charlie's ankle has healed since he rolled it, but he still feels the occasional twinge. He's careful where he steps, the uneven ground littered with jagged rocks. They get closer to the cave. Charlie hears something, faint and distant. A low hum.

"What's that sound?" he says.

"You'll see," Ryan says without slowing or turning.

They reach the mouth of the cave. It's dark and cooler than outside.

"Stay close," Charlie says to Ryan. "It's getting real dark in here, and I don't want to lose track of you."

"There's a corner here, and once we get around that it'll light up."

Charlie places a hand on Ryan's shoulder. Ryan flinches, but he doesn't stop.

"I told you," Charlie says, pointing the gun between his shoulder blades, "I don't want to lose track of you."

They round the corner. Charlie senses Keith and Kayla catching up behind them and sticking close.

As Ryan promised, they soon step into the light. The humming sound that Charlie could hear outside is louder now, and he sees where the sound is coming from. Off to the side, in the corner of the cave, there are generators running which power the hooked up lights. As he looks around, he soon sees that they're powering more than just the lights.

"Here he is," Ryan says, gesturing vaguely off to the side of the cave opposite from the generators. "The man you came cross-country to see."

Charlie picks up on a hint of resentment in Ryan's tone, but he doesn't think too deep about it for now. He looks toward where he motions and sees an older man at a desk, his back to them. The desk is wide, laden with computer screens. Charlie notices that one of them is playing live footage from the drone. He can see part of his arm on the screen, and Keith and Kayla coming up behind. Ryan has kept the drone's camera pointed toward them all the way.

The man at the desk stands and turns toward them. Charlie can see the familial similarities between him and Ryan. He takes a couple of steps forward and then stops, standing awkwardly, giving them a grim-faced smile. He's not sure what to do with his hands and ends up clasping them in front of himself.

"Hello," he says, nodding.

Charlie lets go of Ryan, but Ryan doesn't attempt to move away. Charlie keeps the gun up. He's not taking chances.

"The two of you live here," Keith says, looking around the cave.

Ryan snorts. "I wouldn't call it living," he says. "We *hide* here."

He moves off into the space between the generators and the computers. There is bedding there—a couple of cots spaced far apart. Charlie spots a cooler on the ground between them. Ryan reaches inside and pulls out a soda. He places his drone and its control on the ground under the cot, then props his rifle against the cave wall. He takes a seat, then pops the tab on his soda. He looks like he'd rather be anywhere else.

The older man watches his son, frowning, and then turns back to Charlie, Keith, and Kayla. "I'm Dr. Winston Fallon," he says, holding a hand out to Charlie. "You came here to see me."

Charlie doesn't accept the hand. He regards it warily.

"We don't know *why* we came here," Keith says. "But we were short on options, and you gave us directions."

"Mr. Wright," Winston says, looking beyond Charlie and smiling. "It's very nice to finally speak in person."

"Uh-huh," Keith says. He puts the supplies he's carrying to one side, and motions for Kayla to do the same. "Are you gonna talk straight to us this time, or do we need to put up with more of your riddling bullshit?"

"The riddles were necessary," Winston says. "Can't be sure who's listening."

"You gave us coordinates," Keith says. "If anyone was listening, you led them right here."

"It was necessary," Winston says. "I had to take a risk. And I didn't lead you directly to this cave. But no one else has found their way here—at least, not yet. I keep the area monitored. I have cameras with motion sensor alerts set up far and wide. Usually the only thing that sets them off is a coyote."

Charlie glances toward the computers. He can see that one of the screens is split into many small squares, most of them showing the empty expanse of the desert. He can see road in a couple of the squares.

"You can put the gun down, Mr. Carter," Winston says. "I'm unarmed."

"Doesn't mean I trust you, Winnie," Charlie says, keeping the Glock raised. "And you might as well call me Charlie. You know our names, you might as well use them. It's a lot more than we know about you."

"I intend to be forthcoming," Winston says. "That's why I invited you here, after all."

"You could have been forthcoming long before now," Keith says, stepping forward. "We've spoken twice—in the jail and in Dom's apartment. You hijacked my one phone call while I was locked up—"

"I was *very* clear when you were locked up," Winston says.

"Protect the girl," Keith says. "That's what you said. And I have, and now we're here, and all you've ever done is give us more questions than answers."

Winston smiles. "Tell me, Mr. Wright—*Keith*—have you had to use the words?" He glances at Kayla.

Charlie and Kayla look at Keith. "What words?" Charlie says.

"I don't know," Keith says. "Well, I know the words, but I don't know what he means."

"It's for the best that you haven't," Winston says. "Like I warned you, only use them if necessary."

"What *words*?" Charlie says. "What the hell are you talking about?"

"West," Keith says, remembering. "Clementine, buds—"

"Uh-uh," Winston says, holding up a hand and waving it. "You can't say the words in front of the Prime. We don't know how she might react."

"The Prime?" Charlie says. "What's the Prime?" But then he sees Winston is looking at Kayla.

Kayla is just as confused as the rest of them. She shuffles her feet as all attention turns to her. "I," she says. "I—I don't know what it means either…"

Off to the side, on his cot, Ryan is laughing.

"Oh, he loves this," Ryan says, shaking his head and taking another drink.

"Ryan, please," Winston says.

"He always has to be the smartest person in the room," Ryan says, crushing the drained can and tossing it carelessly to the side, losing it in the shadows where the lights don't reach. "He loves it —feed out these drips of information, keeping you on edge right up until you get so pissed off you want to *throttle* him—"

"*Ryan.*"

Ryan shrugs. "Just tell them what they want to know. Tell them what the seven words do. Tell them what it all means. Tell them about the mess they're caught up in, just like us. Tell them how we're all going to die."

"I don't like the sound of that," Charlie says.

"You should listen to your son," Keith says. "I've wanted to throttle you since the moment I laid eyes on you, so hurry up and give us some answers."

Winston stares at his son. Ryan is unbothered. He shrugs again. Winston turns back to them. "I don't always have to be the smartest in the room." He sighs. "Look, everyone, take a seat. I'll tell you what you want to know. I'll tell you as much as I can."

11

There aren't many places to sit in the cave. The options are either the floor, or the cot not occupied by Ryan. Kayla sits beside Keith on the remaining cot. Charlie stays standing, his arms crossed, but the gun still in his hand. Kayla doesn't think he's going to put it away, and she feels better knowing he has it out.

The chair at the computers is on wheels. Winston drags it across the ground, closer to them, and takes a seat. The ground is not level enough for the wheels to roll freely, and Kayla hears how they scrape. Winston sits and places his hands on his thighs. He smiles at Kayla. He keeps looking at her, like they've met before and a long time has passed. Like he's seeing all the ways she has changed, and he's comparing them with how he remembers her. Kayla feels herself shifting uncomfortably under his gaze.

"I made you," Winston says. "I made you what you are, and I'm so very sorry."

Kayla frowns.

"What's that supposed to mean?" Keith says.

"We told you, mate," Charlie says, "no more fucking riddles."

Winston holds up his hands. "No riddles, I promise."

He lets his hands drop. He stares off into a corner of the cave, into the darkness and the shadows there, thinking.

"Maybe I started in the wrong place," he says, turning back to them. Kayla thinks he looks tired. He's smiling, but it's a sad smile. "I should have built up to that first. Where to start? When I was a younger man, I worked in an asylum. I treated people with damaged minds. People who couldn't control their impulses. People who couldn't help harming others or putting themselves in harm. It's a difficult job." He bites his lip, remembering. "These are the kinds of people that, if you fail them, you *fail* them. Do you understand? They were high risk—to themselves and to others. I started to research alternative, experimental procedures. You have to understand, I wanted to help people. That was all. I wanted to help them to get better. I explored any means that I could to help my patients. I learned hypnotherapy. I looked into ways electronics could help. I left no stone unturned. Anything that could potentially help, I investigated it."

Winston pauses, looking down at his hands. Kayla watches him. He's thinking. Deciding how much to tell, and what to cut out. Where to take his tale next. She glances back at Ryan. It doesn't look like he's listening. He's sitting on his cot, his arms folded and his face lowered, staring at the tips of his boots. She sees how the sinews in his cheek tighten with the clenching of his jaw. She looks toward Charlie, too, and sees that he hasn't moved from where she last saw him. Standing stoic, arms folded, brow furrowed, gun in hand.

"I suppose most of this doesn't really matter," Winston says, raising his head again. "I just needed to give you a little of my background, especially about hypnotherapy and electronics. As you can see, I've always maintained my interest in electricals." He gestures around the cave with a grin. "One day, I was approached by a man who wanted to talk about my work. I didn't know who this man was at the time. I didn't recognize him, but I got the impression he was someone important. There were bodyguards with him, though they kept their distance and tried to make themselves inconspicuous. I saw them, though. Where he went, they followed.

"To cut a long story short, I was recruited. I suddenly found myself part of an organization I had never heard of before, headed by five men most members had never met before and potentially never would."

"*Did* you meet them?" Keith asks.

"Some," Winston says. "Not all."

"What was the organization called?" Charlie asks.

"The Order. The five men were the Quinquevirate—the small council who oversaw The Order."

"The Order? And what were their objectives?"

"Can't you tell from the name?" Winston says. "They want order. They want control. They want *power*. And they're starting with America. And then your country will be next, Charlie. After that? The world. America is just the beginning. They want everything."

"And they're getting that through hypnotherapy and electronics?" Keith says.

"No," Winston says. "They're going to get it through disinformation and chaos. And through the chaos, that's where they'll rise. It's already begun. Our new president, Zeke Turner, he's a member of The Order. All of the death and destruction that has recently occurred, it's their doing. They'll generate fear, so that next they can generate comfort and security. With comfort and security comes complacency, and with a complacent public, well, there's nothing to worry about, right? They won't even notice all the changes that have occurred right under their noses. They won't notice that the world they wake up in tomorrow is so different from the one they fell asleep in tonight.

"The three of you have thrown a wrench in the works, however. You've drawn the chaos out. No doubt it was supposed to be over and done with by now. Plain sailing into the brave new world envisioned by The Order."

"How long has The Order existed?" Keith says.

"Decades," Winston says. "Like all movements, it started small. It's grown over time. Gained influence whilst remaining under most people's radar. When I was recruited, they numbered in the dozens. Now, they're in the hundreds—perhaps even the thousands. Their numbers are hard to gauge. A lot of their members are so low down the totem, they don't truly understand what it is they're a part of. If they've shown promise, if they appear susceptible, they've been drip-fed just enough information to keep them on side. They've been rewarded, too. A healthy bonus that lets them know that life in this new world will be sweet, especially if they get in early enough. That's how it was for me. I was whispered platitudes, and my bank account was bloated, and as I got deeper and deeper into my work, I didn't truly understand what I was working toward until it was too late."

"What were you working toward?" Keith says. "And what's it got to do with Kayla?"

"You have to understand," Winston says, looking straight at Kayla. "I didn't know, not fully. I'm sorry, I truly am. At that time, I was just as brainwashed as you."

"Brainwashed?" Kayla says.

Ryan snorts.

"Sounds like you don't buy it," Charlie says. "Living out here in this cave with your old man, I reckon you've heard this story before. But you sound doubtful. Is he leaving something out?"

Ryan doesn't respond to Charlie. He speaks to his father. "You're such a fucking martyr."

Winston grits his teeth, but Kayla doesn't think he looks annoyed. He's upset. He's sad. He looks pained. "I'm sorry to you, too, Ryan," he says. "I don't expect you to ever accept my apologies, but I'll never stop saying them."

"What were you doing for The Order, Winston?" Keith says, trying to get the conversation back on track.

"I was helping them to create sleeper agents," Winston says. "Like Kayla. Young girls programmed to be living weapons. Young girls who can be sent out into the field to plant bombs, and either escape or disintegrate in the explosion and it doesn't matter either way, because there's a whole pool of new options to choose from. Living weapons who lie comatose between missions, waiting for the next one."

Kayla's throat is dry. Her jaw aches from her teeth clenching tightly together.

"Why?" Keith says.

"Chaos," Winston says. "I told you."

"But why girls?"

"Because they're unexpected. Because boys are anticipated. And mostly because someone at the top had a preference—I didn't make these choices. I didn't make the choice to always name the Prime Kayla Morrow. I don't why those decisions were made. All I knew how to do was my job. All I knew was how to make them susceptible to suggestion. I was part of a large team and we all played our part. We programmed these girls and prepared them for what lay ahead."

"And what *does* lie ahead?" Keith says. "What is this all in service of?"

"Haven't you been listening? *Control. Power.* Their army has started small, and The Order has used every soldier at their disposal—whether they were witting or not." He nods toward Kayla. "The Order grows bigger and bigger through fear and chaos and intimidation."

Keith starts to say something, but Kayla cuts him off. "Wait,

wait—what are you saying? Brainwashing—comatose between missions—this is all too much... My memories—"

"All implants," Winston says. "You have no memories, Kayla, not really. Nothing outside of what you have made for yourself in the last few weeks. There may be some flashes of things you saw between programming, but they won't be anything of real substance."

Kayla swallows. She feels like she's going to be sick. "My parents..."

Winston shakes his head. His face is grim. "I'm sorry. I don't know who your parents are. The two people you know as your parents, as your mother and father, they're no blood of yours. Your true parents are either long dead, or they wonder where you are every day—I'm afraid I don't know. I don't know where you came from. Either an orphanage or stolen from the street would be my best guess."

Kayla blinks. Her eyes are burning. She tries not to gag. Keith reaches out and squeezes her hand to comfort her.

"Jesus," Charlie says, staring at Winston. "You wanna try and sugarcoat it next time?"

Kayla gets to her feet and she paces. "What the—what the *fuck?*" she says. "All of my memories—my whole life—everything is a lie..." She freezes, realizing something. A hand covers her mouth. "I'm a *killer*. I...I planted bombs. I killed the vice-president..." She wheels on Winston. "How many?"

He blinks. "How many what?"

"How many people have I killed?"

"I don't know," Winston says. "I left The Order five years ago."

Ryan snorts. "*Left?*"

"We don't really have time for your family bullshit right now," Charlie says. "Can't you see the poor lass is having a crisis?"

Kayla's chest is tight. She's struggling to breathe. Keith notices. He gets off the cot and hurries to her, placing his hands on her shoulders. "It's okay," he says. "Try to calm. I get it, I do. Try to stay calm. Just breathe nice and easy, nice and slow. In through the nose, and out through the mouth. That's right, that's right, just like that. You're doing it. You're doing great." As she calms and she's able to breathe again, Keith wraps her in his arms and holds her close. "It's not your fault," he says, speaking low into her ear. "It had nothing to do with you. You didn't do a damn thing wrong. None of this is on you."

The front of Keith's shirt feels wet, and Kayla realizes she's crying. Keith strokes the back of her head. She's not sure how much time passes. Other than the hum of the generators, the cave is silent. She wonders if everyone is watching her or if they've turned away awkwardly, waiting for her to stop crying.

Charlie is first to make a sound. He clears his throat. "She knows things, though," he says. "It's not like she's a newborn. She's got at least school-level knowledge appropriate to her age."

"Taught by her handlers," Winston says. "AKA her adoptive parents. And then programmed to make her think she attended school, surrounded by other children her own age. Every lesson she can remember, she was in her home, likely locked away in the basement. That's where they're usually kept."

"How complete is the programming?" Keith says, and Kayla feels his words reverberating through his chest.

"What do you mean?"

"I mean that Kayla broke free of her conditioning, right?"

Winston is silent for a moment. Kayla lets go of Keith enough so she can turn and see the older man as he thinks, a finger curling around his chin.

"I'm not sure if 'broke free' would be the proper term," he says eventually. "I don't know what her programming was for the explosion in DC, but I would imagine it was to go either one of two ways—she was either supposed to die in the explosion or return to her handlers. But whichever it was, the programming should not have been broken."

"Could the explosion have knocked it loose?" Charlie says.

"It shouldn't have," Winston says. "But I suppose it's possible. Kayla doesn't look as though she experienced any severe head trauma, though. I'm not sure why you didn't return to your handlers."

"What about the song?" Kayla says. "What is it? What does it mean? You put everything else in my head, you must have put that there, too. What's it for? Is it just to drive me crazy?"

Winston frowns. "Song?"

"I have a song in my head," she says. "I can't remember the words, I can barely remember the tune, but it's there and I can't shake it out and I don't know what it is."

"I don't know about any song," Winston says. "You must have picked it up since you broke free."

"No," Kayla says, suddenly sure. She sees a flash—lying in a bedroom, stars twinkling on the ceiling cast by a projector in the corner, and she feels very small and very young, but safe and warm and happy, and a song, the song—but then it's gone. "If you got me when I was small, then no. The song came while I was brainwashed."

Winston doesn't say anything to this.

"Well," Charlie says, stepping forward. He raises the gun. "This all sounds pretty fucking awful. I reckon you're gonna need to give me a damn good reason why I shouldn't just shoot you where you stand."

Winston raises his hands. "I'm not with The Order anymore. I'll admit, I was a fool. I was blinded by what they told me—the promises they made, and the money they paid—but when I saw what was happening, the true cost of what they had planned… I left. I didn't know anyone was going to get hurt, and on such a scale. I left five years ago, and things have gotten worse since then."

"What did you *think* they were trying to do?" Keith says. "You thought they were brainwashing these girls to grow up and vote a particular way? You thought you were just manufacturing some Stepford Wives type deal?"

"It doesn't matter anymore," Winston says. "I know I was foolish, and I know what I did wrong, and believe me, I've paid for it."

Again, Ryan snorts.

"All right," Charlie says, "I think it's about time you tell us what this strained dynamic is all about."

"He loves the sound of his own voice so much," Ryan says, "*he* can tell you." He glares at his father.

Winston clenches his jaw. When he speaks, it's to the three, not to his son. His son already knows this story. "You can't just *leave* The Order," he says. "And I knew that. We were supposed to leave quickly and quietly. What I didn't know was that The Order must have been on to me. I don't know what I did to tip them off. I thought I was acting the same as always. I did my job. I gave nothing away. But they *knew*. And I think, looking back, that they had my house bugged. They heard me making plans to run away and live off-grid. I'd discuss it with my wife in bed. We were *whispering*. But they knew, and they came for us." He stops. He tries to continue, but he can't. Kayla watches his face. He looks like he's about to cry. He turns away and covers his eyes with a hand.

"He got away," Ryan says, finishing the story. "But my mom didn't." His lips are pursed. His face is sour. "They killed her. Then *he* turned up at my apartment, rambling—I couldn't get any sense out of him. He dragged me out of my home and to the car and we've been on the run ever since. He couldn't tell me what had happened to Mom until a couple of days later. We all lost a lot that night. We all lost our lives."

"I think I need to go outside," Kayla says. "I need air."

"There won't be much air," Ryan says. "It's gonna be hot."

"I don't care," Kayla says. "I need to get out of here for a while."

"Do you want to be alone?" Keith says.

Kayla nods. "I think I do."

She heads toward the mouth of the cave, her arms wrapped tight around herself. As she goes, she can still hear the men talking behind her. Winston is silent, but she hears Ryan speaking to Keith and Charlie. "The three of you have anywhere else to be? We don't have more beds, but we can work something out for you to stay. Believe it or not, we don't get many visitors."

Then Kayla is too far to hear. She reaches the mouth of the cave and she steps out into the sun. The air is thick and hot. She feels sweat burst on her skin. She doesn't care. She leans against the side of the cave wall, her arms still folded. She closes her eyes and breathes deep. Her mind races with memories. Fake memories. She sees the faces of her parents—her 'parents'—and wonders if they're real. Is that what they really looked like? Are their faces just another implant?

Kayla feels tears run down her cheeks. Her body shudders. Her legs are weak. She slides down and draws her knees up to her chest. She covers her face with her arms. She cries. She doesn't try to hold back the tears. It doesn't matter if she cries. Nothing matters anymore. Nothing matters. Nothing is real. Her whole life is a lie.

She's a killer.

She's a weapon.

She's nothing. She's barely even a person.

12

Jack is sleeping. It's still early evening, but they sleep in shifts to keep watch. Georgia sits out on the porch. The sky is light, but it's gradually darkening. In the far distance, through the trees, Georgia can see its golden edges as the sun goes down.

Jack's Springfield hunting rifle is propped against the cabin wall beside her, within easy reach. Georgia listens to the woods around her. She can hear the occasional rustle of branches and leaves—the darting of small animals, and the landing of birds, but nothing big enough to alarm her.

It was raining earlier, and the smells of damp earth and moist greenery is thick in the air. She breathes it deep. It's peaceful out here. She can understand why Jack likes it.

She's known Jack nearly all of her life, whether she's been aware of it or not. She's certainly known him as long as she's been Georgia Caruso. And twelve years ago, when she was still Kayla Morrow, she knew him then, too. Exceptshe didn't *know* him, not really. As Kayla Morrow, she was barely aware of anyone around her. Jack himself has filled in some blanks since then. Has told her how they first met when she was nine, before she went on her first mission. It was a test run. Her first time out in the field. They'd been training her for four years at that point. Testing her programming. Testing her limits. Making sure she was completely under their control. Making sure their investments had been well placed.

Her first mission was theft. "They wanted to make sure you could get in and out without being detected," Jack told her. "They sent you in to steal some documents. I don't remember what they were pertaining to anymore—it was a long time now and it doesn't matter anymore. But you broke into that facility—shimmied your little body in through an air vent—and you avoided detection. You picked the lock of a filing cabinet, you got the documents wanted, and you got them out. They were very pleased."

They, Georgia thinks now. Always *they*. She's never truly known who she's up against. She's not so sure Jack knows who all of their enemies are, either.

When she was still a sleeper, Jack was her handler. They ran things differently back then. She had her 'parents,' and she had her handler. Jack has told her that now the 'parents' double as the handlers. It was still early days not just for Georgia, but for the whole operation. Working out the kinks. So the 'parents' dealt with her day to day, and Jack took her on missions.

"Did we speak?" Georgia has asked him.

"Speak? No. You didn't speak, not when you were engaged in a mission. You sat like a zombie, eyes forward. Hell, you barely even *blinked*."

"So, we didn't have any kind of a connection?"

"I guess not."

"Then why did you save me?"

Jack was silent for a while when she asked this. He wasn't thinking about his answer. He already knew his answer, Georgia could tell. His brow didn't furrow. He didn't stare off into the distance. He just looked back at her, with a sadness in his eyes. Remembering that night, more than likely. Remembering what happened. "Because you were still just a kid," he said. "And because I'd known you since you were an even smaller kid. And because it was *wrong*. You deserved some kind of a life. And I'd had doubts mounting in my mind for a while about The Order. About what they were trying to accomplish. When they gave the word what they wanted done with you… Well. I guess that was my tipping point."

"Do you regret leaving?"

Jack didn't hesitate. "No."

Georgia looks through the trees while she remembers. Her memories may wander, but her focus remains sharp. She stays aware. She's always aware.

She stands and twists side to side, stretching out her spine. The light is fading, and it won't be present for much longer. She picks up the rifle and does a quick sweep of the immediate vicinity. It gives her a chance to stretch her legs, too. She doesn't like to stay static for too long. It's important to remain limber. To always be prepared to jump into action at a moment's notice.

She returns to the porch and takes a seat. Again, her memories roam. They return to twelve years ago, when she was sixteen, soon to be seventeen. Again, she doesn't remember most of this. The information has been relayed to her via Jack. She has flashes of memory, but they're weak and blurry, and influenced by what she's been told. Like a newborn opening its eyes for the first time. The images don't make sense to her.

Sixteen going on seventeen, and her programming was beginning to falter. Her will trying to impose itself, perhaps. Jack tells her that has been rectified since. The programming goes deeper. It is regularly updated, and checked. If any signs of disruption occur, the girl is immediately removed from the field. Georgia knows what this means—the girl is eliminated. Destroyed, like a dangerous animal.

That had been the plan for her. She was becoming a liability. They couldn't send her out into the field anymore. She was slower than she used to be. Unfocussed. She was waking up.

There was no more use for her. Her 'parents' were supposed to put her down. And they would have, too, except Jack knew of the plans.

Georgia's most vivid memory from that time is of rain. Of being carried like a child much younger and smaller than she really was. Of Jack's face. Her first *true* memory of Jack.

Her thoughts are interrupted. She hears a sound, and it isn't an animal. A whirring sound, coming closer.

Georgia grabs the rifle and drops to a low crouch, raising the scope to her eye and swinging it in the direction of the approaching noise. It's high. She looks for it through the trees in the dying light. It comes closer, and closer, and as it does, it gets louder. It's taking its time, though. It's searching the area. Scouring the ground below.

She spots it. It's practically above the cabin. A drone.

Georgia doesn't hesitate. She shoots it down. The drone jolts and turns on its side. It crashes to the ground less than ten feet away from the porch. Georgia hurries over and smashes what remains with the butt of the rifle. She sees that she managed to destroy the camera when she shot it. Her bullet tore through it. There's no way of telling whether the camera was able to spot her or the cabin before she shot it down, but that doesn't matter. It saw enough. Whoever is flying it knows enough. If they're here looking for Georgia and Jack, they know where they are.

Behind her, the porch door opens. Jack has been awakened by the shot. He's alert. Concerned. "What is it?" he says, unable to see the drone, blocked by Georgia's body. "What you shooting at?"

Georgia steps aside so he can see the drone. She looks through the woods, and listens for approach. There's no one coming, not yet. There are no other drones in the air. She turns back to Jack. His face is grim.

"We've been found," Georgia says.

13

The day has passed in the cave. Charlie and Keith stayed to one side for most of it, discussing what to do next.

"I'll ask him directly, but I don't get the impression this guy knows where The Order are holing up," Keith said.

Charlie nodded. "If we want this over, we need to find them. We need to find the people running this thing. Just going to the news with this far-fetched story isn't going to be enough. We're gonna have to bring it down from the top."

Keith looked toward the cave's entrance. Kayla was still out there. She stayed out there for a long time. They left her alone. She had a lot to process. "We'll stay here tonight," Keith said. "Kayla needs some downtime. In the morning, we'll figure out what we do next."

It was hours before Kayla rejoined the rest of them in the cave. She hasn't said a word since then. Keith has offered her food and water, and she's taken them, but he didn't try to force her into conversation.

Winston and Ryan have stayed separate. Charlie has kept an eye on them both. Ryan has spent most of the day on his cot. He's read a book. Something by Raymond Chandler. Charlie spotted a small case with a dozen tatty paperbacks on it, most of them crime fiction.

Winston has sat at his desk, at his computers. At times his fingers have ran over the keys, punching in codes, his cursor running over the screen. Charlie tried to watch what he's been doing. There was a lot of distance between them so Charlie couldn't make out the details, but it looked like Winston was looking up news headlines, and searching sites Charlie had never seen before. The dark web, perhaps? Other than that, he sat and watched the security cameras he had scattered and hidden around the surrounding area. The motion sensors have gone off a few times. Whenever they have, Ryan has sat up and reached for his rifle until Winston has checked the source of the noise and then signaled to him that it's all right. Winston never said what caused the noises, but sometimes Charlie could see the creatures on the screen—usually coyotes, and a couple of times smaller animals that he didn't recognize.

It's getting late now. Charlie is feeling antsy after being cooped up all day. Keith comes to see him. "I'm going to try and get some rest," he says. "And I'll suggest to Kayla that she does the same, but I don't know how she'll take it. Are you okay to keep watch?"

"Aye," Charlie says. "I'll keep an eye on these two."

"You don't trust them?"

"Do *you*?"

"Can't get a bearing on them just yet," Keith says. "But I'm open to giving them a chance to prove themselves. It's tiring not being able to trust *any*one."

Charlie nods but says, "Better safe than sorry. I'm gonna find a spot and pretend to sleep. Give them a chance to reveal themselves, but I'll be watching."

"Good thinking." Keith holds up a fist and Charlie bumps it, and then Keith goes to talk softly to Kayla.

Ryan hands them some blankets they can use to rest on. Charlie balls his up and lies down in a corner opposite Keith and Kayla, where he has a clear view and can keep an eye on both Winston and Ryan. He rests his head on the balled-up blanket, laces his fingers across his stomach, and watches through half-closed eyes. The Glock is in his waistband at the front, within easy reach. Ryan has returned to his cot, and his book. Winston hasn't left his computers. Charlie watches him, slowing his breathing so it seems like he's sleeping.

He's careful not to actually fall asleep. He squeezes his interlocked fingers to remain alert. He balls and wriggles his toes inside his boots to keep his blood flowing. He flits his eyes between Ryan and Winston, watching them closely through his lashes. He looks toward Keith and Kayla, too, and sees that they're both fast asleep. Poor Kayla is emotionally drained and physically exhausted. She's had a long day. He can't begin to imagine what she's going through.

Charlie will give Keith a couple more hours and then he'll wake him and he can stay on watch. A couple more hours is long enough to see whether Winston and Ryan are up to anything. By then, they should both be asleep, too.

Looking from father to son, Charlie becomes aware that Ryan is watching him. He's put the book down, and is staring intently. Charlie doesn't move. He stays cool. Keeps his breathing the same. He doesn't close his eyes any tighter. He watches Ryan right back.

A couple of minutes pass. Charlie doesn't budge. He can see the doubt on Ryan's face. He's checking that Charlie is asleep. Nothing has made him suspicious that Charlie is pretending. He shifts his attention toward Keith and then Kayla, watching them both for just as long. Charlie cuts his eyes left, looks toward Winston. Winston is still at his computer. He's not watching anyone. He leans back in his chair and rubs at his eyes, then yawns. He's tired.

Ryan gets off his cot and goes to his father. Winston hears his approach and turns to him, but he remains in his seat. Ryan lowers his voice when he speaks, but Charlie can hear him.

"You're getting us too involved," he says.

Winston looks at his son for a while before he responds. "You knew what was going to happen. I directed them here."

"And I tried to talk you out of *that*," Ryan says. "But you went ahead and did it anyway. You said you would answer their questions and send them on their way, but I get the feeling you're not going to send them on their way. You're going to drag us in deeper."

"You invited them to spend the night."

"That doesn't mean I want to go where they're going next."

"We don't know where they're going to go next."

"Yeah, but you're going to try and help them find their way, aren't you?"

Winston doesn't respond.

"That's as much answer as I need."

No one speaks for a while, and Charlie expects Ryan to turn and return to his cot. Before he can, Winston says, "I'm sorry about your mother, Ryan." His voice is very low, and not just because they have sleeping guests. It's pained. "More than you could ever know. She was *my* wife. I..." He almost chokes up. He swallows hard before he continues. "I saw her die. I saw them kill her, and I wanted to give up then and there, let them shoot me down, too, but I didn't—I *couldn't*—because they knew I'd spoken to *you*, too, and I knew they'd come for you next. I miss her, Ryan. I miss her more and more every day. All that keeps me going is the hope that one day I can make them *pay*—that I can make them suffer for what they did."

Ryan opens his mouth, but before he can speak, one of the

computers makes a sound behind Winston. It's an alert, but it's not the same kind of noise as the motion sensors.

"What is that?" Ryan says.

Winston turns to the computer and presses some keys. Ryan is in the way and Charlie can't see what comes up on the screen. "It's Jack," Winston says.

Charlie gets to his feet, Glock raised. Winston and Ryan both turn to him, startled. "Who's Jack?"

Ryan has left the rifle by his cot. He and Winston raise their hands. "You're awake," Ryan says. "Have you been listening to us?"

"Of course I've been fucking listening," Charlie says. Keeping them covered, he edges his way toward Keith, tapping him with his foot to wake him. He kicks him harder than he intends but Keith comes bolt upright without complaint. He's on his feet, taking in the scene. "Who's Jack? I'm not going to ask again."

"Just calm down," Winston says, "you don't need to be alarmed. I'll read the message to you. Jack is a friend. He's in the same boat as the rest of us."

Keith wakes Kayla.

"You better read it quick," Charlie says.

"It's a warning," Winston says. "He's been hiding out—I don't know where, and he doesn't know where we are, either—but he's been found, and he's warning us. He says he's been careful, but they've still managed to track him down, so he's telling us they could be coming for *us*, too."

Charlie looks at the computer screen beyond them. "Move over," he says. "Keith, I'll keep them covered. You go read it."

Keith goes to the computers when Winston and Ryan have moved to the side, hands still raised. He reads it then turns back to Charlie. "It's like they said," he says.

"I would have woken you and told you," Winston says.

Charlie ignores him. "Are you keeping a close eye on your cameras? Is anyone coming for us?"

Winston returns to the computers. "None of the alarms have sounded," he says. He goes through the cameras. "I don't see anything out of the ordinary." He turns back, remaining in the chair. "But Jack is right. If they've managed to find him, we should be worried. We need to be extra vigilant, and we should probably get on the road soon."

"And by we, you mean *all* of us," Charlie says. "I heard everything."

"I was hoping for more time to convince you all that our sticking together is our best option."

Ryan glares at his father.

Charlie and Keith exchange glances. "No one's coming yet," Keith says. "We've got a little time, and we're open to suggestions as to where we go next. I figure if anyone here is gonna have a good idea as to our next destination, it's you." He nods at Winston.

"This is pointless," Ryan says. "There's nowhere to fucking go. The Order are a secret to *themselves*. We'd just be running around on a wild goose chase, wasting time on the road. If they've found Jack, we need to find somewhere new to hide out. The three of you can do whatever you want." He turns to his father. "This is because you contacted them, it has to be. We were never at any risk before you did that. Did you tell Jack what you were doing?"

Winston doesn't answer. He's thinking. Charlie watches them both.

Ryan throws up his hands. "Jesus Christ," he says, exasperated. "Just tell them you don't have any idea where to go next."

Winston bites his lip. He looks at Kayla, still blinking herself awake. "There might be someone we can go see."

14

Georgia was ready to flee, but Jack surprised her by running back inside the cabin. "What are you doing?" she said, following him in.

"First of all, I'm checking the cameras," Jack said without turning. He checked the security footage. "No one's coming yet. I'm gonna start writing a message, ready to send as soon as they turn up."

"Send to who?"

"An ally. I've mentioned we have allies."

"We're going to have to talk more in-depth about our allies later." Georgia watched the cameras over his shoulder while he typed. Her eyes flickered from screen to screen. No one appeared. She ground her jaw, stopping herself from bouncing on her heels, feeling agitated. They weren't being proactive. She didn't like it. "You're being very leisurely about this, Jack."

"I'm not taking anything leisurely," Jack said. "You know me better than that. We need to be sure the people flying that drone are our enemies. People fly drones recreationally. I know it's unlikely, and especially at this time of night, but we have to at least entertain the possibility. If it's our enemies, and they've managed to find us, there's a risk they've tracked down everyone else, too. As soon as they show themselves, I hit send on this message."

"As soon as they appear, we're stuck here fighting them."

Jack looked at her. "Then we'll make them regret coming to find us."

Georgia doesn't like it. She waits out on the porch, the rifle in her hands, ready to swing up and use when and if necessary. She stares through the darkness. Her eyes have adjusted, up to a point. She can only see so far before it's nothing but inky blackness. She tenses at every slight sound. While she waited, she brought out more weaponry from Jack's armory. An M16 and a couple of AR15s are standing nearby.

Jack appears beside her. He's wearing night vision goggles. He holds a pair out for her. "They're coming in hot," he says. "We've got about five minutes."

Georgia nods and slips on the goggles. "How many?"

"I counted two dozen, but I'm looking to reduce those numbers." He holds up a switch. "Brace yourself. Soon as they're close enough, I'm setting it off."

Georgia crouches in the corner of the porch, rifle raised and resting on the railing. She doesn't look through the sight, not yet. She'll need to lift the goggles up to do that. For now, she looks out into the trees. She can see movement, coming closer. The men coming are slowing down, now that their target is near.

Jack is crouching at the other end of the porch. "Fire in the hole," he says, then presses the switch.

Georgia closes her eyes to avoid being blinded by the flare of the explosion. She hears it, and then the screams of the men as the bombs planted at the base of the trees blow up in their faces. She opens her eyes and quickly scans the area, eyeing who is still standing and who has fallen, then lifts the goggles and raises the scope. The men are dressed like they're black ops. They wear

89

night vision goggles, too. She picks them off, aiming for those who are standing first.

She lands three headshots before they start falling back and heading for cover. Some of them fire back wildly and without aim, but their bullets all fall short. Georgia turns her attention to the men caught up in the explosion, the ones who are still living. She ignores the ones who are badly injured and trying to crawl away. There are two who have propped themselves up and are trying to get to their feet. They're shouldering their weapons. Georgia puts them both back down. Two more headshots.

Jack is no longer beside her. He's left the cabin porch, armed with the M16 and one of the AR15s slung over his shoulder. She hears him out in the woods, opening fire on men he has seen approaching from the side via the security cameras.

Georgia crouches low and moves, slinging the other AR-15 over her own shoulder, then leaves the porch and catches up with Jack. He's stopped firing and is waiting for her to join him. He looks down at a monitor in his hand, showing the various cameras dotted through the woods.

"They're regrouping," he says. "We've caught them by surprise."

"They won't regroup for long," Georgia says, sweeping the area with her goggles. "They'll attack again soon."

"Let's get moving. There's a few of them have tried to get around the back of us, but if we head north-east we should avoid them."

"What about the cabin? They'll search it."

"I'm going to blow it," Jack says, already walking.

Georgia follows, continuing to scan the area. "What do you mean? When did you plant the bombs?"

He chuckles. "They've always been there. Under the floorboards."

Georgia blinks. "You didn't tell me about *them*."

"What difference would it make? I was comfortable enough walking around on top of them."

"A heads-up would be nice."

Jack ignores her. "Come on. Let's pick up the pace."

They start jogging through the woods, aiming to avoid another firefight. Jack continues to watch his monitor. When they're clear, he presses the detonator for the cabin. It erupts in a fireball that reaches up into the sky, beyond the tops of the trees. Georgia can feel the heat of it.

"Jesus," she says. "That wasn't a small amount of explosive."

"Had to be sure everything was destroyed," Jack says. "Nothing left behind for them to sift through."

"You weren't worried about setting the rest of the woods ablaze?"

"This close to Seattle?" Jack snorts, digging a heel into the moist ground to illustrate his point. "Not really."

15

"Who?" Kayla says, returning Winston's gaze. "Why are you looking at me like that? Who can we go and see?"

Winston turns away from her. He takes a deep breath.

"Are you going to answer her?" Charlie says.

"I'm not sure the young lady is fully prepared to join us," Winston says. "I'm not sure she can go where I'm about to suggest."

"She stays with us," Keith says.

"It's her father," Winston says. "Her 'father.' Derek Morrow —or whatever his name really is. I know where he is. I've tracked him."

Kayla feels a fist squeezing in her chest. She clenches her jaw and swallows. In her mind, she sees her father, laughing as he throws her overhead, the sunlight streaming through the trees in the park—a fake memory. She shows him a picture she's drawn of the two of them and Mom, and he proudly sticks it onto the refrigerator—a fake memory. She sees herself wrapped up against winter cold, with hats and scarves and a thick coat, and her father holds her mittened hand as she kicks through the brown and red leaves, and splashes in the muddy puddles—another fake memory. All fake. All implanted. All dreamt-up scenarios of an idealized, picturesque, fictional childhood.

In all of these memories, she is young, so much younger. A small child. She tries to remember things more recent, from her teenage years. Nothing as standout. The three of them, as a family, sitting around the dinner table. Or in a car, she in the back, a long journey but she doesn't know where they're going. She tries to remember a single conversation. She can't.

In the back of her head, the tune amplifies. A song with words she can't remember. Notes she cannot align. The noise of it fills her skull, threatens to overwhelm her.

"What do you mean?" she says. "You know where he is, right now? What about—what about my…" She hesitates. "What about the woman I thought was my mother?"

"I know where the man is," Winston says. "After things went south in DC, I knew they'd have been told to disperse. I was able to track Derek, but Heather—Heather Morrow, your 'mother'— was more elusive. I don't know where she's gone."

Georgia feels like she's spinning. She looks around the cave, into all of the four faces turned her way. Winston is grim, but his son watches her with interest, curious of her reaction. Charlie's face is blank, unreadable. Keith, however, is more empathetic.

"Kayla," he says, his voice soft. "This is a good lead for us. But if you don't want to see him, that's understandable. We can find somewhere for you to hide out. If you want, I'll stay with you. Charlie can go and talk to him."

Kayla shakes her head. "No. If we go to see him, I'm going, too."

"Not so fast," Charlie says. "The doctor here didn't think to tell us this sooner—is there anyone else he knows the location of? Anyone that might be pertinent? Mate, I don't wanna have to keep asking what you know and what you're holding back. I don't want another day to pass where you suddenly click your fingers and realize you forgot to tell us something relevant."

Winston holds up his hands. "It's only been a day. I told you everything relevant at that time—everything I could think of. The location of Derek Morrow would have occurred to me sooner rather than later."

"*Is* there anyone else?" Keith says.

Kayla doesn't care if there's anyone else. She wants to go and see her—she wants to go and see Derek Morrow, or whatever his real name is.

"I don't know where anyone else is," Winston says. "Only Derek."

"How were you able to track him?" Keith says.

"Hacking into security cameras," Winston says. "I followed him that way. He wasn't as careful as the others I've tried to track—and I've tried to track them all. A point came when Derek disappeared into the wilderness, but Ryan took a drive out there and was able to locate him."

"You've been *out* there?" Keith says. "You've seen where he's staying?"

"I was careful," Ryan says. "He never saw me."

"We know where he is," Winston says, "but there was no worth in approaching him at that point. Better we knew he was there for if a moment came and that information could prove useful."

"Uh-huh, well, here's a question for you," Charlie says, "since it seems like we might need to anticipate anything that might be of worth. What do you know about this ARO I keep hearing about? They got the blame for what happened in DC, but we know it wasn't them. Are they on the same page as The Order? Are they rivals?"

"The Anti-Right Outreach?" Winston says with a smirk. "Oh

yes, I know all about them. To answer your question, they're very much on the same page as The Order."

"In what way?"

"In the way that they don't exist. They *are* The Order. The ARO are a false flag. Fictional scapegoats. A bogeyman to blame all of America's problems on."

"They've made up a fall guy?" Keith says.

"Exactly."

"What's the endgame?"

"They'll keep the ARO in existence as long as they're useful—"

"I don't care about any of this," Kayla says, unable to contain herself any longer. "*Where* is Derek Morrow? Wherever he is, *that's* where we're going, and I'm coming with."

They all look at her again. Their expressions aren't so pitying this time.

"All right," Keith says, placing a firm hand on her shoulder and then looking around at everyone else. "We go to see Derek. Everyone agree?"

Everyone does.

16

Shira sets out from the apartment in the early morning, before the neighborhood has come fully alive. Before the road is too busy. Before there are too many people on the sidewalks.

She wears a baseball cap, the peak pulled down low to obscure her face. She's made a mental note of all security cameras in the area, from the apartment building to the supermarket, and she avoids them all. She has to go far out of her way and down a couple of back alleys to avoid some cameras, but she won't take any risks.

There are cameras outside and inside the supermarket, of course. These are unavoidable. Shira keeps her face lowered as she makes her way around the store, filling her basket with supplies for Noam and herself. She pays cash, keeping conversation with the clerk to a minimum. The clerks here are disinterested, just making it through the day, praying the place isn't going to get robbed on their shift. The lack of interest from the staff and the lack of conversation is one of the reasons she comes here.

She bags her groceries and leaves the store. Keeps her head down until she's reached the end of the block, out of view of the nearest camera. From here, she takes a subtle look around. She checks the road and the sidewalk behind her.

Someone gets out of a car parked on the opposite side of the road. Shira watches out the corner of her eye as she crosses over and turns a corner. There are two men, both of them dark-skinned, shaven heads, and broad, wearing turtlenecks and dark jeans. Shira can't tell if they're armed. One of them looks at her, and Shira keeps her eyes straight. She can feel him watching her. She doesn't quicken her pace, as much as her legs will her to do so. It's important to stay casual. She gets around the corner and keeps walking. She listens for steps behind her, listens for if they follow her around the corner or go straight on.

She hears them. They're following. She grits her teeth but doesn't turn. Looks straight ahead. She has to stay calm. Her mind is racing, but she manages to marshal her thoughts. She needs to make a plan.

The two men are following. They're holding back, keeping an inconspicuous distance. They're bigger than Shira, and outweigh her by a hundred pounds each. There's an alley up ahead, over the road and on her right, part of her route to avoid security cameras. When she reaches the alley, she needs to make a decision. She can run, or she can fight. If she runs, they could gun her down. If they want to take her alive, they could easily run her down. If she chooses to fight—well, she'll have a better idea of what she's up against when that moment comes. If she slows in the alley, she could catch them by surprise. She's armed, her handgun concealed under her jacket, but it would be best to keep things as quiet as possible. Throw the grocery bag in the face of one to momentarily distract him, and kick the other between the legs as hard as she can. That should put him down. Shira is trained in Krav Maga. She wonders if these two men are trained. She wonders what they know.

She crosses the road. She turns her head only to check the

road for traffic. She glimpses them in her peripheral vision. They cross, too. Shira takes a deep breath. Braces herself. Things are about to get violent.

She reaches the alley. She pauses to readjust her grip on the grocery bag. To anyone watching, it's a regular move, just someone struggling with the weight of their groceries. In reality, she's shifting the weight more to her right hand—her throwing hand. Readying herself to launch the bag and its contents into the closest man's face.

When she starts walking again, she's slowing. Luring them in. Drawing them closer. She can hear their footsteps. Soon, they'll reach the entrance to the alleyway. They'll be right behind her. She listens.

A car goes by on the road, and drowns out the sound of their steps. Shira curses silently. Unable to hear, they could be gaining on her. She spins on her heel, ready to launch the bag.

The alleyway is empty. The two men have not followed. She returns to the entrance and peers out. The two men are walking away down the sidewalk. Neither of them looks back. Shira watches until they're out of sight.

It takes a moment to decompress. Her limbs and tendons are coiled, ready for action. She breathes deep, easing out the tightness. She walks slowly the rest of the way down the alley, giving her blood pressure a chance to lower, and waiting for the tension to calm. She doesn't let go of it entirely. She can't. It's impossible. It's a part of her now. It keeps her alive.

She gets back to the apartment. She dumps the grocery bag on the counter and, before she empties it, she goes straight to the windows and checks the streets below.

Noam is at his laptop. He looks like he's showered while she was out. He watches her. "Everything okay?"

"I'm fine," she says. "There was just a moment I thought I was being followed, but it turned out to be a false alarm."

"It's easy for us to become *too* paranoid in our current situation."

Shira goes to the kitchen. "I don't believe there's any such thing," she says and blows air through pursed lips.

"Before you do that," Noam says, seeing her reaching for the grocery bag, "I have something to show you. I'm not sure yet, but it could potentially be of interest."

Shira goes to him. "What is it?"

Noam sets up footage, pausing it to explain before he plays it. "There was a private jet coming into Dulles airport. Its departure information wasn't available, but I've got my ways. I traced its route back, and that's where I started to find that I wasn't just wasting my time. That's when things started to get interesting. The flight departed from Newcastle, England."

"Newcastle?" Shira says. "Isn't that where Charlie Carter's from?"

"I double-checked to be sure, and yes, he is."

"Okay, but that doesn't necessarily mean anything."

"Perhaps not, but that's where this footage becomes important. And you need to remember, I've been working backwards. I came across this footage before I knew where the jet was coming from."

Shira stares at the screen. The paused footage looks like it's been taken from a security camera. She can see the small jet in the foreground. There's a man standing at the foot of the ladder coming down from its open hatch. The man wears a suit, looks like private security. Leaning closer to the screen, Shira can see he's wearing an ear piece. He's likely armed, a concealed handgun in a shoulder holster.

"Okay," she says. "Hit play."

Noam does.

An armored truck pulls into view. The guard at the foot of the stairs was watching its arrival. As the truck stops, figures appear at the top of the steps. Two men, dressed the same as the man standing guard. They're wearing ear pieces, too. Between them is a smaller figure. It looks female. The two men each have a hand upon a shoulder. The female's hands are cuffed in front of her, and her head is obscured with a dark towel that hangs down low, past her stomach, only her cuffed hands poking out the bottom. They bundle her along and put her into the back of the armored truck. The three suited men climb into the back with her. A moment later, the truck pulls away.

"Do you know where they go?" Shira says.

"Not yet," Noam says. "But I'm working on it."

"Do you know who she is?"

"I'm working on *that*, too. And I'm trying to find who she's been taken by—there's no guaranteeing she's been taken by the same people we're looking into."

"It would be a big coincidence at this time that someone from Newcastle has been brought to America in cuffs, concealed, and transported in the back of an armored truck," Shira says. "My guess is that she's someone important to Charlie Carter. Is he married? A girlfriend? Does he have sisters? Hell, it could be his mother."

"He's married," Noam says.

"Then maybe look into her whereabouts first."

Noam nods. "I'm on it."

17

It's raining, but it's not just the rainwater that drips onto Georgia. There is blood, too. It lands on her face. She can taste it. It gets into her eyes and blurs her vision. Blinking it out, she looks up into Jack's grim face. He's looking ahead, escaping, carrying her in his arms. She's a small child. Except, that's not right. She wasn't a child. She was a teenage girl.

But Jack has her, and they flee into the night, and into the rain. It washes the blood from them both. But it's so wet that Jack's grip on her begins to slip. He trips on the wet ground and loses his hold on her. He falls, and Georgia is flying through the air, getting smaller and smaller, younger and younger, becoming a baby—

Georgia wakes with a start. Jack is driving beside her. They're in a truck he had stashed and fully fueled outside of the woods. He had vehicles parked and hidden at various exit points. The truck was the nearest to their escape route. They've been driving through the night. Jack has let her sleep. So far, there has been no direction in mind. Their priority has been getting clear.

"It's morning," Georgia says, narrowing her eyes as she looks out the windshield. She shifts her weight in her chair. Their weapons are stuffed behind their seats, and she feels them sticking into her back. "You let me sleep a long time."

"You must have needed it," Jack says, watching the road. "You didn't get to take your shift resting last night, and then we were real busy."

"Where are we right now?" The road is thickly lined with trees on either side. Georgia can't see any vehicles ahead or behind them. It's a quiet area. A backroad.

"We just passed into Oregon about an hour ago."

"Is there anything for us in Oregon?"

"Just passing through. Keeping on the move while we figure out our next move."

"What have you got so far?"

"Still thinking. We're at a delicate crossroads. We can't just go back into hiding. We're beyond that now. Seems to me The Order are heading into their endgame." He takes a deep breath. "Did you sleep well?"

"I had a dream," Georgia says. "Except, it was more of a memory."

"Oh yeah?"

"The night you rescued me."

Jack doesn't say anything to this. She glances at him, sees him staring straight ahead. His jaw is tight.

They drive in silence for a while. Jack looks ahead, blinking against the rising light.

"I can drive if you want to sleep," Georgia says.

Jack doesn't respond. He clears his throat. "Your dream," he says, surprising her, "if it was of that night, it sounds like more of a nightmare."

"I was a child in it," Georgia says. "In the dream, I mean. That's pretty weird, right?"

Jack chuckles. "You were light, but you weren't *child* light."

"At the end of my dream, you also fell over. I don't remember you falling over."

Jack shakes his head. "I didn't drop you. Dreams don't mean anything. They're just dreams. That's all. You weren't a child and I didn't drop you. People pay too much attention to their dreams."

Georgia pauses. "We've never really talked about that night."

"What's there to talk about?"

"I only have vague memories of it. All I really remember is looking up into your face. While you carried me out into the rain. And there was blood, but it wasn't either of ours. That's what I remember. I can barely remember my parents—"

"They weren't your parents."

"I know that. They were my *handlers*. Same as you were a handler. But I barely remember their faces, and I spent *years* with them."

"Years under hypnotic suggestion."

"I don't understand why you're being so standoffish."

They drive in silence for a while before Jack sighs. "They weren't your parents, but they were my friends. I'd known them for years. I knew them before you were born."

Georgia did not know this. She stares at Jack, surprised, feeling her eyes widen.

He doesn't say anything for so long that she doesn't think he's going to follow up. When he eventually does, she listens intently. "Your programming was waning. You know that. You were outgrowing it. I've heard they've improved on it since, but who knows? Nothing lasts forever, and nothing is perfect. But back then, when it started to happen to you and you weren't as suggestible anymore, they knew it was time to move on. Otherwise you were just going to become a liability. Word came down that you were to be disposed of. I couldn't just let that happen. I was already pulling away from the organization. What they were doing hadn't sat right with me for a very long time. Your death sentence meant that all of a sudden it was time for me to make my move."

"You must have come straight to the house," Georgia says.

He nods. "I did. I had no idea whether you'd still be alive when I got there. It was a storm that night. I drove so fast I was sure I was going to skid off the road, that I was going to kill myself before I had a chance to save you. But I didn't. I made it. They were taking you down into the basement when I got there. They were surprised to see me, bursting through the door like I did, already soaked from head to foot just from running from my car to the house."

"I don't remember you getting there," Georgia says. "I remember them trying to take me down into the basement. I was phasing in and out. Like you said, their hold was waning."

"They'd gotten the basement ready," Jack says. "Lay plastic sheeting all across the ground. Do you remember them setting that up?"

"No," Georgia says, feeling sick at the thought, despite how long ago it was now.

"Keep it all nice and clean," Jack says. "They weren't armed. Not yet. Their gun was down in the basement, too. I wasn't armed, either. I've thought about that a lot. I should've gone with a weapon, but I didn't."

"Why didn't you?"

"That's what I've thought about. That's what I've wondered. I think a part of me hoped I could have reasoned with them. That I could have talked them out of doing what they were planning to. That maybe they'd see things my way. Realize how wrong it all felt. Maybe they'd even come with me—with *us*. As soon as I saw the look in their eyes, I knew they wouldn't. They were too far gone. They were going to kill you, and there was nothing I could say to stop them. But I still tried,"—he pauses—"didn't do any good."

Georgia doesn't speak. She wants to hear what happened next. It's a mystery that has always eluded her. Of course, she *knows* the broad strokes of what occurred. She knows the two people who portrayed her fake parents died. She doesn't know how. She doesn't know what happened. She won't ask Jack to continue. If he wants to tell her, that's up to him.

He doesn't speak for a while. He drives. The only sound is the engine. "I have another vehicle near here," he says. "Another ten miles or so. It won't take us long. So long as no one's found it and vandalized it, we'll swap out and keep going."

"Do you have many more cars stashed?"

He shakes his head. "That'll be the last one. After that, we need to decide where we're going next." He clears his throat and sighs. "I can tell you're waiting for me to continue. About that night from your dream."

"Only if you want to."

"There's not much more to say. You remember their names, don't you?"

"Only what you've told me," Georgia says. "Bruce and Tilly."

"Those were their real names. They weren't fake names or code names or anything like that. Well, Bruce came at me. Tilly tried to hurry you down into the basement so she could finish what they'd started. Bruce grabbed a kitchen knife out of the rack and he charged. I took the knife off him and I...I killed him. It didn't take long. And then I ran down into the basement as quickly as I could. Tilly hadn't reached the gun yet. She was nearly at it, though. Do you know what happened?"

"What do you mean?"

"Do you remember what you did?"

Georgia frowns. "No?"

"You stuck a foot out. You tripped her. The rest of you stayed perfectly still. Your face didn't show a damn thing. Another sign of the programming failing. You tripped her up and I caught up to her before she could get back up and get at the gun. She wouldn't just give up. She jumped at me. We fought. I don't even know how it happened, but…but the next thing I knew, the knife was in her stomach." He grunts and runs a hand down his face. "And then I grabbed you and I ran. Out into the rain. Dripping blood that wasn't mine. And I didn't trip, and you weren't a child. You were light, but not *that* light." He tries to grin, but it's twisted by his memories. By the remembrance of Bruce and Tilly, and what he had to do. "I got us as far away as I could from that house, and then I started changing up cars and plates. We just kept driving. We went down to Georgia. You remember much from that time?"

"No," Georgia says. "Not really."

"Just the two of us for about three months. Did my best to try and break the conditioning. Got through a little. Some days you were clearer than others. You just seemed lost. First thing I knew I had to do, though, was change your name. Since we were in Georgia I figured that was as good as anything, so Georgia you were.

"I couldn't take care of you, though. Not like a real parent. I tried my best, but I wasn't any kind of a father. You needed a real family. Took me a while to find one, and when I finally did, I took you straight to Florida and to the Carusos. You remember *them*, right?"

She does. She smiles sadly. The sweet old couple who took her in. The closest she came to ever having a family. She was with them for four years.

"And they knew all about your past. They knew what had happened to you. Didn't matter to them. They had a lot of love to give."

Georgia nods. She tries not to think about the Carusos much. Her eyes burn. They feel wet. She blinks. "And you became Uncle Jack."

"I didn't care for Florida much," he says. "Too hot for me. But I knew I needed to stick close. To help you out."

Helping her out consisted of training her in hand-to-hand combat. She took to it like a fish to water. She'd had training already, while in her sleeper state. Her muscle memory retained most of the movements and greatly assisted in teaching her awakened self the keys to defense. Jack taught her how to hunt, too. Taught her how to camp, and how to survive out in the wild. He taught her how to shoot. He taught her everything she would need to stay alive, should she ever be found.

Right up until they *were* found. They'd never know who was tracked—whether it was Georgia or Jack. When they found her in Florida and killed the Carusos, they didn't know her name. She was still Kayla Morrow to them then. Ten years later, judging by what the men said to her in the library back in Alaska, they finally knew her as Georgia.

Georgia and Jack had to escape again. They were out when the Carusos were killed. They'd been fishing. When they got back to the street, Jack noticed something was wrong. He saw the men arranged, trying to look casual, parked in cars and pretending to jog. He didn't return to the house. He pulled away from the street and kept going, breathing hard, his eyes watching the mirrors. The men waiting hadn't seen them. They weren't following.

The next day, they saw in a paper that the Carusos had been killed, though they already knew. They'd been stabbed to death, and police were treating it as a burglary gone wrong. Georgia wept for them when she read the report. Her time with them was the closest her life had ever come to normalcy. She would never get that back.

Jack drove her to Alaska. She was old enough to take care of herself, and he had taught her everything he could. He told her she should change her last name, too, but she couldn't bring herself to do it. The Carusos were a part of her, an important part, and their name was all she had left. They'd never adopted or fostered her officially. There were no records of her ever having lived with them. She took the risk. She was so careful in all other regards, she took this one risk.

"I have to go back," Jack said, leaving her in Alaska, close to the town of Minnow. "They're going to keep coming for us. This is a war now. I need to find a way to take the fight to them. I need to find people who can help."

He embraced her and told her to take care of herself, and to always be careful, and he left, promising he'd let her know how she could find him.

Georgia thinks about him living alone in the woods in Washington. Hiding away from the war he told her would always be searching for them, always looking to swallow them whole. He was still fighting it, and always prepared for it. That much was clear. But Georgia wonders if he'd grown weary of it, and was more happy hiding. Away from it all. She wonders if the overwhelming adversarial numbers had worn him down. Tired him out.

Georgia doesn't ask him. He looks old. He looks older than fifty. He looks tired, too. Very tired.

"Y'know," Georgia says, "those are my happiest memories. When I was with the Carusos, and Uncle Jack would come to visit every weekend."

He takes a deep breath. "I think those are probably some of my favorite memories, too." He looks at her now, briefly, keeping most of his attention on the road. He smiles.

18

Matt Bunker enters the Oval Office, a folder tucked under his arm. Zeke wonders if this is a genuine document, or if it's just for show. Matt is here to discuss Order business, and it's unlikely he'd have written anything pertaining to that down.

Zeke runs both hands down his face and slaps his cheeks. He's been awake all night. When he took the office he had no idea how little sleep he would be getting. It's early days, though, and things are busy right now. He should have expected this. Over time, things will calm down, he's sure. At the minute, he's averaging about three hours a night, and even then he's tossing and turning, expecting a wake-up call at any second.

"Tired?" Matt says.

"What gave me away?"

Matt chuckles. Zeke eyes him with envy. He seems to have been awake just as long as Zeke—longer in fact—but he's not showing any signs of wear. If anything, he looks as alert as he ever does. He's younger, sure, but that will only get him so far. The man's a machine.

Anthony Tomasson sits nearby, arms folded, chin upon his

chest while he grabs a catnap. "Shall I wake the vice-president?" Matt says, tilting his head in Anthony's direction.

Zeke nods, rolling his neck until it pops. He takes a sip from his coffee. An aide brought it in ten minutes ago and it's still hot. Matt takes a seat and nudges the bottom of Anthony's foot with his own. Anthony wakes with a start and a snort. He blinks and widens his eyes while he pushes himself up in the chair. He clears his throat.

"I'm awake," he says.

He looks at Matt, then at Zeke, and then around the rest of the office. They're the only three present. Anthony remembers why Matt is here. He leans forward, alert, waking himself up completely. Zeke hands him a coffee and Anthony takes it gratefully.

Matt checks the time. "We still have a few hours before the funeral," he says.

Zeke is well aware. The funeral for President Frank Stewart. Zeke's predecessor. The man he killed for this position. For this chair. The man he was selected to replace.

"Is your speech ready?" Anthony says.

"I've read it and made notes," Zeke says. "I'm waiting to get the final draft back. Should I expect any last-minute amendments needed?" He looks at Matt.

"Potentially," Matt says.

"Let's forget about the funeral for now. Are you bringing good news?" Zeke says.

Matt's face is solemn and Zeke feels like he already has his answer. "Afraid not," Matt says. "Naturally we're continuing to work on it, but Georgia Caruso and Jack Athey got away."

"Did it get violent?" Zeke says.

Matt nods.

"How many did we lose?"

"Just over a dozen. The woods were laden with booby-traps

and the cabin was loaded with explosives. They got away after they set it sky-high. We were able to track down the vehicle they escaped in but it had been abandoned and burned out. Seems like Jack was careful and he had something else stashed. We don't know what it is yet. But he knows how we work. He was ready for us."

"I'm sorry," Anthony says, raising his hands. "There's a lot going on right now and I have a lot of names running through my head—who is Georgia Caruso?"

"She used to be Kayla Morrow," Matt says.

"But she's not the *current* Kayla Morrow, no?" Anthony says.

"No, she's not," Zeke says, leaning back in his chair. He casts a steely gaze over Anthony, expecting better of him.

Anthony wilts under the glare. "I apologize," he says. "It's not like I can write anything down, and I'm struggling to keep everything straight."

"Then you're going to have to do better," Zeke says. "I'm relying on you, Anthony. We all rely on each other." He taps the side of his head. "You need to get it right up here."

Anthony nods, suitably chastised.

Zeke turns his attention back to Matt and raises his eyebrows for him to continue.

"We've currently lost track of Shira Mizrahi, too," Matt says. "Since the death of her boyfriend, she's disappeared."

Zeke leans forward. He's been giving a lot of thought to Shira Mizrahi, and her status as ex-Mossad. "Do we have anything to worry about from the Israelis?"

"No signs so far. They maintain that Shira has nothing to do with them. They could be lying, of course, but they don't have anything currently happening on a large scale. If Shira *is* working for them still, she's out here on her own." Matt smirks. "But if they placed her here as a sleeper agent, she would have expected their denial. She knows she'll be flying solo. She'll be prepared for it."

Zeke knows Matt was the one to kill Shira's partner. A man Matt was a long-time friend of, but he was getting too close. Shira will want his blood. They all know it. Matt appears unconcerned.

"There's still no sign of our main three," Matt says. "Charlie Carter, Keith Wright, and the current Kayla Morrow. It's as if they've disappeared off the face of the earth."

"I don't like the sound of that," Zeke says.

"Nor should you. But I have confidence they'll turn up sooner or later. They have to. They'll be laying low for the moment, but they can't stay that way forever. The second they come up, we'll be on them."

"I would prefer *sooner* over later," Anthony says.

"We all would," Zeke says and takes a deep breath. "I would like to have some good news for when I meet with the Quinquevirate."

Anthony whistles low. "You've been holding out on me," he says and looks at Matt. "Did you know about this?"

Matt nods.

"Of course he did," Anthony says. He laughs. "You probably set it up, right?" He shakes his head and slaps his thigh. "This is a big deal, Zeke. It's *huge*. I assume it's after the funeral?"

Zeke nods. "And I'd be looking forward to it a whole hell of a lot more if I wasn't going to see them with my tail between my legs to tell them how much we're all fucking up. So. Does anyone have anything that could save me from that embarrassment?"

Matt and Anthony are silent. Anthony can't look at him.

"Marvelous," Zeke says.

"I'm on things," Matt says. "You can count on me, Mr. President."

"What do you have planned?"

"Well, as you know, we have someone very important to

Charlie Carter. This could be where those last-minute speech amendments come into play. I think it's time to coax them out from where they're hiding. Rather than us trying to go to them, we'll find a way to bring them to us."

Zeke pinches his chin. "It's better than nothing. What about the rest of them?"

"We'll find Georgia and Jack the same way we'll find the other three. We'll find a way to draw them out—I believe the three will be the key to doing that. I'll figure that out later. As for Shira, I know exactly who to send after her." He grins a dark smile. Zeke has a feeling he knows what he has planned.

"You'd best get to it," Zeke says.

Matt stands. "I'd best. I'll see you at the funeral, but in case we don't get a chance to talk more candidly before then, good luck with your meeting, Mr. President. I'm sure it'll go well." They shake and Matt leaves the office.

"How do you think it'll go?" Anthony says after he's left.

"It has to go well," Zeke says, staring at the door Matt went through. "We can't afford for it to not, or else before we know it we'll be consigned to the history books along with Frank and Jake."

Anthony swallows. The color drains from his face.

"I don't want that either, Anthony," Zeke says and taps the side of his head. "Get this in the game. You need to take this situation seriously. Getting here, into this office, into these positions, that wasn't the finishing line for us. It was the starting point. Our heads are on the line, and I mean that literally."

19

Harlan takes a video call from Matt Bunker. The computer is in the back room. The curtains are drawn tight. The only light comes from the screen. Despite this, Harlan keeps his sunglasses on. The glow is too much for his eyes. "Do you have something for us?" Harlan says. There's a bite to his tone.

"Are you getting stir crazy out there?" Matt says, grinning.

"Not yet," Harlan says. "I've been in smaller places for longer times, but you told me there was a mission, and I was very excited to partake in that mission. Thus far, I've been sat on my ass. Feels like I was moved from one prison to another."

"Then I have good news," Matt says.

"It's time?"

"It certainly is, and I have a feeling you're going to like what I have for you."

"I'm all ears."

Matt holds up two fingers. "Two things. Firstly, Shira Mizrahi. Ex-Mossad. We need her found."

"A Jew?" Harlan feels a smile split his face.

"I knew you'd like it."

"Where are we supposed to look?"

"I'll send over all the information we have after this call has ended. I'll be sending some extra help your way, too. Hackers, analysts—people who can help find her. If we're all working together, we can cast our net wide, and faster."

"What's the second thing?"

"The second is a little more vague, but we're hoping things should start moving soon. The three who have disappeared, the three who are responsible for what happened to a couple of your men in a DC jail, we're going to try and coax them out of hiding. When they show up, I want you there to greet them. How does that sound? That make you happy?"

Harlan claps his hands together. "I'm ecstatic, Agent Bunker."

"Good. I live to spread happiness and cheer. I'll send over what we have in an encrypted email. I'm sure I can count on you for this, Mr. Thompson?"

Harlan shows his teeth. "For this? There's no one you can count on more."

20

With two extra bodies, it's a tight squeeze in the car. Kayla is in the back, sat in the middle between Winston and Ryan. They're both wider than she is. They take up more space. As if that wasn't enough, they both sit with their legs spread, their thighs pressed up against hers.

Keith drives. Charlie is beside him. The cave is far behind them, now. They're back on the road, heading out of Death Valley. The trunk has their supplies already, and now it also has what father and son have brought with them. Some of Winston's electronics, and one of Ryan's drones, as well as his rifle. Ryan sits to Kayla's right. He seems antsy being unarmed. Kayla stares at his knee, watching the way it bounces. His elbow rests on the windowsill and he stares out, absently chewing on the skin around his thumbnail.

Winston is to her left. He has his laptop open, scrolling through news sites. Kayla watches over his shoulder. He doesn't try to conceal it from her. Nothing catches her eye. Nothing seems to catch his eye, either. He closes one page and opens another and resumes the process. "The former president is being buried today," he says suddenly, looking up, addressing everyone in the car.

Charlie turns his head a little, but Keith doesn't react.

Winston shrugs. "Thought it might be of interest," he says, then returns to the screen.

Kayla lays her head back on the rest and closes her eyes. Once again, they're criss-crossing the country. They have another long drive ahead of them, made even longer by the fact they'll be sticking to back roads, avoiding cameras and built-up areas wherever they can. A return to the ultra-careful trips to gas stations, pulling baseball caps down low over their faces, wearing sunglasses if possible.

They're going to Texas. Or, to be more precise, they're going to the border with Mexico. That's where Derek Morrow is, according to Winston. That's where he's hiding out. Kayla hears the familiar tune playing in her head. The music she can't place. The words she can't decipher.

"What's his real name?" Kayla says, opening her eyes and looking at Winston.

He looks at her, confused. "Who?" he says.

"Derek Morrow," she says. "My *father*." She says the word with disdain. Yet another lie.

Keith glances at her in the mirror.

"I told you," Winston says. "I don't know."

"How can you not know?"

"That was the point. None of us were supposed to know."

"But—"

"Kayla," Keith says.

"I'm fine," Kayla says. "I'm just hot, and agitated, and it's very tight back here, and neither one of these *fucking* men seem to be able to keep their legs to themselves."

Winston and Ryan both give a start. They close their legs, providing her with a little more space. It wasn't so much that they were touching her that bugged her—though she wasn't a big fan of that—it was the heat that the contact generated. She's already hot enough. She's sick of feeling so hot.

"Sorry," Ryan mumbles.

Kayla ignores him. She ignores all of them. She closes her eyes again. The music plays. She lets it. She's already got enough to be annoyed at, one more hardly matters.

21

Shira and Noam have the television on. The funeral of deceased President Frank Stewart is starting soon.

Shira sits by the window. She yawns. Noam has left his laptop running at the desk. "How many people do you think are watching this right now?" Noam says.

"A lot," Shira says. "Millions. Maybe more, internationally."

"You think people are bothered enough internationally to watch it live?"

"I don't know. Maybe they'll just catch the highlights on the nighttime news." Shira looks down at the road. It's quiet out there. There are still some people on the sidewalks, and vehicles passing by, but not as many as there usually are at this hour. "What are you hoping to see?"

"I don't know," Noam says. "But anything could happen, wouldn't you agree? Whoever we're up against, they've been hitting anything and everything. It stands to reason that they might strike here."

"Even if they do, it'll be on a delay. And we've talked about the new president potentially being a part of this. If he is, why would they strike at him?"

"To make him look good. Like when Reagan was shot. His approval rates went up after that. I'm not saying they're going to shoot him, but a potential assassination could do wonders for his numbers." Noam watches the screen. The funeral is starting. He turns the volume down while the national anthem plays. "There's a lot of security."

"I'd be more surprised if there wasn't."

They watch the funeral play out in silence. Shira remains on the windowsill, glancing outside every so often and moving from room to room so she can look out of the other windows. "Listen," she says, coming back through to the living room, "I'm gonna do a sweep of the neighborhood."

"Ever vigilant," Noam says, nodding.

"Most of the country is distracted right now—would be a perfect time for them to try and move in." She glances at the screen. The camera pans across the somber crowd gathered in DC, undeterred despite the recent bomb attack. The area is swarming with police. There are snipers atop buildings, though attention is not drawn to them. The presence of all this security likely comforts the crowd. Sets their minds at rest that they will not be attacked today. "Let me know if anything important happens."

Shira heads outside and circles the block, scanning the few people and vehicles she sees. The area is clear. It's quiet. She wonders how many people in the neighborhood have gone to the funeral in person. She's not sure how many people in Petworth care enough.

Before she goes back inside the building, she presses her back to the wall and takes a deep breath. She looks up and down the road. There's no one around. She's all alone. There's no one to see her cry.

She closes her eyes and thinks of James. If he were still alive, he would have been working the funeral. He'd have been on crowd control. Cool, calm, and collected. Always in control of the situation.

Shira hasn't had time to grieve. She hasn't allowed herself to, but even if she wanted, she couldn't. She's too busy, and Noam is always around. The tears roll hot down her cheeks. They drip to the sidewalk. She watches them land, splash, dark on the ground like raindrops.

She sniffs and wipes her eyes. She takes a deep breath and finds a window to check her reflection in, seeing if it's obvious that she's been crying. It's not. She straightens herself out and then goes back inside. When she gets back to the apartment, Noam is sitting forward, staring intently at the screen. He's turned the volume up.

"What's happening?" Shira says, coming closer.

"The new president is giving a speech," Noam says, motioning for her to be quiet.

Shira stands beside the sofa and watches the television. The president's face is hard. He looks serious, his eyebrows have narrowed and his eyes are unblinking. He wears the somber look of someone in mourning, but at the same time, there is a driven air about him. There is something about his demeanor that goes beyond grief.

He stands at a podium and grips it with both hands. Behind him, Shira can see brickwork that she assumes is the church where the funeral is taking place. The president is not inside the church. He's outside. He's addressing the crowd. The camera does not pan over them. Does not show their reactions. It stays with the president. He fills the frame. His speech is almost over. "America has faced down more than its fair share of adversaries. We've never bowed down before, and we're not going to start now. We are a nation united in this cause against our collective enemy, and whether that enemy comes from abroad or from the interior, we shall tackle it together. And together we say that not on this day, nor any other, will terrorism destroy who we are, nor our way of life, nor our great country."

"I think he's one of them," Noam says, turning down the volume as the people applaud. "At this point, I'm pretty certain." He keeps an eye on the screen to see if anything more is said, but the speech is over.

"We already had our suspicions," Shira says, "but what makes you say that?"

"What he's just said, and how he said it."

"What have I missed?"

"Well, for a start, I think I know for sure who they were taking off the plane."

Shira frowns. She takes a seat beside him. "He said who it was? In his speech?"

"Basically," Noam says. "Those soundbites, they're going to be on the news, they're going to be all over the internet—and I think that was the point. I think that was *his* point."

"I'll watch it later, but for now, tell me what he said."

"Like we suspected, they've captured Niamh Carter—Charlie's wife. He said they caught her trying to sneak into the country. They said she was in touch with the ARO, trying to meet up with them. That confirms it—the woman we saw them bringing into the country was Niamh. She didn't try to sneak into the country. I doubt she's had any kind of contact with the ARO. She was brought here."

"She's bait," Shira says.

"Exactly," Noam says. "That's why it's going to be everywhere. They don't know where Charlie and the rest are, but they want them to see that they've got his wife. They're trying to draw them out of hiding."

"And this makes you believe the president is a part of everything going on here?"

"It was in his face, Shira." Noam looks at her. "When you

watch, you'll see for yourself. It was in the tone of his voice. You'll see. I know it's vague, but I can't explain it. But also, when they brought him news that they'd captured the wife of one of their runaways trying to sneak into the country, don't you think he'd have wanted to see that footage? Wouldn't he have wanted all the information they could give? Her sneaking in isn't what the footage shows. One way or another, I believe he's involved."

Shira grits her teeth. "They could already have the White House."

"They could," Noam says. "We have no way of knowing for sure."

Shira clasps her hands in front of her face, staring at the television but not really seeing it. She's thinking.

"We can't remain passive, Noam," she says, turning back to him. "We've been cooped up and hidden away here for too long. We need to take a more active role. We need to participate. The longer we take, the larger their organization grows." She pauses. Noam doesn't say anything. He watches her, waiting for her to continue. "We need to find the others. We have mutual enemies, and that makes them our allies. We need to find them before they can."

22

The diner is silent. There aren't many people inside. Maybe a dozen, not including the waiting and kitchen staff. No one is eating. No one is serving. Right now, everyone's attention is turned toward the television behind the counter. One of the waitresses has turned the volume up so everyone can hear.

They're watching the former president's funeral. They've been listening to the new president's speech.

Georgia and Jack sit at the back of the diner. They've stopped eating, too, so as not to draw attention to themselves. As the speech comes to a close, people return to their food, and to their jobs. The waitress turns the volume back down. Hushed conversation fills the room.

Jack turns to Georgia, an eyebrow raised. "What do you make of that?"

"They want Charlie to do something stupid," Georgia says. They keep their heads low while they talk, leaning close to each other across the table.

Jack points a finger, thumb cocked back like a gun. "Bingo."

Georgia regularly looks around the diner, checking out the other patrons. She knows that Jack is doing the same. There's a window to Georgia's right. She looks out of it, too. Checks the parking lot. Checks their vehicle. No one approaches it. No one approaches them.

"We need to find them," Georgia says. She has a chicken salad, but she's not very hungry. She picks at it, knowing that she needs to eat. "We need to find Kayla and the others."

Jack grunts. He has a beef sandwich. He doesn't look at her. He's concentrating on his food.

Georgia watches him. He's guarded. Keeping something from her. "What?" she says, not wanting to raise her voice too loud.

Jack takes his time chewing. He blows air out of his nose before he speaks. "I know where they are," he says. "Or, more precisely, I know where they're going."

Georgia frowns. "How?" She thinks on what he said back at the cabin, before they were attacked. How he needed to warn someone. Wonders if it's connected.

Jack sucks on his teeth. He takes his time answering. "I'm in contact with someone they're with."

"The person you alerted at the cabin."

Jack nods.

"Who is he?"

"It's not important," Jack says and takes another bite of his sandwich.

"You're keeping something from me," Georgia says. She leans closer, looking into his eyes. "This is no good, Jack. You can't keep anything from me."

"You won't like it."

"I already don't like it. That doesn't matter. Tell me."

"They're with Dr Winston Fallon."

"I don't know who that is."

"He made you, Georgia. He made all of the sleepers."

Georgia blinks. She feels her teeth grinding, though she's not aware she's doing it. "I think we need to leave," she says. "Right now."

Jack wears a solemn face. "I'll go pay."

Georgia leaves him in the diner. She returns to the truck, opening and closing her fists. She's shaking. She presses her hands down on the top of the passenger door and takes deep breaths. Jack soon comes out. He avoids looking at her. He unlocks the truck. Neither of them says a word until they're inside. Georgia turns to him.

"What the *fuck*?" she says.

Jack holds up his hands, motioning for her to stay calm. "You trust me, don't you?"

"What does that have to do with anything?"

"Answer the question—you trust me, don't you?"

She stares at him for a long time. She does, but it's hard to say so right now, so soon after his revelation. "Yes," she says. "So you better have a damn good explanation."

"He's not part of The Order anymore," Jack says. "He hasn't been for a long time. He's with us."

"How long have you been talking to him? How long have you known *they* were with him?"

"We've talked for years," Jack says. "And Kayla and the others reached him a couple of days ago."

"And you didn't think I'd want to know about him? About them being there? Jesus Christ, Jack."

"Was there really a good time to tell you about him, and who he is? What he's done? What he helped do to *you*?"

Georgia seethes. She looks away and stares straight ahead at the diner.

Jack gives her some time.

"Why didn't you tell me you knew where Kayla and the others were?" Georgia says.

"I was going to," Jack says. "But things started happening. We needed a chance to catch our breaths. And after I sent them the warning, they started moving, too."

"All this time we've been running away, I didn't think we had any idea where we were supposed to go next. You were holding out on me."

"I had my reasons."

"And what were they?"

"Look at me, Georgia."

She does.

"Once we start," Jack says, "there's no stopping. There's no going back. It's going to be war, and most likely for the rest of our lives. I..." He sighs. "I hesitated, Georgia. The thought of it...it wore me out. I'm already so tired. I've given my life to fighting against The Order, and they just grow and grow and grow. They get stronger. No matter what I've done, it's never been enough to stop them. And if we keep going now, chances are we're charging to our deaths." He pauses. He reaches over and takes one of her hands. He squeezes it. "I didn't want this for you. I didn't want you to lose so much, the way I have. I wanted you to have an actual life."

"It's too late for that," Georgia says, but her words are not cold. She understands what Jack is saying. She understands his concerns. "We don't have any choice anymore."

Jack nods, a sadness on his face and in his eyes.

"We need to go after them," Georgia says. "We need to find them."

Jack swallows. He starts the engine. "It's going to be a long drive."

"Where are they?"

"On the move, but I know where they're going. Texas. Right down to the border."

"All right," Georgia says. "Then start driving. And on the way, you can tell me all I need to know about Dr Winston Fallon."

23

Charlie is putting gas into the car when he finds out about his wife.

He's paying at the pump. He's wearing a cap pulled low. There is a television screen on the pump. It's broadcasting the former president's funeral. In the car, on the radio, they heard the live updates. The new president was taking to the podium as Charlie got out to fill the tank. He's not paying attention to the screen. He can hear it, though. He hears his wife's name.

He looks up and freezes. He listens to the president's words. The fuel is forgotten. Charlie grits his teeth. He balls his hands into fists. He doesn't snap back to what he's doing until petrol begins to overflow and splash onto the ground below.

Keith leans out of his door. The radio is still playing. He's heard. "Charlie, get back in the car."

Charlie tears himself away from the screen. He puts the pump back and steps over the petrol that has spilled. He gets in on the passenger side. They wait for Ryan to return. He was inside, paying. He climbs into the back. His eyes are wide. The television was clearly on inside the station. Keith drives away. The president's speech is over. The people who gathered for the funeral applauded him.

"They were talking about you?" Ryan says, leaning forward. "That's your wife?"

Kayla nudges him with her elbow. The look on Charlie's face should be answer enough.

He swallows, feeling the world open beneath him. He can't think straight.

"Listen, man," Keith says, "he could be lying. It could be bullshit, to draw you out. It could be a trap."

"It's definitely a trap," Winston says. "But that doesn't mean they don't have her. We have no way of knowing for sure, but I believe they do. He's announced it publicly. It would be too easy for people to fact-check."

"Where will they be keeping her?" Kayla says.

"She could be anywhere," Winston says. "But my guess would be DC. They don't know where you all are, but they *do* know that you've been active in the capitol. It stands to reason they'd hold her as close to your last known location as possible. If they were keeping her somewhere else, I think they would have said. It *is* a trap, and for a trap to work you need your victim to know where to go."

"Pull over," Charlie says. He feels like he's going to be sick.

"Charlie—" Keith starts, but Charlie cuts him off.

"Pull over," he says again. "Right now." His mouth fills with spit. His stomach clenches.

Keith pulls to the side of the road. They're passing through a small town. The road is quiet. There is no sidewalk, but Charlie gets out of the car and paces on the grass verge. He bends over with his hands on his knees, his throat raw, but nothing comes up. He coughs a couple of times and spits to the side. He straightens and laces his fingers on top of his head, staring off into the distance.

Behind him, Keith and Kayla get out of the car. They don't come close, don't try to pat and stroke him, to comfort him. They give him time. They give him space. They wait.

Charlie feels something inside himself akin to grief. As if he has just been told of Niamh's death. But she's not dead. She's captured. Because of *him*. He's put her in danger, because of this mess he's got himself caught up in. Up until now, he thought she was safe. Overseas, back in England, he thought she would be safe there. He just needed to straighten out what was happening here, and then he could return. Now she's a part of it. They have her—they've *taken* her—and he has no idea where she's being held, or what they might be doing to her.

He turns. Keith and Kayla are looking back at him. In the car, Winston and Ryan remain in the backseat, peering out.

"I'm sorry, Charlie," Keith says. "It's messed up. They've brought your family into this…"

"What are you going to do?" Kayla says.

"I need to go after her," Charlie says. "I need to get her back from them."

"Do you want us to come with you?" Kayla says.

"I can't ask you to do that."

"Of course you can," Keith says. "You've had our back, and we've got yours."

Charlie shakes his head. "You need to find Kayla's fake father. You need to find some answers. I don't know where they have Niamh, but I'm going to find out. Chances are, it's going to be dangerous. I could get captured, too. I could get killed. If that happens, you need to be out here still."

The rear door of the car opens and Winston steps out. "What's happening?"

"Charlie needs to go and find his wife," Keith says.

"That might not be a good idea," Winston says. "We shouldn't divide like this. We need to stick together. We need to stay the course."

Keith glares at him. "He can't leave her with them."

"It's a trap—how many times do I have to say that? What kind of fool walks into a trap *knowing* they're doing it?" Winston holds out his arms, exasperated.

"I don't care," Charlie says. "I'm not going to go in one direction when there's a chance she's in another." He steps closer to Winston. Winston flinches. "Get on your laptop," he says. "Find me the fastest way back to DC."

"Train would probably be your best bet," Ryan says, leaning over. "I'm not saying it would be the fastest way—flight would be your fastest option, but you don't want to risk going through airports, especially not right now. There might be security at a train station, but it won't be anywhere near as tight as at an airport. Likewise, if you were driving—it could potentially be faster, but there are probably still blockades around DC. The train gives you more options."

Charlie nods at this, then looks back at Winston. "Then invent me a name and book me a ticket."

Winston's eyes flicker toward Keith. When he sees that there's no support for him there, he gives in. "All right," he says. "*All right.* I'll get straight on it. But we're going to have to double back on ourselves; I hope you all realize that. There's not going to be a cross-country train station anywhere around here."

"Then so be it," Keith says.

Charlie nods his gratitude to Keith and Kayla. His throat feels tight, and he doesn't think he can speak anymore. He can barely think straight. His thoughts are on Niamh, on where she could be and what she could be going through. Wherever she is, he can't leave her there alone. He has to get her out.

24

Niamh is alone.
She doesn't know if it's day or night. She doesn't know how long she's been in this cell. Embedded into the ceiling are four small round lights. They never switch off.

They drugged her before they put her on the plane. Up in the air, she started to come 'round, but she remained dazed and groggy. When they noticed she was waking up, they gave her another dose. When they landed and bundled her into the back of some vehicle she never saw, they drugged her again. She's been in and out of sleep since then. Only now does she feel like whatever they pumped into her is fully working its way out of her system.

She's in a cell. It feels like it's underground, but she has no way or knowing for sure. She thinks this because of the lack of windows. The walls and ceiling are concrete. There is a mat on the floor in the corner, with a thin blanket. No mattress. Beside it, a bucket. The door is made of steel, with a flap in the bottom through which her meals are delivered, and a slat at the top for the people outside to look in at her. The only time they do is when they bring her food. She doesn't see anyone else. She can't hear anyone outside, either. Dumped in the basement. Locked up and forgotten, save for the bringing of food.

She's tried pounding on the door, but no one answered. She can't hear anything outside, beyond this room. She sits on the mat with her head in her hands and waits for whatever comes next.

Coming down from the drugs was hard. Her limbs felt leaden. Her brain was swimming, and she saw double. Food would be shoved through the slat, but she didn't have the strength to crawl across the ground and go to it. Some indeterminate amount of time later, the slat reopened and the untouched food was taken away.

Niamh has strength enough to get up and eat, now. She has strength enough to pace the floor and wonder where the hell she is, and what's happening. It has something to do with whatever Charlie is caught up in, no doubt. She remembers the men who attacked her in her home. Remembers their American accents. They took her on a plane. Does that mean she's in America now? She wonders if they left the house a mess, or if they cleared it up after they had her—if they made it look like they were never there. Does anyone realize she's missing? How long has it been?

Niamh waits. She paces to avoid her muscles growing stiff. It's impossible to judge from her meals what time of day they are being brought—they're not distinctly breakfast foods, and it's nothing like a light lunch. She's brought gruel. She's brought bread. Once, she got an apple to go with a sweating piece of meat that looked like a burger without the bun. Her stomach did somersaults at the sight of it, but she pinched her nose and ate it. Whatever is happening here, she needs to keep her strength up. She can't afford to be choosy.

The eye slat opens without warning. Niamh did not hear anyone approach. She never does. The eyes search her out. Niamh calls out as the slat begins to close.

"Wait!" she says. "Wait, please!"

The eyes ignore her. The slat closes. The opening in the bottom of the door is pulled up. Her tray of food is pushed into the cell.

"Talk to me!" Niamh says, dropping to her knees before the hatch can close. "Where am I? Why am I here?"

She sees a pair of combat boots and, above them, a flash of combat fatigues. The hatch falls back into place. It's locked.

Niamh sighs and presses her forehead to the cold of the door, closing her eyes. She's tried talking to them before, but they never answer. She turns and sits with her back to the door, slamming the side of her fist against it. "Arseholes!" She doubts they can hear.

On the tray, there is a hotdog without a bun. She touches it with the tip of her index finger. It's cold. There is a juice box next to it, and a dollop of something that could be pudding. She sniffs it. It smells faintly of chocolate. There's nothing to eat it with. There never is. She has to use her hands.

In a while, someone will return for the tray. Niamh has tried to draw them into the cell, to open the door all the way. She kept the tray out of reach. It didn't work. When they noticed it wasn't close, they shut the hatch and left. Niamh ended up with three trays. They didn't care. They left him with her. There was nothing she could do with them. She could snap them, sharpen their jagged edges, but then what? The only person she could hurt was herself. None of them were coming close enough for her to pose any kind of threat. Eventually, she gave up and put the trays back next to the door. They were taken without a word.

Niamh isn't hungry. She leaves the food on the tray by the door and goes to the mat to lie down. She stares up at the ceiling. There's no way of knowing how long they're going to keep her here. She doesn't know if they'll ever let her out. This latter prospect terrifies her. It makes her chest tight and her breath come quick. She tries not to linger on it. She can't think like that. She has to believe that one day, she will see the outside of this cell.

That one day she will be free again. If she loses hope, she's lost everything. She can't let them break her. If they do, they've won.

Niamh wishes she knew what kind of game they were playing. Wishes she knew what they want. As time crawls on, and she doesn't know whether it's day or night, or what day it is, or how long she's been here, it gets harder and harder to hold onto her hope. To hold out that she'll ever get out of here. The longer this goes, the closer they get to breaking her.

She closes her eyes. Slowly, piece by piece, sleep takes her.

25

Zeke feels a level of nervousness and excitement that he has not felt since he was a child. He does not think of himself as a man who is easily intimidated, but he has to admit to himself in this situation that he is daunted.

He rides in the back of an SUV with blacked-out windows. The rest of the vehicle is filled with security. There is no motorcade. There is no flag standing erect on this vehicle. There is nothing to indicate that anyone of importance travels within. The aim is to be as nondescript as possible.

They've come straight from the funeral. They've left DC and headed north-west. They're in Maryland now. Zeke has not been told where he's being taken. He's had to rely on the traffic signs to let him know where he is. Matt Bunker rides up front, in the passenger seat. He refers to directions that have been transmitted to him on a burner phone, motioning to the driver where to go.

Zeke concentrates on keeping his breathing level. He concentrates on *appearing* calm, despite how he feels inside. He doesn't want to show himself up in front of his security detail. Doesn't want them to snicker between themselves later at how ragged his breathing might sound, or how his hands were shaking or his legs were bouncing. He keeps his limbs still, and his breathing controlled. He keeps his mouth shut and he doesn't ask questions. Makes it seem like this isn't a big deal to him.

Of course, it *is* a big deal. It's a huge deal. Most members of The Order go their whole careers—their whole *lives*—without being invited to meet the Quinquevirate.

They reach Bethesda. Zeke has been to Bethesda before. He recognizes the area. They stay on the outskirts, though. They don't go to where it's built up. The road here is surrounded by trees, as if they're heading toward a hiking trail, except through the woodland he's able to spot expansive driveways that lead up to grand houses. The Secret Service either side of Zeke do not look. They stare straight ahead.

Matt flicks through the directions, then turns back. "Not far now, Mr. President," he says. "We'll be there soon."

Zeke nods. He doesn't risk speaking for fear of how his voice might come out. His throat feels dry. He swallows, not wanting the first words out of his mouth to crack when he leaves the SUV.

Matt points ahead and to the right. "That's our stop," he says to the driver. "Take your time. Nice and slow."

The vehicle begins to slow as it turns. Zeke stays casual, despite how much he wants to lean forward to get a better look at what they're heading into.

The trees are thicker here. Their branches interlock in a canopy overhead that turns the day to sudden night. The SUV rolls to a stop in front of a closed, wrought iron gate. Atop the brickwork pillars either side of the gate there are cameras pointing at the SUV. Beside the driver's door, there is an intercom. The driver puts his window down and waits, but no one speaks to him. The driver glances at Matt. Matt shrugs and holds out his hands.

The driver turns back to the intercom. "Hello?"

There's no response. Instead, the gates begin to open. The driver hesitates.

"Go on through," Matt says. "Just take your time."

The SUV begins rolling down the drive. There are trees on either side here—a mix of oaks and maples. Zeke wonders if there are more cameras there, hidden in the woodland, watching them make their way through. Zeke wonders if there are men out there, too. Armed men, watching them go. He wonders too, if he were to look back, if the gate would still be open. He doubts it. It likely closed promptly behind them, locking them in.

They get clear of the trees and the grounds open up. Acres of freshly mown grass. In the center of it all, a mansion, far larger and grander than any of the others Zeke spotted along the road coming here. There are turrets at either end of the house. Its exterior is brickwork, and its roof is slate tile. There is a large balcony area off-center, looking out over the drive on the way up to the house. There is no one currently upon it.

In front of the house, there are armed men standing guard. Zeke counts a dozen. They carry automatic rifles. They stare down the SUV.

The vehicle stops. No one tries to get out. A couple of the armed men come forward, motioning for the doors to be opened. One of them peers in, looking each of the men over. He settles on Zeke. "Zeke Turner," he says, "come with us. The rest of you, wait here."

Zeke does as he's told. The guard who didn't talk pats him down. Zeke spreads his legs and holds out his arms. He has nothing to hide. Satisfied, the guards motion for him to go inside. They point to the front door. They don't accompany him as he makes his way over. The armed men remain outside, watching the SUV and the security detail within.

Zeke walks tall, shoulders back and chin up. Makes it so he looks like he belongs here. He reaches the door and steps inside.

A man is waiting for him. He looks like he could be the butler. He wears a suit, and stands with his hands behind his back. He smiles at Zeke. "Mr. President," he says. He's American, but his accent is clipped, like he's imitating a British voice. Wherever he's truly from, he's disguised all trace of it. "It's a pleasure to finally meet you. Please, follow me."

Zeke follows him down the hall. The inside of the house is just as majestic as the outside. Paintings hang from the walls. The floor is carpeted with thick, patterned rugs that disguise the sounds of their footsteps. Zeke does not look around in awe, despite how much he'd like to. He faces forward. Stays focused. He wishes he had Matt with him. Wishes he wasn't alone in here.

The butler leads Zeke deep to the rear of the house, and then up a flight of stairs. Zeke wonders if there are security cameras in the house. If so, they are well concealed. He hasn't seen any guards inside, either, but he assumes they must be here somewhere.

Upstairs, they make their way down a short hallway to a closed double-door. There are guards here. Two men, one either side. They look like Secret Service. They wear all black with white shirts under their jackets, and Zeke can see ear pieces. They each eye him as he approaches. Their faces are stern and unchanging, betraying nothing. The butler steps in between them and stops in front of the double-door. He turns to Zeke, still smiling. "This is as far as I go," he says, motioning for Zeke to go ahead. "I'll be waiting here when you're through. The house can seem like a rabbit warren when you're not accustomed to it. I'll guide you back to your vehicle."

"Thank you," Zeke says, not sure what else he can say.

The butler opens one of the doors for him. As he does so, leaning forward so that his jacket flaps open slightly, Zeke notices that he's carrying a concealed weapon—a handgun in a shoulder holster. He straightens and stretches an arm to guide Zeke through.

Zeke steps inside, realizing that he's holding his breath. As the butler closes the door after him, Zeke exhales slowly and takes in the sight before him.

The room is overwhelming. It seems too large for the size of the house. The ceiling stretches above him in a dome shape, a fresco painted there. Zeke does not know a great deal about art, but he recognizes many of the images contained therein, taken from other famous works: he sees elements of Gustav Dore's 'The Fall Of The Rebel Angels,' and Goya's 'Saturn Devouring His Son.' The others it has taken inspiration from—or else outright plagiarized—he doesn't know the names of, or the artists, but he still recognizes aspects of them. He's seen the two women pinning down the man and beheading him with a sword, except here they are all nude, and he's sure the women at least are dressed in the original. The whole thing connects and weaves together in a nightmarish scene straight from Hell. Whatever it might be trying to say, Zeke does not understand it.

He realizes that since he's entered the room he has been looking up, staring into the painted dome. His jaw feels slack. He closes his mouth tight, hoping it hasn't been like that for long, and lowers his face.

The walls enclosing him are cream, but there are paintings with gilded frames mounted upon them. These paintings, however, are tamer. Portraits of men and women posing either in fields, or upon chairs in front of fireplaces. The time periods vary from frame to frame, from the distant, European past, to the last century. As with the portraits he saw in the rest of the house as the butler led him here, Zeke does not recognize any of the people painted. At the far end of the room, there is a marble fireplace and a roaring fire within. Beneath him, the ground is interlocked wood, herringbone style. To his left, there are three interspaced windows. Through them, Zeke has a view of the grounds at the rear of the house. They stretch as far as he can see, but this isn't what catches his attention. He sees men out there. Lined up, ranks of them, over and over. They're all armed. They stand at attention, in formation. An army.

Zeke forces himself to tear his attention away from the outside. In the center of the room, there is a large round table made of Amazon Rosewood, varnished to a high sheen. There are five men spaced around it. Four of them are sitting. One of them is standing. Four of the men are white, including the one standing. One of the men is Black. They're all looking at him. The Quinquevirate. Zeke notices that there is no sixth chair. He's going to be standing for the whole meeting.

"Mr. President," says the man standing directly opposite him, at what could be considered the head of the table. He grins. He knows as well as Zeke does that this is just a title. They are the real power. He is their representative. When he speaks, it is with their voice. When he has a thought, it's not his own. It's *theirs*.

Zeke isn't sure how to respond. His mouth is dry. He swallows and nods, then looks around the table. "It's an honor to be here."

The men stare back at him, unblinking. Their average ages look to be between mid-sixties and mid-seventies. They all look well, though. Healthy. However old they really are, they could all pass for younger. Save for the man who is standing, they wear no expressions. It's impossible for Zeke to decipher what they make of him. He shifts his weight from foot to foot and hates himself for doing so, feeling like a child called before the principal.

The standing man sits. "We're glad to hear that," he says. He clasps his hands together and pops his knuckles, then tents his fingers. "Do you recognize any of the men sitting around this table, President Turner?"

Zeke looks around again just to be sure, then shakes his head. "No, sir."

"Gentlemen," he says to the table. "Introduce yourselves."

The one on the man's immediate left turns to him. "Are you

sure?" His accent is not American. Zeke recognizes it, though. He's Canadian.

"We've invited him here today," the man at the head of the table says. Zeke wonders if this is his home. His understanding is that each of the five members of the Quinquevirate operate equally, but the others seem to be deferring to him. "If we're going to invite him into the inner sanctum, the least we can do is share our names. We don't have anything to worry about. Either he does his job and he does it well, or he doesn't, and… Well. We all know what happens if he doesn't."

The man closest to Zeke's right smirks.

The Canadian seems satisfied with this. "Timothy Jacques," he says.

"Gregory Ruby," says the man beside Timothy and on Zeke's right, still smirking. American.

"Lord Alred Walmsley," says the man to Zeke's immediate left. British.

"Milton Redding." The Black man. American.

Zeke recites their names over and over in his head, not wanting to forget them. He keeps their faces in mind, too, and lines them up with their names.

Finally, they're back to the man who has so far led the meeting. "And I am Douglas Morrow," he says, "and this is my humble home."

Zeke frowns at the name. *Morrow.*

"Ah," Douglas says, raising a finger, "I can see the recognition. Do you spot it, gentlemen?"

"We all see it," Lord Walmsley says.

"It's a popular name right now," Milton Redding says. "On everyone's lips."

"I'm sure it's just a coincidence," Zeke says.

"Is it?" Douglas says.

They're all looking at him. Their gazes feel mocking, like

they're in on a joke Zeke knows nothing about. Zeke isn't sure if he should speak. They're already treating him like a fool, he doesn't want to give them any further reason to believe it. None of them speaks. They all stare, expectant. They're not going to allow Zeke the escape of silence.

He clears his throat. "Kayla Morrow," he says. "She's the Morrow on everyone's lips." They're still looking at him. Zeke racks his brain, thinking over everything he knows about the sleeper program—which isn't much. It's not his department. The sleepers are a weapon to be drawn on when needed. He doesn't concern himself thinking about them at any other time. He does know, however, that the Prime is always called Kayla Morrow. Always.

He takes a chance. "She's named for you," he says. "The Morrow. That's after you?"

"It's after my daughter," Douglas says. There is a grimness to his expression that he tries to hide, but Zeke sees it. The same kind of grimness that comes with mourning. Zeke does not think that Douglas Morrow's daughter is still alive.

"Let's move on from this," Milton Redding says. "We're through with the introductions. He doesn't have to know more than he needs to. Let's get down to what's important."

"And what would you say is important, Milt?" Douglas says.

"His performance review," Milton says.

They're all staring at Zeke again. He stands his ground. Keeps his chin held high. He won't shuffle his feet again. Won't be made to feel like a child.

"I'm sure it goes without saying, young man," Lord Alred Walmsley says, "that you're in a very important position now, and you have a very important job to do."

"We're on a delicate precipice," Timothy Jacques says.

"Our balance relies upon you," Gregory Ruby says, speaking

for the first time since revealing his name. "Unfortunately, thus far, we have not been impressed."

Zeke feels his stomach sink. "I'm...sorry to hear that."

Douglas holds out his empty hands. "I told them to go easy on you," he says. "I reminded them you haven't been in the position for very long." He leans forward, resting his forearms on the table. "They disagreed. They say it's been long enough."

"More than," Timothy says. "Our objectives are falling into place. They can't fully be positioned while we have all of these problems running around."

"Sleepers wide awake," Milton says. "Ex-military. Former members of our *own* organization have turned against us. And foreign agents to top it all off. And they're all still out there. Running wild."

"You can't even catch a bloody Geordie?" Lord Alfred Walmsley says.

Zeke frowns. *A Geordie*? He'll look up what it means later.

"I would have expected this to be nipped in the bud *very* quickly," Gregory Ruby says. "I had high hopes for you, Zeke. We all did."

"Some of us still do," Douglas says. "But even we have to admit, the string of our hope is growing frayed. We're becoming as concerned as the others."

Zeke worried he would be walking in here to admonishment. He'd hoped he'd be mistaken, and that potentially he would be drawn deeper into the inner circle, become a greater asset to their machinations. He doubts that this latter is going to happen. Not any time soon. Certainly not today.

"I can only apologize," Zeke says, "and make assurances that things will improve going forward."

"Assurances are just words," Milton says.

"I'm aware," Zeke says, "but I promise you, you will see a great change coming. I've been easing myself into my new role—

I've perhaps not been coming down on mistakes and inadequacies in the way that I should have been. That will change as of right now. The runaways will be found, and they will be handled."

The five men look at him. Zeke stands firm. To falter is to show weakness. He needs them to know that he means what he says.

Douglas leans back in his chair. He doesn't look at Zeke anymore. Instead, he looks up. Toward the domed ceiling. The fresco there. He takes a deep breath and then turns back to Zeke. He watches him for a silent moment before he speaks. "When we decided that you were to be president, Zeke, that was our decision to make you *our* face to the rest of The Order. That was not a decision we made lightly. There were others who could have taken your place, but we chose *you*. You became our spokesperson. You became the very embodiment of the Quinquevirate. You're aware of this, aren't you?"

"Of course."

"Then bloody well act like it," Lord Walmsley says, but Douglas raises a hand for him to calm down.

"He knows, Al, he knows," Douglas says. "And he *is* going to do better. Isn't that right, Zeke?"

"Yes, sir," Zeke says. "I've made my promises, and I intend to stick to them."

"Good." Douglas claps his hands together. "Don't be afraid to delegate, Zeke, just always remember—the buck stops with you. Use what's at your disposal, and give your men everything they might need. But the *buck stops with you*. Is that clear?"

It's very clear. If things aren't resolved soon and satisfactorily, Zeke will be replaced. He knows his replacement won't be a case of him simply stepping aside. He'll go out the same way as his predecessor. He won't see it coming.

"I won't let you down again," Zeke says. "Any of you. Like I said, I stand by my promises."

"We're very glad to hear that," Douglas says. His is the only smiling face. The others stare at him. Lord Walmsley appears outright hostile. "We're done for today, Mr. President. Hopefully we won't need to see each other again for a long time."

"I'm counting on it, sir," Zeke says.

"Good. You can leave now. My butler is waiting outside. He'll show you the way out. I know this place isn't easy to maneuver when it's your first time."

Douglas is smiling at him, but it's a cold smile. Douglas wears the friendliest face out of the five men, but Zeke does not mistake this for weakness. He saw how the others deferred to him. How he led this meeting. The Quinquevirate may be equal, but Douglas Morrow appears to be a little more equal than the rest of them. He's a man who Zeke would not like to be on the wrong side of, and he doesn't intend to be.

It's been a brief meeting, but they've made their point and it's done now. Zeke flashes one last glance out the window, toward the small army standing to attention on the fields out there, and then he turns and walks as calmly and confidently as he is able from the room. He doesn't look back. He doesn't dare.

26

Keith drives Charlie to Los Angeles. They go to Union Station. Winston came through. He booked the tickets under a fake name. He created a false online identity for Charlie.

"Can you do an accent?" he'd asked in the car, typing away on his laptop.

"What kind of accent?" Charlie said.

"I don't know. Any kind. It's probably not wise you travel as a Brit."

"Can you do American?" Ryan said.

"Maybe," Charlie says. "For a little while."

Keith chuckled. "Let's hear it."

Charlie cleared his throat. He did his best American impression. "What do you want me to say?"

Keith laughed. "Was that supposed to be Elvis?"

Ryan laughed, too.

"I liked it," Kayla said. "It was very believable. I would buy you as American."

Winston coughed. "Well," he said. "All going to plan, you shouldn't have to talk too much."

Keith pulls around the back of Union Station and parks as

close to the building as he can get. Charlie stares up at it. He's going to go inside soon, as close to the train's departure as he can leave it. It will take three days to get back to DC. It's longer than he'd like—far too long—but he can't fly, and the journey will give him time to formulate some kind of a plan. As it stands, when he gets to DC, he doesn't yet know what he's going to do. He's not thinking straight. The only clear thought he has right now is to get Niamh back. The rest he can work out on the train.

Charlie has a sport bag resting on his knees. They stopped at a store for him to grab a change of clothes, and a bag to conceal his Glock in. It's in the bottom, wrapped in a T-shirt. He has a baseball cap on already, but it's currently pushed back so the others can see his face.

"The train will be here soon," Winston says. He's still on his laptop. "It's on time. You've got ten minutes."

"I'd best head in," Charlie says.

Keith and Kayla get out of the car with him. Winston and Ryan stay behind, giving them a chance to say goodbye.

"The two of you be careful," Charlie says.

"Same to you," Keith says.

"*You* be careful," Kayla says. "You're going out there on your own—*you* need to be careful. Extra careful."

"Who dares wins, pet." Charlie winks at her. "Make sure you look after the big man until I get back, all right? He's gonna need you if I'm not around."

"You know I will," Kayla says. "And you *are* going to come back, aren't you?"

"Gonna do my best."

"If you get her out and you get the chance," Keith says, "will you go back to England?"

"I'm not sure we can," Charlie says. He's given this a lot of thought already. "That's where Niamh was when they took her. It would be just as dangerous for us there as it is here. I don't think we can go home, not until this is over."

"Could take a long time," Keith says.

"Then we're locked in." Charlie looks at the time. "I'd better be going." He holds his hand out to Keith. "Take care of yourself. I wanna know I've got people to run to when I get Niamh out."

They shake. "We'll be out here," Keith says.

Charlie offers his hand to Kayla. She hugs him. Charlie pats her back. "Take care of yourself, too," he says.

"She'll look out for me and I'll look out for her," Keith says. "We've got each other. And when you and Niamh catch up to us, we'll have your backs, too. Now go and get your train. You don't wanna miss it."

Charlie grits his teeth and nods. He walks into the station and doesn't look back. It's hard to depart without Keith and Kayla. To leave them behind. They haven't known each other for long, but they've already been through so much together.

Charlie pulls down the peak of his baseball cap and steps into the building. It's cooler here. He looks around, getting his bearings but keeping his face low. This place looks familiar to him. He's seen its art deco design before, in movies or television shows, music videos—perhaps all three. He prints out his ticket and then makes his way toward his platform. Over the speakers he hears that his train is arriving.

Someone bumps into him from the side, and Charlie stiffens, feeling instantly defensive and ready to fight. His bag is knocked from his shoulder.

"Oh my God, I'm so sorry!" the woman who has bumped into him says. Charlie sees her phone in her hand. She was clearly lost in it, not looking where she was going. He can see a map open on her screen. "I should have been paying more attention—are you okay?"

Charlie picks up his bag and reshoulders it. He pulls his cap back down. The woman is young. She wears slacks and a loose blouse. She's not armed. She's not about to attack him. In her face, in her wide, round eyes, there is nothing but apology. There's no recognition, though. She's too embarrassed at bumping into him to realize who he is.

"That's okay," Charlie says, slipping into his Elvis impersonation. "Don't worry about it." He continues on to his platform, and behind him the young girl hurries away. Charlie steps outside and sees his train. It's long and sleek and gleams in the sunlight. He counts nine cars. He looks up and down the platform. He doesn't see any police. Doesn't see anyone that could potentially be undercover. The only people he sees in uniform work here.

Charlie gets into the train.

27

Noam sits bolt-upright in his chair, causing Shira to start. "What is it?" she says. "What's wrong?"

Noam turns to her excitedly. "I have a hit! I've found one of them!" He turns back to the screen.

Shira leaves the window and hurries to him, watching over his shoulder. "Who is it?"

"Charlie Carter," Noam says.

Shira sees footage on the screen. Noam rewinds it, then lets it play for her. She sees a woman bump into a man. The man wears a plain black baseball cap pulled low to disguise him. The woman is not looking where she's going. She's striding fast and staring two-handed at her phone. They collide. The man drops his bag. His cap rides up a little. The woman is apologetic. As the man turns to her, the camera catches a glimpse of his face.

Noam pauses the screen. "We got him. He's in LA currently, but he's getting on a train."

"Do we know where he's going?" Shira says.

"No—he obviously didn't book the tickets under his own name. There's a lot of stops on the journey, but one of them is right here in DC."

Shira considers this. "His wife. He's coming here to look for her."

"That's what I think too."

"Any sign of the others? Keith? Kayla?"

Noam shakes his head. "The facial recognition software hasn't picked up on them. Wherever they are, it doesn't look like they're traveling with him. But this is good, right? It looks like he's coming right to us."

"We don't know that Niamh is here."

"I can try and find out before he gets here. I mean, I don't know what his plan is, but—"

Noam stops talking. An alarm sounds from his laptop. "*Shit.*" He leans forward and starts typing. His movements are harried. Something about them concerns Shira.

"What's happened?" she asks.

"Oh shit, oh shit," Noam says.

"Noam!" Shira places a firm hand on his shoulder. "I need to know what's happening."

He looks up at her, his face ashen. "Someone's hacked me," he says. "It must be when I got into the security, they must have picked up on it and—"

Shira cuts him off. "Then we need to go."

28

With Charlie gone, Kayla sits up front with Keith. Winston and Ryan, father and son, ride in the back.

Kayla watches the side mirror, seeing Union Station growing smaller behind them. "It doesn't feel right," she says.

"What was that?" Keith says, his focus on the road.

"I said it doesn't feel right," she says, "leaving Charlie behind."

"He should already be on the train by now," Winston says. "Where he's going now, we couldn't all go with him. It's too risky."

"I know that," Kayla says. "But that doesn't mean I like it. That doesn't make it feel right. In fact, that's why I hate it. We've sent him off alone and he could get killed. His wife could be killed, or else they'll be locked away forever and no one will know where they are."

Winston looks back at her. He doesn't know what to say.

"I just don't feel good about it, okay?" Kayla says, and she turns back around.

They drive in silence for a while. Ryan is the first to break it. "The three of you have got close, huh?"

"I guess we have," Kayla says.

"What was it you said, Dad, when they were on their way to us?" Ryan says. "You remember?"

Kayla turns again so she can see them both. Winston is looking at his son. "I remember," he says.

Ryan waits, but when his father doesn't share, Ryan does instead. "You said Kayla was like a newly hatched bird, opening her eyes for the first time. She was imprinting on these two—on Charlie and Keith—like a baby bird does on her mother."

Winston doesn't say anything.

"What's that supposed to mean?" Kayla says.

"It means it's no surprise that you miss Charlie," Ryan says. "He and Keith, when you look at them, you see comfort. You see protection. Now, half of that is gone."

"You don't know what you're talking about," Kayla says. "You just like to hear yourself talk."

Ryan chuckles, and Kayla turns away from him, facing front again. Out the corner of her eye she glances at Keith. He's looking up into the mirror, at father and son, and frowning. He turns away from the mirror and drives. Silence falls in the car once again. They drive like this for a long time.

Eventually, Keith glances at the mirror again. Kayla peers into the back. Ryan is sleeping, the side of his head pressed against the glass. Winston is looking out the window. With neither of them listening in, Keith talks.

"I'm gonna miss Charlie too," he says, looking into her eyes quickly before turning back to the road. "But he can take care of himself. We've seen it first-hand. Remember when he jumped between the buildings? He nearly broke his damn ankle, but he still did it." He chuckles, and Kayla laughs too.

"He never let us hear the end of it," she says.

"No he did not," Keith says, smiling. "My point is, they're gonna have a hard time catching him. He knows what he's doing.

And if his wife's in danger, I don't think there's a thing they can do to keep him from her." He reaches over and pats Kayla's leg. "He'll be okay. We'll see him again. I'm almost sure of it."

"Almost?" Kayla says.

"All right then," Keith says. "I'm *certain*. How about that?"

"Better," Kayla says.

"Good. And listen, the best thing we can do to help him and to help ourselves, is to stay our course. It's the only chance we have at taking the fight to The Order, and solving all of our problems. If we're lucky, the next time we see Charlie, we could be ready to put all of this behind us."

Kayla watches the side of his face as he says this. She's not sure he believes his own words. They were for her benefit. He's trying to make her feel better. Trying to assure her—and maybe persuade himself—that this will all be over soon enough.

Kayla wishes she could believe it. She wishes it were true. Except, what then? If they free themselves from The Order, if they expose them for who they are and what they've done, if they bring them down, where does she go from there?

That's another problem for another day. Another in a long line of many.

29

Shira and Noam grab their things and flee from the apartment. Shira leads the way, her bag strapped tight to her back. Her Glock is not in her hand, but she keeps it close, tucked down her waistband and concealed under her jacket. They don't run, but they walk fast, making their way toward the stairwell. Noam is behind her. Shira can hear him breathing hard. He's nervous. He's never been in the field before. More used to sitting behind a desk. He's not a fighter. The thought that they've been tracked down, that someone could be coming for them right now, scares him.

"If they got into my computer," he says, keeping his voice low, "and they know where we are, then that means they know where Charlie is, too. They know he's on that train."

"We'll deal with that later," Shira says.

She can't think about other problems, or the future. Right now, she needs to concentrate on the present, on this one big problem that has suddenly confronted them. They need to get outside of the building. They need to get to the car and they need to get clear.

Shira hears a door swinging closed down below. She hears footsteps coming up. She thinks two sets. No one's talking. She motions for Noam to slow and stick close. She keeps her hand close to her gun. The footsteps get louder, drawing closer. They're not running, though. There doesn't seem to be any kind of rush. Shira doesn't know if this is a good sign or not. If they are coming here looking for her and Noam, they could be conserving their energy. It would make sense not to come running up these steps. If it were her, she'd walk them. Especially since chances are good there are probably men coming up the elevator, too, and more waiting outside.

Shira keeps this in mind as she and Noam get closer to the men on foot. She can see them now, coming around the corner. Two men. Both white. They're big guys. They work out. One of them has a shaved head. The other has close-cropped hair, like he's in the army. They wear dark jeans and heavy boots, and jackets over T-shirts—the skinhead wears a white T-shirt, and the one with cropped hair has a blue one. The latter has a tattoo on the side of his neck. An equal symbol with a slash through it. Not equal.

Shira knows what it means.

The two men are looking up. They've seen their approach. They haven't attempted to rush forward. They have their prey in sight. There's no need to hurry. Shira and Noam can't go anywhere.

Shira doesn't intend to go anywhere. She slows, but she's not going to turn. Shira doesn't know if these Nazis are involved with the people after them. It seems like they could be. Regardless of whether they are or not, they're clearly a threat. Behind her, she can feel Noam's nervous energy. He's buzzing with it. *He* wants to turn and run. He's desperate to bolt. It's the worst thing he could do. Shira reaches back and squeezes his arm. He's vibrating, and her touch is not enough to calm him.

The man with hair locks eyes with Shira. He must feel the way her eyes burn into the tattoo on his neck. He smirks. He reaches into his jacket. Shira sees a flash of shoulder holster. The skinhead reaches into his jacket, too.

Shira moves first. She moves faster. She has the high ground. The advantage. She lets go of Noam and places one hand on the stairwell railing and the other against the wall. She can reach her gun, but she doesn't want to shoot. Doesn't want to draw attention, bring others running. Instead, she hoists herself up and drives her boots into the chests of both men, knocking them back and stopping them from pulling their guns. They need their hands to scramble for purchase. To keep themselves upright and prevent themselves falling down the stairs. The skinhead is closest to the railing. He's able to grab it with both hands. The one with hair is next to the wall. He has nothing to grab onto. He falls back, tumbling backward down the stairwell, head over heels.

Shira goes after the skinhead, pressing her advantage. He's still working on his balance as Shira swings an open-palm shot at his throat. He gags, choked. As his hands go to his neck, Shira slams her elbow into the side of his head, then reaches down and grabs his legs. She flips him over the railing. He can't scream as he drops down the center of the stairwell, his throat too damaged from the earlier blow.

The other Nazi has stopped rolling. He's gone down half a dozen steps. He looks dazed. He's trying to reach for his gun. Shira advances on him, descending two steps at a time. She swings a kick into the side of his head. The other side of his head bounces off the wall. He falls back, unconscious, sliding down a few more steps on his back.

Shira turns to Noam. He hasn't moved from where the fight began. He stares wide-eyed, clutching his laptop case to his chest. "Come on, let's go!" she says.

Noam hurries down after her.

At the bottom of the stairwell, they come across the Nazi Shira flipped over the side. He's landed on his front. He's unconscious, too. His left leg is twisted at a bad angle. It's broken. Shira can see bone poking through. Blood seeps out from under his face. They leave him where he lies and exit the building.

Shira puts an arm across Noam's chest to stop him from rushing off toward the car. "Stay behind me," she says. She moves carefully toward the front corner of the building.

"Were they Nazis?" Noam whispers.

Shira nods without turning.

"What was that? Are they part of this, or is this just some kind of crazy coincidence and they could tell we were Jewish?"

"I don't know," Shira says. She peers out from the corner of the building. There's a van parked not far from them, in front of the main entrance. She retreats back into cover. "Back in the jail cell, Nazis went after Kayla, remember? That was when Keith and Charlie got involved."

"They've been hired? They've been involved all along?"

"I don't know, and it doesn't matter right now. They were already our enemies." She looks around. Their car is parked around the corner, away from the building. "We go down the block," she says, pointing. "Stick close to me and don't look back. Just walk straight, got it?"

Noam nods. He swallows. "Don't look back."

"If they come after us, I'm going to have to start shooting. I'll lay down covering fire, you run ahead and get the car. Clear?"

"Clear."

"Hopefully it won't come to that." They leave the alley and start walking. They stay calm. Their pace is brisk, but they don't hurry. Every fiber of Shira's being wants to look back at the van to make sure no one has seen them and no one is following them. She doesn't turn. She grits her teeth and they get around the corner and to their car. She gets inside, behind the steering wheel. She glances in the mirrors. No one is coming. Shira starts driving.

Noam is breathing hard. "Shit," he says, wiping his brow. "What now?"

"We meet up with Charlie," Shira says.

"We wait until he reaches DC?"

"No. We're not waiting for him here. We won't be the only ones waiting for him. They might go after him on the train, too." She bites her lip. "We need to leave the city, catch up to him on the line. It's better if we meet up with him on his way here, rather than we wait and we all get caught up in an ambush together."

Noam starts pulling out his laptop. "I'll work out where we can cut him off. It might take us a while to drive there, though. He's coming from the other side of the country."

Shira nods. She turns the car west, heading out of the city. "Do what you can."

30

Zeke sits alone in the Oval Office. His back is to the room. He stares out the window, but he isn't really looking. He doesn't see. He's lost in thought. Thinking about the Quinquevirate. Of what they said to him. Of their veiled, and not so veiled, threats. He pictures their faces, and runs through their names, keeping them fresh in his mind. It's important that he remembers who they all are, especially if he's to see them again.

Lord Alfred Walmsley. Timothy Jacques. Gregory Ruby. Milton Redding.

And, of course, Douglas Morrow.

Zeke runs his hands down his face and he sighs. Recently, there has been more bad news. The Israelis, Shira Mizrahi and Noam Katz, evaded capture. They're at large. Yet another failure. Another black mark next to his name. There is *some* good news that has come out of this situation, but until these problems are either all dead or in captivity, it doesn't matter. Finding where the Israelis or any of the others are doesn't matter if they can't catch them. Until they do, this is all chase. It's gone on long enough. Zeke needs this chase to be over. Until it is, he can't breathe easy. He can't rest.

He feels useless, sitting here, waiting. There's nothing else he can do. He's sent out everyone at his disposal. He's given financial carte blanche. The faces of the core three are everywhere—in newspapers, and regularly appearing on the news cycle. Hell, they even have one of their *wives*. If Keith Wright was in any kind of relationship, they'd have his partner, too. Zeke has pressed the importance of a quick clean-up upon all the people who answer to him—on the Nazis and the mercenaries and everyone else. Bonuses have been promised. There is nothing more he can do. Just wait.

He hates the waiting. He hates everything being out of his hands. He hates having to rely on others.

There's a knock at the door. Zeke takes a deep breath and turns the chair around. He becomes aware of the impatient bouncing of his right leg. He conceals beneath the desk and concentrates on forcing it to stop bouncing. He calls for the knocker to enter.

It's Anthony Tomasson. He's alone. He's smiling. He looks pleased with something. "Mind if I take a seat?"

Zeke gestures toward a chair.

Anthony sits directly opposite him. The grin is still on his face. He's trying to suppress it, but he can't wipe it away entirely.

"Is something amusing?" Zeke says.

"Not amusing, no," Anthony says.

"Then what the hell are you smiling at? You look like a damn fool."

The insult does not falter Anthony. He clears his throat. "How was your meeting?"

"What meeting?" Zeke says, though he has a feeling he knows exactly which meeting Anthony is referring to. He's not going to come out and tell him, though. Anthony will have to work for it. "I have dozens of meetings each and every day. You're going to have to be more specific."

"You know which one," Anthony says. There's a gleam in his eye.

Zeke doesn't say anything. He stares at his Vice-President. Anthony finally relents, though his smile never fades. "With the Quinquevirate."

Zeke pauses a little longer, then says, "It was fine."

Anthony raises an eyebrow. "That so?"

"What are you getting at? Do you know something I don't? Have you heard something? I don't appreciate you playing coy like this."

"Are you sure you would describe it as *fine*?" Anthony says.

"What's that supposed to mean?"

Anthony shrugs and leans back in the chair, crossing one leg over the other, making himself comfortable. He looks around the room, as if casting an appraising eye over the décor. As if he's thinking about how he would redecorate. Finally, his eyes settle back on Zeke. "I heard it perhaps *wasn't* so fine."

Zeke feels a lump of ice in his chest. His jaw clenches. He stares at Anthony. "Who told you that?" He thinks of everyone who accompanied him to Bethesda. He thinks about Matt Bunker. Would they talk? Except, none of them know anything. None of them were there in the room with him. Zeke thinks about how he may have come across in the car after, returning to Washington. He was quiet, of course. He had a lot to think about. But the other men were quiet, too. No one tried to engage him. They were quiet on the way there. He wonders what his face could have been doing. If it betrayed him, if it revealed his thoughts. Could his silence and expression have been enough to alert everyone in the vehicle that the meeting had not gone well?

"I'm not at liberty to divulge that information," Anthony says smugly. Zeke doesn't like it.

Zeke leans forward. "And neither was whoever has spoken to you," he says. "What was discussed in that room was *private*. No one outside of it should be privy. So listen to me, Anthony, unless you want to get yourself in a whole world of trouble, you need to tell me right now who it is that has been whispering stories in your ear."

Anthony does not look concerned. He makes a show of inspecting the crease of his trousers, and picking off a piece of lint. "It was a private meeting, certainly," Anthony says. "Between you, and the Quinquevirate. So if I'm telling you I'm not at liberty to divulge who has been talking to me, who do you *think* the message came from?"

Zeke feels his face drop. He can't stop it. "They've spoken to you?"

"Indirectly," Anthony says.

"A messenger."

Anthony nods.

"Who?"

"I've told you already," Anthony says, "and I'm not going to repeat myself again."

Zeke's eyes narrow. "What did they say?"

"Ezekiel," Anthony says. He's gloating. In this moment, Zeke hates him. It's a burning hatred. He despises the smug man sitting before him with all of his being. "You had a private meeting, and I received a private message."

"Then why are you here talking to me? You felt like rubbing it in?"

"I just wanted to make you aware, Zeke. That's all. But I also wanted to let you know that when the time comes, I won't be the one holding the knife. Or the needle, as the case may be." He smirks. "I won't be getting my own hands dirty."

"You little prick."

"Just confident, Zeke."

"Confident in what?"

"That you've already fucked things up. That it won't be long before that seat is mine."

"You should have kept your mouth shut," Zeke says, gripping the edge of the desk. "You should never have let me know. I still have time to turn things around, and when I do you're going to regret coming here to gloat."

Anthony doesn't appear concerned. "If you say so. And it's not gloating, Zeke. I came here to give you a sporting chance. But this is politics, after all. Do you think I became a politician because I *don't* want to be president? I want what you have. President Tomasson has a nice ring to it, doesn't it? I'm sure my wife will agree. First Lady Michelle Tomasson. She'll like that. It's what she wants, too. That's why she hitched her wagon to my train in the first place. Remind me, Zeke, who is the current First Lady?" There is a wicked look on Anthony's face.

Zeke is unmarried. Anthony knows this.

"It strikes me that the Quinquevirate is realizing already that they made a mistake," Anthony says. "You're not the right man for this job. You never were. Let's put Order business to one side for a moment. Let's put what the Quinquevirate think about *you* to one side for a moment. Are you paying attention to the polls, Zeke? Are you paying attention to what the ordinary American citizen thinks about you after just a few short weeks in office?"

Zeke has no idea. He's been too busy to concern himself with such things.

"No?" Anthony says. "They don't like you, Zeke. They didn't vote for you. They didn't elect you. You came into this position through death. You've come in amidst all this chaos, and they don't see things getting any better under you. And you're not married. You're not even widowed. Do you know the last time America had an unmarried president? James Buchanan. 1857 to 1861. And *he's* not exactly fondly remembered."

"Well done," Zeke says, unimpressed, "you went online

before you came to see me. Buchanan's being unmarried had nothing to do with his popularity, or lack thereof."

"If you think so. But the facts remain, you're not married. You're not widowed. Hell, you're not even seeing anyone. Do you know what the optics of that look like? You're not a popular man right now, Zeke, not with anyone." Anthony begins to stand.

Zeke realizes he's still gripping the edges of the desk. He lets go. His wrists and fingers are aching from squeezing the wood.

"I didn't come to gloat," Anthony says. "I mean it when I say that. I really didn't. I came to give you a chance. If you go back to the Quinquevirate now, tell them you're not the man for this job, there's a good chance they could be lenient with you. You'll lose your position, but you'll keep your life. Or, continue on as you are, and you'll never see it coming. It's your choice, Zeke. But one way or another, I *am* going to be president."

Zeke stares, struggling to keep his breathing under control. He feels his mouth twist into a sneer. "Fuck you," he says. "Get out, you treacherous little prick. We're done here."

Anthony chuckles. He's already leaving.

After he's gone, Zeke has to catch his breath. Has to calm his pounding heart. He rubs his hands together, trying to get rid of the cramping pain there. He needs to be calm. There's no use in letting Anthony push his buttons. There's no benefit to rushing into anything just because his blood is hot. He's no good if he can't think straight.

He closes his eyes and takes deep breaths. He does think on some of the things Anthony said, but he does so now from a calm, measured distance. If nothing else, he was right about Zeke's being unmarried. He was right about how it might look to the public. If a man is in the White House, they like to see a First Lady beside him. There's the saying, behind every great man there is a woman. People believe it, whether they're aware of it or not. It's ingrained into their subconscious. Zeke worries now that without a wife, perhaps he looks weak. From what Anthony was saying about the polls, it would certainly appear so. Of course, that has to do with more than just his lack of a First Lady.

The simple fact is, Zeke has never been interested in taking a wife. He's always been too busy—first with his political career, and that was soon coupled with his duties to The Order. And also, and mainly, he has a general disinterest when it comes to women —to being in a relationship with them, that is. He treasures his personal time too much. He's never had trouble hooking up with them, he just doesn't want them to still be around after it's over. His flings have never been an issue before, but things are different now. He's president. He's the mouthpiece for The Order. For the Quinquevirate.

And the Quinquevirate are already bored of him. The majority of them made that clear to his face, but now they're already reaching out to a potential replacement. The message is loud and clear—he's just a puppet, and he can be replaced at any time, and with ease. His succession is already lined up.

Zeke isn't prepared to go down without a fight. He's not going to roll over and take it, not when his own life is at stake. He was determined to prove the Quinquevirate wrong. To show them that he is more than capable. However, if they're already making premature decisions, if power moves are being played, then Zeke needs to get in on the action. He can't stand by the sidelines, twiddling his thumbs and hoping for the best. He needs to shore up his own powerbase.

Zeke contacts Matt, tells him to come to the office. He's feeling calmer now, though his anger continues to simmer beneath the surface. He continues his deep breathing until Matt arrives.

Matt looks around the empty room, making sure they're alone. "Everything okay?"

Zeke doesn't offer Matt a seat. He clasps his hands together atop the desk and stares at him. Matt frowns.

Zeke takes his time. He sits back. "Are you aware that the Quinquevirate have contacted Anthony Tomasson?"

Matt tilts his head. "In person?"

"No. They sent a messenger. Were *you* that messenger, Matt?"

"No," Matt says, and there's no hesitation in his voice or on his face.

Zeke believes him.

"What's happened?" Matt says. "You seem angry."

Zeke can't admit to this. Can't admit to anything. He has to appear strong. He *always* has to appear strong. He has to *be* strong. "Everything's fine," he says. "Matt, let me ask you a question."

"Okay."

"Are you loyal to me?"

"Yes," Matt says, though it's clear he's confused by the question. "Of course."

"And you're loyal to The Order?"

"Yes. What has Anthony said?"

"You don't need to be concerned about that right now, but there's something I need you to do for me. Keep an eye on him. In his security detail, make sure there's always one of our people. Someone you trust. I want updates on everything he's doing. *Everything*. Who he sees and where he goes. Hell, I want to know what he has for breakfast."

Matt hesitates. "Do you have doubts about *his* loyalty?"

"Yes," Zeke says. "I do." Not to The Order, but to himself. Matt doesn't need to know this.

"But you said the Quinquevirate contacted him?"

"And that's why I'm concerned about his loyalty now more than ever. I need certainties, Matt. Assurances. I've been placed in an important position. The future of The Order counts on me. I can't have someone like him cause it to come crumbling down."

Matt nods, clearly perturbed. He prepares to leave, but Zeke stops him.

"I trust you, Matt," he says. "If Anthony is causing a schism within The Order, I know that I can count on you to be on the right side of it."

"Thank you, sir," Matt says, but he can't hide his alarm.

"I want you to know, you can trust me, too. We may not be able to rely on everyone, but I believe it's important that we can at least rely on each other. I'll always remember your loyalty, Matt. I will repay it. Do you hear me?"

"I hear you."

"I'll always keep my word."

"I appreciate that."

Zeke nods. He breathes a little easier. He can trust Matt. He just needs to keep him on his side. He's confident he can do this. "Keep in touch."

Matt leaves.

31

It's the morning of the second day of his train journey. Charlie keeps his head down. Sticks to his cabin in the sleeper car at the front of the train. It's not big, but it's more than spacious enough for one man. It could fit a family. Wherever Winston pulled his funds from, he wasn't afraid to splash them around in order to give Charlie some privacy.

Charlie has used that privacy well. He's shaved his head in the small bathroom, his elbows bumping against the cramped walls as he did so. He shaved his face, too, getting rid of most of his stubble but leaving himself with a goatee. Minor changes to adjust his appearance.

The rest of the time, he's tried to busy himself to keep from going crazy. He's stripped and cleaned the Glock. It's loaded with one full magazine, and has another spare. Nowhere near enough for what he might have to do.

He thinks a lot on *that*, too. He spends most of his time thinking on that. Thus far, he's no further forward. He has no plan for getting his wife out. It's going to be hard for him to formulate one until he knows where she's being held. *That* is his priority. Finding out this crucial information. That's all he has so far.

Airing that she had been arrested was to get him to come to them, and that's exactly what he's doing. He has to be smarter than them. Has to be smarter than to do what they want, and what they expect.

Like he told Kayla, and like it was drilled into him in his past life with the SAS, *who dares wins*. He has to believe that now more than ever. All those platitudes—*fortune favors the bold*, all that kind of stuff—if ever he needed fortune to be on his side, it's coming up very soon.

He sits by the window and watches the scenery go by. This is the most he's ever seen of America. With his plagued mind, he's not really taking it in. Looking without seeing. Every so often, he exercises on what little floor space is available to him. There's enough for him to do push-ups, so long as he keeps his elbows tucked in. He can do squats and sit-ups. They're more than enough. They keep him sharp. Keep him in shape. Keep him focused on something other than where he's going.

The train begins to slow, nearing a station. A voice comes over the system, telling the passengers that the train is pulling into Atlanta, Georgia. Charlie stays away from the window, angling himself in the seat so he can see outside onto the platform but so the people waiting aren't able to see him. He checks to see if there are any cops out there, or anyone else he should be concerned about. He sees a lot of civilians. No one leaps out at him as someone of concern.

He sits and he waits for the train to start moving again. For them to leave Atlanta and draw ever closer to DC. Back to DC. Where all his problems first began.

Time passes. The train remains still. It's different at every station, Charlie has noticed, but this feels especially long. He keeps an eye on the time. Fifteen minutes pass. Twenty. The wait soon reaches half an hour. Charlie wonders if they're changing crew. If they're getting a new driver. He hasn't seen much of the people who staff the train. He orders food and they bring it and outside of that he doesn't see anyone else.

The only time Charlie has seen the rest of the train was when he first got on. He took a quick walk through all of the cars, getting an idea of the layout. If everything goes well, he shouldn't need to see the rest of the train again until he reaches DC. Being stopped in Atlanta for so long is starting to concern him.

As he's about to get up to investigate, a voice comes over the system. "This is a notice for all passengers. We're currently at a standstill due to unforeseen maintenance work on the lines ahead of us. We're monitoring the situation closely and will hopefully be moving again soon. We apologize for the inconvenience and will do our best to keep you updated."

Even through his closed door, Charlie can hear the groan that ripples through the train. He glances out at the platform again. It's empty. He closes the curtains. This sudden stop makes him uncomfortable, but there's nothing he can do about it. He sits tight, and waits for them to start moving again.

32

Shira and Noam are in Atlanta, heading toward Peachtree Station. Noam stopped the train. He got into the system and made it seem like there was an electrical fault. He can see that the train has been stalled since. Shira sticks to the speed limit, but it's hard. She rides it, being careful not to go over.

"How far out are we?" Shira says.

"Ten minutes," Noam says. "Take the next right. It looks like a small station. We probably won't see it until we're close to it."

"How long has the train been held up?"

"Closing in on an hour now." Noam is typing. "I'm booking our tickets."

Before long, Shira can see the station. It's quiet outside. She goes to the parking lot and finds a space. "Are we good?"

"We're booked," Noam says.

Shira gets out and grabs her bag. She passes Noam's bags to him. Chances are, they might never see this car again. They take out everything important to them. It isn't much. Just their bags containing their scant belongings.

Noam closes his laptop and slips it inside its case. They go to the station to check in. The tickets are on Noam's phone. The ticket inspector checks them. He raises an eyebrow. "Looks like you folks have got lucky," he says. "Your train ain't left yet."

Noam nods. "We saw that!" he says, then laughs. "We were running late—we came here thinking we were gonna have to get the next one. I couldn't believe it when I saw ours hadn't gone."

"Just a minor issue on the line," the inspector says. "Shouldn't be much longer now."

Noam thanks him and he and Shira head to the train. They're in the fifth car. "He has no idea how long it's going to take," Noam says as they climb aboard, chuckling under his breath. "Only I know that."

"Give it another ten minutes," Shira says. "We don't want it to look like we've just on and suddenly it's moving. That's too obvious."

The people inside look bored. They're reading magazines and books, or they're playing on their phones. None of them look up or bat an eyelid at the new arrivals.

Shira and Noam find their seats. The chairs are positioned on a slant, so they face out of the windows. The chairs on either side of them are empty, allowing them some privacy. They don't store their bags overhead. They keep them close, at their feet. Noam keeps his laptop case on his thighs, but he doesn't take the computer out yet. He checks the time.

Shira looks around, but she keeps it subtle. There are cameras. She doesn't want them picking up on her face. Noam notices and leans closer, whispering to her. "I've put them on a loop. They won't pick up on us. As long as we're in this car, it was like we were never here."

"What about Charlie?" she says, turning back. "Have you picked up on him?"

"I know where he is," Noam says. "Last I checked, he's never left his cabin as long as he's been on this train."

Shira nods. "All right. Then we'll sit tight for now. We don't want to spook him. But keep an eye on his cabin. Make sure he doesn't give us the slip. And make it so only you can see. Loop the rest of the cameras. Every car. Erase Charlie from the footage, too."

Noam takes his laptop out. They sit and they wait, allowing more time to pass. Noam hasn't started work yet. It's quiet in the car and they don't want his typing to draw attention. Shira knows that when he removes the fake fault from the train line, they won't instantly start moving. It'll still take a little while before the train can go again, the driver making sure everything is right.

"Okay," she says. "Turn it off. Get us moving."

33

It feels good to be free.

Now that things are finally happening, Harlan can relish his new life outside of the prison. Now that he has an objective, he feels alive again. Reborn. He feels truly free.

Smuggling orders out when he was in solitary was one thing, but being here in the field is completely different. Now, he feels like a real leader. A general. He's always preferred leading from the front. When his new government-funded hacking team got into the Jew's computer and saw that he'd found out where the Brit was, it was time to get into action. He sent men direct to where the Jews had been hiding out, but he didn't get ahead of himself. He knew there was no point rushing out to Union Station. The train was already leaving. Instead, he got his hackers to check the cameras in the surrounding area, to see if they could find the rest of the runaways.

They did. The Brit's friends dropped him off, right outside the rear entrance to the station. Kayla and Keith and a couple of new bodies in the back who he didn't get a good look at. Whoever the two new arrivals were, they didn't matter. If the group had found friends, well, that sucked for their new friends. They were about to get themselves caught up in a crossfire. It's no skin off Harlan's nose. He doesn't care what happens to them.

"Keep an eye on that vehicle," he said. "Don't fucking lose it, whatever you do. You lose it, I'm gonna take your balls."

He had a meeting with Earl Borden. "I'm going after the girl," he said. "Get me a team."

"You want me to come with?" Earl said.

Harlan grinned. "Of course I do."

"What about the Brit?"

"He's doing exactly what they wanted, right? They got his wife, and he's going to her. DC, right? Get in touch with our boys out there, except I don't want them to wait until DC. Tell them to get on board that train early. A few stops before. They said he's ex-military, right? I doubt he's stupid. He might not get off in DC. He could get off before and find another way there. I want our boys on that train. They get him that way."

That was a couple of days ago now. The Jews managed to hurt a couple of his men and give the rest of them the slip, but he's not sweating it too much. They'll get theirs. They're as much a part of this as he is, and they're all locked in together.

Harlan and his team didn't have to start moving straight away. It seemed like the group comprising Kayla and Keith was coming their way, down to Texas. "Let's just wait and see how things go," Harlan said. "Keep the team on standby. When they cross into the state, that's when we move."

The group reached Texas and Harlan and his team moved out, looking to catch them up.

He rides up front in a black van, another sticking close behind them. Earl is driving. Harlan has his window down. Behind his sunglasses, his eyes are closed. He feels the warmth from the sun on the left side of his face as it shines through the windshield, and on the right, he feels the blowing wind keeping him cool.

Freedom.

In the back of the van, there are five men, cramped but uncomplaining. Heavily armed. It's the same in the van behind. Fourteen, all told. They're not messing around. When they catch up to the girl and the others, they're taking them in. Harlan has been presented with a great opportunity to be part of The Order, and he's not going to squander it. Great things are coming for the Vanguard Whites. They just need to play their cards right. They just need to do things *properly*.

One of his hackers is in the back of the van. He keeps in touch with the others back at the compound. So far, the hackers have not let Harlan down. He's pleased. They want to keep their balls, he's sure. It's incentive enough.

Harlan turns, calling back to the hacker. "Still got them?"

"We've got them," he says, looking up. "We've never lost them. Never gonna lose them."

It hadn't taken long for Kayla and the others to get out of reach of security cameras. The hackers were prepared for that, though. By that point, they weren't using cameras anymore. They were using satellites.

"Where they now?"

The hacker glances at his laptop. "Looks like they're heading down to the border."

"Mexico?" Harlan says. "Think they're looking to hide out, put this all behind them?"

"Could be," the hacker says. "Hard to tell for sure. Right now, they're out in the middle of nowhere. They're not even on the road."

34

Texas is big, and Texas is hot.
 It feels to Keith like they've been driving through it forever. It's not as hot as Death Valley, though. He reminds himself of this as he wipes sweat from his brow. The A/C is running at full. Keith has his window down. The closer they get down to the border, to Mexico, the hotter it feels. It's early evening, and Keith had hoped that the lateness of the day would bring coolness. So far, this has not been the case.

They haven't spoken much since they dropped Charlie off. Splitting like that, it seems to have sucked the air out of the car. They've taken the long route, sticking to quiet roads, same as always. Passing through towns so small they probably didn't have names. When they needed to rest, they didn't check into a motel. They pulled off the road, concealed themselves under trees, and slept in the car. They kept watch in shifts. Keith, and then Ryan, and then Winston. They'd let Kayla sleep through, despite her objections.

Kayla sees a sign for the Mexico border. Thirty miles. She turns to see Winston. "How far away are we? How much longer?"

"Down to the border, and then we head west," Winston says.

"How long do we go west?"

"It'll be about two hours."

"It'll be dark soon," Keith says. "It'll be dark when we get there."

Winston grunts.

"We're not going straight in when it's dark," Keith says. "We need time to watch the place in the light."

"Whatever you think is best," Winston says.

"How close to the border do you want me to get? We don't want them to see us."

"We're going to have to go off-road," Winston says. "I'll tell you when."

"I don't know how many more times we can take this car off-road. It's not built for it. It's already feeling heavier. It's got sand gumming up the works from back in Death Valley."

"It is what it is," Winston says.

Keith frowns at him in the mirror. "I'm not sure what you expect me to make of that. If the damn thing dies and we're in the middle of nowhere, what then?"

"I'm just saying, we have to do the best with what we have."

Kayla tries to stretch out her legs. "I'm sick of being in this car."

"We're all sick of it," Ryan says. "But have you thought about what happens when we *do* stop?"

Kayla doesn't answer. She doesn't turn.

Ryan leans forward. "Have you thought about what you're going to say to him?"

Kayla stares straight ahead.

"Just leave it, Ryan," Winston says.

"Why? I'm not trying to be a dick. I'm just curious. Have you thought about it, Kayla?"

"Of course I've thought about it," she says. "And I don't know. I don't *know*."

"Listen," Ryan says, "I'm not trying to upset you. I just want to make sure you're prepared. If we get out there and you freeze up, what then?"

"We're not going out there for Kayla to have a confrontation with this man," Keith says. "We're going there to get answers. We're going there to figure out our next move. This guy is the only decent lead we have."

"Ryan's right, though," Kayla says. "I *am* going to have to talk to him. It'll be impossible not to. And when I see him, I don't know what will happen. I don't know how I'll feel or what I might say. I might just freeze up, and I don't want to do that."

Keith hears the way her voice breaks a little when she talks. She's close to tears.

"Whatever happens when we get there," Winston says, "it is imperative that we do not allow him to speak the words. If he does that, then we've lost Kayla. Is that clear?"

"What do the words even mean?" Kayla says.

"I'm not going to tell you them," Winston says.

"That's not what I'm asking. I'm asking what they *mean*. Why they were selected."

"I don't know that," Winston says. "I was told what the trigger words would be. They probably mean something to the man who passed them down to me, but I don't know what that is."

Keith remembers the words. He's wondered what the meaning behind them might be, too. "Kayla," he says, his voice soft.

She looks at him.

"I'll be there with you," he says. "No matter how bad you might feel, I'll be right there with you. He can't hurt you. Not anymore."

"I don't want to think about it," Kayla says. "The closer we get, the worse I'm going to feel. I know it's going to happen. I just want to get there, and then… I don't know. I'll deal with it when I have to."

The car falls silent.

Keith drives, waiting for Winston to tell him where and when to turn off. He watches the road. There are other vehicles around. Most of them are heading in the opposite direction. There's one behind them, but it's far back.

"Pull over," Winston says. "This road is quiet. We should let it clear. It doesn't look like it'll take too long."

Keith pulls to the side of the road. The sun is lowering. Keith can see it setting out of the corner of his eye. It'll be dark within the house. It's going to be difficult for him driving off-road as the night sets in. He'll have to be careful. He'll have to take his time.

The car behind them draws closer and then continues past. Soon after, a truck follows after it. It's clear behind them. Up ahead, a few more cars pass from the opposite direction. The area is clear.

"All right," Winston says. "Off-road. Take us west."

35

Shira is tired, but she forces herself to stay awake, despite the swaying of the train. To stay alert. To stay focused.

It's dark outside. Others in their carriage have either left to go to the sleeper car, or else they've dozed off in their seats. Noam is snoozing beside her. His laptop is closed and back in its case. Shira had to put it away. Noam fell asleep with it illuminating him. The lights are off overhead now. She didn't want the light of the laptop to disturb anyone else, or draw attention to them.

Shira yawns. She stretches in her seat, twisting side to side. She'd like nothing more than to fall asleep right now. She could do with the rest. She can't remember the last time she had a good night's sleep. She runs her hands down her face and slaps her cheeks. In the window opposite, she can see her reflection. She looks gaunt. Her eyes are sunken. There's nothing there but darkness. She looks like a skull. She's sure it's just the lighting. She doesn't feel like she's lost that much weight, though when she thinks about it, she's not sure when the last time she had a decent meal was, either. On the move, she and Noam grabbed what they could when they could. Even in the apartment, they ate small meals that could be quickly put together.

She leans closer to the window so she can see her eyes. Up close, she doesn't look so bad. She's tired and she's hungry and she's stressed, and to top it all off she's in mourning, too. She looks about how she should. The lighting's not great, either.

She hasn't gone to speak to Charlie yet. Noam has kept the security camera feed live on his laptop, and they've seen that he hasn't left his cabin yet. When he finally does, they assume it will be because he's preparing to get off. That's when they'll intercept him. That's when they'll introduce themselves. Explain who they are. They'll be very careful. He's liable to be jumpy. They don't want to alarm him. They're getting close to DC, and Shira assumes he'll try to get off the train soon.

The train begins to slow. Shira thinks about nudging Noam to wake him up for when they pull into the next station. They're in Virginia now. It won't be long until they reach DC. Just a couple more hours. She leaves him. Lets him sleep. One of them should. She pulls his laptop out and turns it back on and keeps an eye on Charlie's cabin. She goes back through the footage to make sure he hasn't already left. His cabin door remains closed.

The train stops. Shira sits facing the opposite platform. She has to turn to see the one they've pulled up to. At this time of night, it's quiet. There are more people getting off than those getting on.

Shira freezes. She sees a group of men that make her heart race, and not in a good way. Alarm bells are ringing. She sinks down in her chair to stay out of view of them.

She counts seven. They're not in uniform, but they're dressed so similarly they might as well be. Jeans and plain T-shirts and dark jackets that could easily conceal weaponry. Most of them have shaved heads. Some of them have tattoos on the sides of their necks. Some of them have them on the backs of their hands, or covering their forearms where they've rolled up their sleeves. They remind her of the men she and Noam ran into in the stairwell back in DC. She recognizes some of the symbols they have inked onto their skin, the same as she did in the stairwell. They're Nazis. They're getting on the train.

Now she wakes Noam up.

36

It's been a couple of days since Anthony came to see him, and Zeke thinks he's slept a grand total of six hours since then.

His nerves are fraught. Despite everything, he thinks he manages to give the impression of being calm and in control. He hasn't snapped at anyone, not even Anthony himself when they've been in meetings together. And he sees the looks that Anthony gives him. The sly smirks. They're hard to miss. Anthony is just waiting for Zeke to fail. Picturing himself where Zeke is.

Outside of what is absolutely necessary, Zeke does not spend much time with Anthony anymore. It's only now, in his absence, that he realizes how much time they were spending together before. How much Zeke had come to rely on him, thinking they were in this together. How wrong he was. He thinks he understands now what it must have felt like for Frank Stewart when he realized Zeke had killed him. Had betrayed him. That's how this feels. A betrayal.

No one is on his side. Even his own side is against him. The men who put him here, they're already tired of him.

Zeke is in his room. It's late. Things are never fully asleep in the White House, but right now, it's as quiet as it ever gets. He isn't in bed. The bed is still made up, untouched, from when the maids last put it together a few days ago. Any sleep Zeke has managed to get has been in the chair he's currently sitting in next to the window. He has a clear view of the door, should anyone try to sneak in on him. He starts at every unexpected noise.

It's so hard for him to think. He'd expected that fearing for his life would put things in perspective, would make them crystal clear and his focus would become razor sharp, but this has not been the case. It's more like a fog has descended. It's like he's wading through treacle. He knows that if he doesn't clear his head then he's as good as dead, but this just makes things worse.

He's one man. How can he be expected to go up against The Order, up against the Quinquevirate? It's a fool's errand. These people they're chasing down, they don't understand how hopeless it is for them. They might keep slipping through his fingertips for now, but they can't forever. There's nowhere they can go. Nowhere they can hide. Eventually, they *will* be caught. Most of them won't survive their capture. Zeke doesn't need them to. In fact, it would be a hell of a lot easier for him if they were already dead.

He knows that his people are closing in on them, that the Vanguard Whites are showing their worth, but it's not enough to be close. They need to be on top of them. They need to have them. Only then can Zeke relax. If he gets lucky, they capture the runaways and this is all over by tomorrow. He can't just assume this is going to happen. Not until it's done, until it's over, will he be satisfied. That will get the Quinquevirate off his back. Then Anthony will see who is smirking.

The alternative...

The alternative doesn't bear thinking about, but he must. He has to be prepared. Failure to prepare is preparing to fail.

If things don't go his way, he needs to be ready for what happens next. It might not come tomorrow, or next week, or even next month, but if the Quinquevirate continues to be displeased with him, they *will* send someone for him, and he won't see it coming. So what can he do? He won't go down without a fight. He's willing to fight for this cause, for everything The Order believes in and everything they want, but not at the cost of his own life. Nothing is more valuable to him than that, and certainly not some belief in an authoritarian future.

He has to consider things from that angle. He's looked into the five men who make up the Quinquevirate since he had the meeting with them in Bethesda. They have no real records to speak of. For all five of them, their occupations are listed as 'businessman' and 'entrepreneur.' The only one he was able to find anything of real substance on was Lord Alfred Walmsley, though even then his occupation was still listed the same as the others. He was born into his peerage in an upper-class British family located in Surrey. He's a distant cousin to the Royal Family, and in line to the throne—though only if more than a hundred people die ahead of him. Zeke wonders if this is potentially a future ambition for The Order.

The Order don't just want America. This is clear. This is known. They want the world. America is a stepping off point. When they have America, Canada will soon follow. Zeke assumes Timothy Jacques is already weaving webs up there. Then Britain, likely through whatever machinations Lord Walmsley has playing out across the pond.

If they want the world, and they're prepared to take it, what can he do in turn?

He strokes his chin and considers this.

There's a knock at his door and Zeke nearly falls from his chair. He stares. Stares at the handle. The door is locked. The handle doesn't turn, doesn't rattle. There's another knock, though it's softer this time as if it's realized he might be asleep and doesn't want to wake him.

Zeke swallows and then takes a deep breath. Steadies himself. "Who is it?"

"It's me, sir." Matt's voice.

Zeke thinks he can perhaps breathe a sigh of relief, but he doesn't. He wants to trust Matt, but he can't fully commit. He goes to the door and unlocks it, but opens it only a little. He's wearing pajamas with a robe and feels suddenly exposed. He pulls the robe tight at the front. Looking out, he notices his bodyguards are not outside his room. He frowns. There's only Matt and, behind him, a woman. Zeke doesn't recognize her. She wears a charcoal-grey dress with tights, and pumps with a sensible heel. She has red hair and pale skin, and looks a little younger than Zeke, maybe ten years at a guess. She's attractive, though. She gives Zeke a small smile, her eyes sparkling, and for a second, he wonders if Matt has brought him an escort.

"Can we come in?" Matt says.

Zeke eyes them both, then steps back and holds the door wide. They enter. Zeke closes the door. He checks the time. "It's very late, Matt," he says. "What are you doing here?"

"I came *because* it's late," Matt says. "I wanted us to have privacy. I had a feeling you wouldn't be sleeping."

Zeke eyes the woman.

Matt sees where he's looking. "This is Sarah Cuthbert," he says. "She's going to be your new aide."

"She is?" Zeke says. "What was wrong with the last one?"

"Sarah is one of us," Matt says and leaves it at that.

"I see," Zeke says.

"I wanted the two of you to have a chance to get acquainted, away from everyone else," Matt says. He tilts his head and draws Zeke to the side, away from Sarah and out of earshot. "I've been thinking about what you said the other day." His voice is low, conspiratorial. "I believe in The Order, Mr. President. I believe in its aims. But I can still think for myself, and I'm not so sure I believe in Anthony Tomasson. From what I've seen, there is only one man who can be the face of The Order, and follow through on their mission plan if they start to falter. That's you. I'm *your* ally, Mr. President. You can count on me. But I'm just one man. We need more allies. I've vetted Ms. Cuthbert myself. She will make a good friend for us."

Matt takes a step back and smiles at Sarah. "I'll leave the two of you to get to know each other. When you're ready to leave, Sarah, call me and I'll escort you out. We don't want anyone to see you creeping out of the president's bedroom in the middle of the night."

She grins at this, then she and Zeke wait until Matt has left. When he's gone, she holds her hand out to Zeke. "It's a pleasure to finally meet you, Mr. President." Her voice is soft, but has a hard edge to it. She's not afraid to get firm if she has to. Not afraid to raise her voice. From the expression she wears, too, Zeke can see she's used to getting what she wants.

Zeke takes the hand. They shake. Her grip is strong, her fingernails biting into the back of his hand. "Ms. Cuthbert," he says, glancing at her left hand. There is no wedding ring.

"Please," she says, "call me Sarah."

"And call me Zeke," he says, motioning for her to take a seat. Zeke sits in the chair close to her, their knees almost touching. "Well," he says. "I wasn't expecting company tonight. You already have the job, and I trust Matt's judgment, so I'm not sure what to say."

"Say whatever you like," Sarah says. "Ask me anything. We should get to know each other before we face your cabinet together."

Zeke nods at this. She's right. "Okay. Where are you from?"

"New Hampshire."

"You don't have an accent."

"I haven't lived there in a very long time."

"Irish?"

She grins and flicks a strand of her red hair. "Everyone always thinks so, but no. Scottish."

"Ah, same," Zeke says. "How old are you, if you don't mind my asking?"

"I don't. Forty-six. I know you're fifty-five."

"You've done your research."

"Of course I have. I always come prepared."

"I'm very glad to hear that. Sarah is a very nice name. It means 'princess,' doesn't it?"

She nods. "So my parents told me."

"They must have had high hopes."

"All parents do. Or at least they should."

"Do you have any children?"

"No."

"Ever been married?"

"No."

"Any reason why?"

"I could ask you the same thing."

"It's never appealed to me."

"Likewise."

"Your work came first?"

"To an extent."

"Do you have interest in men? Women? Or perhaps neither?"

"I like men, Zeke." She grins. "But just because I like them doesn't mean I've ever felt the need to pin myself down with one. I assume it's the same for you."

"I'm glad you can understand that." Zeke shifts in his chair. He glances toward the closed door and then leans closer.

"This looks serious," Sarah says.

"It is serious. How long have you been part of The Order?"

"Seven years. And you've been a member for ten."

"I don't know how you would have found that out, but I'm impressed."

"I have my ways. That's why Matt Bunker chose me to be your new aide."

"What else did he tell you?"

"He told me your concerns regarding Vice-President Anthony Tomasson."

"Mm. I'm concerned about his loyalty."

"His loyalty to The Order," Sarah says, tilting her head, "or his loyalty to you?"

Zeke doesn't answer.

Sarah smiles. "You don't need to be shy, Zeke. You can be open with me. That's why I'm here."

He decides that silence remains his best option. He's only just met this woman. It doesn't matter how well Matt has vetted her, he still needs to play this meeting careful. This is more about getting him to know *her*. The less she knows about him for now, the better.

"I've been thinking about Anthony," she says. "I assume that if he's making a move against you, he's not doing that of his own accord. Correct? He's got the go-ahead of the Quinquevirate. Am I right? Otherwise, he'd need some really big balls, because he wouldn't just be going up against you. He'd be going up against *them*. And I don't think he has the testicular fortitude for that kind of a move."

Zeke says nothing, but he can't help a smirk.

"It's understandable for you to be coy," Sarah says. "But here's something you need to know about me, Zeke. I'm not really concerned about the wants of five old men I've never met, who pass their judgments down from on high."

"How do you know they're all men? Did you manage to find that out, too?"

She gives him a look, as if asking him how he could be so naïve. "Just an educated, unsurprised guess. I'm not here in service to them, Zeke. And as much as I might believe in The Order, I'm not here in service to that, either. I'm here in service to *you*."

Zeke studies her.

"So I suppose the question now is, what exactly *is* The Order that we both serve? And is there a way in which it can be improved?"

Zeke likes what she's saying, but still he doesn't respond.

Sarah leans forward. "You know what I think, Mr. President?"

"What?"

"I think that *you* could have the balls. Right now, you're just not sure of yourself. That's why you're still awake this late at night, and why you don't look like you've been sleeping. That's why you look like you've got so much on your mind. You're worried, aren't you? And it's more than that. You're *scared*. You're scared for your life. I don't blame you, Zeke. I know how you got this position."

Zeke grunts. "Who talks to you?"

"Anyone and everyone, but I'll never name names. If I want to find something out, I will. If I want something, I'll get it. If there's something I need, there's nothing can stop me. You want me on your side, Zeke, because the last thing in this world that anyone wants is to be going against me."

Zeke studies her in silence, and she looks right back at him. She's relaxed. Calm. She meets his eyes with ease.

"Let me ask you something," he says.

"That's why I'm here."

"If you were in my position, and your life was in danger… If you had to go up against The Order, up against the Quinquevirate, what would you do?"

Sarah is silent in thought until she says, "I would schmooze."

Zeke blinks. "I don't understand."

"I would consolidate my own power. I would grow my own army. The only way to do that, is to schmooze. To kiss ass. It doesn't matter if I'd feel degraded doing so—all that matters is the outcome. And in doing so, in ingratiating myself to these people, I'd find who was on my side, and who is against. And then, for those who are for, I would show them that I can offer them something greater than what they already think they're getting."

Zeke folds his arms and strokes his chin, considering what she has said. "What could they be offered?"

"I don't know. That would take some thinking. But I suppose I'd have to consider, what do people want more than anything else? What is it they can never get enough of?"

"Power?" Zeke says. "Money?"

"You can't give away the former," she says. "Not when you're consolidating it for yourself. But money—that's certainly something everyone wants." She sits back. "And I think that might be your answer."

"I don't have money to just give away."

"No, but you're certainly more than capable of presenting people with the opportunity to make more for themselves. How familiar are you with oligarchy, Zeke?"

"I'm very familiar with it. The Quinquevirate are an oligarchy."

"Exactly. You need to create an oligarchy—a Quinquevirate—of your own."

Zeke grins. "The word oligarchy has always reminded me of *monarchy*. I suppose, again, it's the same thing. The meaning behind your name is shining through, Sarah. Perhaps you really are a princess."

She shakes her head. "I'm no princess," she says. "I'm a queen."

"Not yet," Zeke says. "But soon." He holds out his hand and she takes it. Once again, they shake. "This has been an enlightening conversation, Ms. Cuthbert. I can see that I'm going to enjoy working with you very, very much."

37

At the window, Charlie sees the seven men getting on the train in Virginia. They've stuck close to each other while on the platform. They're clearly here together. He doesn't like the look of them. They look like a gang. They set off alarm bells. He sees their tattoos, too. The symbols. He knows what they represent. He knows what these men believe. It concerns him. The thought occurs to him that they could have some connection to the men back in that DC cell, the men he and Keith had to rescue Kayla from shortly after the explosion that killed the Vice-President and so many others. Has The Order recruited them? Were they always a part of this?

As they come aboard, the group splits. Five of them head toward the rear, but it looks like they could be separating further, entering the train in different cars. The remaining two men get on at the front.

If they *were* here sent by The Order, that means they're looking for him. All those different sections of the train they've stepped into, they won't remain there. They'll be on the move. Searching.

Right now, he's just making assumptions. They could be

nothing more than seven white supremacists looking to get a late-night train to DC. They might not know about him at all. They might not care. Charlie isn't going to take the chance, though. His paranoia is what keeps him alive. When it speaks, he listens. Always.

Charlie pulls his cap on and tucks the Glock down the back of his jeans. He grabs his bag and leaves the cabin, closing the door quietly behind him. He doesn't want to draw the attention of the two who got on a little further down. It's late. It's quiet. A lot of passengers are already sleeping.

The train starts moving.

Charlie keeps his balance, pressing his shoulder against the wall. He straps the bag to his back and pulls it tight. Starts making his way down the train. If they're coming, they're coming from both directions. For now, he heads toward the rear. It gives him more options. No matter which way he goes, if they know his face, he won't be able to slip by them. Not in this narrow tube. Instead, he'll try to find somewhere to hide. Somewhere he can lay low and then get past them. After that, he'll keep moving. Get to the very back of the train. It's not far to DC. His intent had been to get off before then. If he can make it to the back, away from everyone else, he can get outside. As the train slows, pulling into the station, he can jump from it and disappear into the dark.

He reaches the second car. The lights are low. The seating here has tables. There aren't many people present. No one sits together. The few people he sees are using the tables to do work. They have the overhead lights on. Most of them are men in suits, top buttons undone, looking tired. There's a teenage girl to his left sitting on her laptop. It looks like she's playing a game. She's wearing headphones. To the rear of the car, a man is on his cellphone. He doesn't attempt to lower his voice. He talks loud and clear enough for everyone to hear the details of the deal he's trying to make.

Charlie keeps moving. He looks ahead, between cars. He can't see anyone coming this way. He has to be careful. The last thing he wants is to bump into anyone who could be looking for him.

Before the third car, there is a toilet. Charlie pauses, looking ahead. He waits, watching through the glass. The next car is similarly made up of tables, but there are fewer people here. He sees an old couple sleeping, the wife's head resting on her husband's shoulder.

Charlie sees two of the men from the platform coming. He glances back the way he came. The two who got on at the front are not on their way, not yet. If they're checking each of the cabins in the front car, it could take them a while.

The bathroom is unoccupied. Charlie slides the door open and slips inside. He closes the door but doesn't lock it. He keeps it open just a crack, his left hand holding it in place, enough to see out with one eye. His right hand reaches back, resting on the Glock's handle. He hears the door open from the third car. The two men have arrived. They're in the vestibule with him. One of them glances at the bathroom door, but they're only checking the lock. They see that it reads vacant and they keep going.

They pause at the door through to car two, swaying with the train's movement. They steady themselves against the wall. "You see them?" the man on the right says.

The man on the left leans closer to the glass. "They're not here yet."

"Well, he ain't in these cars. Should we keep going, help them look?"

The man on the left checks the time. "Suppose we should," he says. "They might only be about halfway done by now. If they haven't hollered, they haven't found him yet. Might be worthwhile having us there in case they do."

"Strength in numbers," the man on the right says.

Charlie slides the bathroom door open. He pulls out the Glock and points it at their backs. "Who you looking for, lads?"

Both men stiffen.

Charlie could have let them go. Let them travel down to the first car and then continue on his own way toward the back of the train, but that would be putting a band-aid on a bullet wound. It covers it up, sure, but it doesn't deal with the problem. The men would still be out there, on the train, looking for him. There'd be nothing stopping them from turning around and coming back the other way, catching up to him down the line. Hearing them talk, certain now that they're looking for him, he's decided to take his opportunity to deal with a couple of them, at least.

"You didn't check the fucking bathroom?" the man on the left says.

"It wasn't locked," the man on the right says. "Who doesn't lock the fucking door?"

"Am I gonna have to ask again?" Charlie says.

The man on his left snorts. "Reckon you know exactly who we're looking for."

Charlie steps out of the bathroom, moves into the wider space of the vestibule. "You armed?"

Neither man answers.

"Throw them over. Nice and slow. You first." He nudges the man on his left with the barrel of the Glock.

They each do as he says in turn. They're both carrying Glocks. Charlie is glad to see this. He takes the magazines out of both and slips them into his pocket, then drops the frames into the built-in trash can in the wall opposite the bathroom.

"Give me your belt," Charlie says. He nudges the man on the left again.

The man is confused, but he does as he's told. He doesn't have any other choice. As he takes it off, Charlie looks left and right, through the glass doors leading into the two cars. No one is coming.

"In there," he says, taking the belt. "In the toilet. Both of you."

It's a cramped fit, but they do as they're told, squeezing into the bathroom together.

"Should've taken the shot while you had the chance," the man on the right says. "You ain't gonna get it again."

"Y'know," Charlie says, holding the door open with his foot. "Maybe you're right."

Both men freeze. The one on the left shoots the other a look. The man on the right's eyes bulge. He was talking tough. He didn't expect anything to come of it.

Charlie doesn't shoot them. He slams the handle of the Glock down onto the tops of their heads, knocking them dizzy, subduing them both. It'll keep them quiet for a while. Blood runs down the center of their faces. Charlie uses the belt to lock the bathroom from the outside, looping it through the door handle and the balance rail on the wall next to it. He loops the two ends together and knots them tight. He looks back the way he's come. It's still clear. He puts the Glock away and keeps moving.

The elderly couple are still asleep. There wasn't enough noise to wake them. No one else is looking his way. He presses on through the third car, checking the faces of the people who are sitting here, making sure none of them are the men from the platform, that they're not friends of the two men he just locked in the bathroom. He looks ahead, too, through the glass. He reaches the end of the third car. Enters the vestibule. Waits. Looks into the fourth car.

The seats here are angled toward the windows so people can watch the scenery they pass. There isn't much scenery to see at this time of night. Everything is in darkness.

And the car is empty. The seats are unoccupied. There is no one sitting here.

Charlie doesn't go inside. He can't see anyone who could be waiting for him, but the whole situation stinks of a trap. He starts to head back the way he's come, his mind running through what he can do to deal with the other two men he knows are down there.

He doesn't get far. Doesn't get through the door and back into the car. The two men from the front are on their way up through the train. He can see them inspecting the people sitting at the tables. Before long, they'll reach the locked bathroom.

Charlie turns back around. He needs to take the risk. He steps into the empty car and slides to the side, looking it over. He keeps a hand pressed to the handle of the Glock. He watches and he waits. He rocks with the train, staring unblinking at the door at the other end. The vestibule is in darkness. Another cause for alarm. He can't see movement. He doesn't see anyone looking back out at him.

Looking back, he sees the two men from the front of the train are in the vestibule. They've seen the locked bathroom. They're untying it.

Charlie pulls out the Glock and gets down, monkey running through the car, heading for the next door. Despite his rush, he remains careful, moving from angled chair to angled chair.

Halfway down, the door at the end of the car opens. Three men step inside. They're all armed, carrying handguns. The man in the middle is smiling.

"Well," Charlie says, looking them over. "Suppose I might as well stand up."

"Do what you want," the middle man says.

Charlie straightens. He keeps the Glock out. The men have already seen it. Charlie is outnumbered. It's a small space. He hears the door open behind him. He glances back. Four more of the sons of bitches. The two he bundled into the bathroom have blood streaming down their faces. One of them wipes it out of his eyes. They're furious. They're also the only two out of the seven who aren't armed. Their fists are balled. They're shaking.

Charlie turns back around. He's a quick draw. He's fast. He knows he's fast. But not fast enough against five armed men. Definitely not, especially in a train car. There's cover behind the chairs. He could keep moving and shooting, make it difficult for them to get a clear shot at him, and take a few of them out before they put him down. He takes a deep breath and grips the Glock tight.

Of course, there might be an alternative. They might not have been sent to kill him. They could have been sent to capture him. If they capture him, where then? Will they take him to the same place they're holding Niamh? When he looks into their faces, he's not so sure they have capture on their minds.

"All right then, lads," Charlie says. "How we gonna do this?"

38

Shira and Noam kept their heads down as the Nazis made their way through the car. They pretended to be asleep. The men were inspecting everyone they passed. Shira watched them through half-closed lids. They didn't linger long when they reached Shira and Noam. It was clear neither of them was who they were looking for. After that, more than ever, Shira was certain they'd come aboard to find Charlie Carter.

The Nazis moved on. There were three of them, but one held back. He took a seat close to the door leading through to the vestibule. He wasn't resting. He was watching. Shira and Noam continued pretending to sleep, but Noam brought up the security footage in the cars on his phone. He dimmed the screen and held it low between them. They were able to see the man sitting at the front of their car. They were able to see all of the others, too, moving through the train.

And they could see Charlie Carter. Cap on, pulled low, making his way toward them.

"We don't move yet," Shira whispered. "We wait."

The two men who had left the car went to the back of the train, checking the passengers in the other cars. They returned and rejoined with the third man. They went through to the fourth car. A moment later, the people through there were ushered into Shira and Noam's car.

The Nazis weren't being so quiet anymore. Two of them blocked the door. They flashed their guns. "Everyone sit tight and make yourselves comfortable," one of them said. "And so long as everyone stays quiet, there won't be any trouble. If you have a phone, I would advise against trying to call out. It won't work. We have a scrambler onboard."

"What's happening?" someone said, a man near the front, someone they had dragged through from the fourth car. "Is this a hijacking? Are you taking us hostage?"

The Nazi shook his head. "Nothing like that. We're just looking for someone is all. Keep out of our way and no one gets hurt. This isn't difficult to understand. Just sit tight, and this will all be over before you know it." He turned and left.

Once he was gone, a murmuring rose in the car. People kept their voices low, not wanting to anger the armed men, even in their absence. They turned to each other, trying to work out what was happening.

Minutes pass. Shira watches the door and waits to see if any of the men return. They don't. "Was he telling the truth about the scrambler?" she says, turning to Noam.

"He was," Noam says. "It's at the front of the train. I've found them planting it. Look at this." He angles the phone toward her. She sees Charlie stuffing two of the men into a toilet cubicle, and then binding the door behind them with a belt.

"He's coming this way," she says.

Noam nods. "And they've set a trap for him."

Shira looks toward the door again. It's clear. The men are inside the vestibule. She notices it is in darkness there, despite the lights previously being on. The men inside have turned them off, in preparation for their ambush.

"Two from the front are coming up fast," Noam says, showing her the screen again.

"We need to help." She reaches into her bag and pulls out the Glock. She conceals it in her jacket pocket. "If we don't intercept, he's a dead man."

Noam's face is grim.

"Stick close to me," Shira says, preparing to move.

"I'm not a fighter," Noam says, "but I'm with you all the way."

Shira and Noam slip out of their seats. Shira crouches low. She doesn't look back but knows that Noam will be directly behind her, doing the same. He's not stupid. He knows to do as she does, and knows to give her space. She makes her way to the door, silently praying none of the men inside decide to look back and spot her coming.

Noam tugs on her elbow. "Charlie is in the car," he says. "They're heading through. The others are coming up behind him."

Knowing that the three in the vestibule are no longer there, Shira speeds up. She gets to the door and rises, looking through the window. She can see the backs of the three men. Beyond them, the view of Charlie is blocked by their bodies.

"Hey—what are you doing?"

It's the man who earlier questioned the Nazis. Shira shoots him a look. He needs to keep his mouth shut.

"Sit back down," he says, looking around the car. "They said they were just looking for one guy—don't get involved!"

"Friend, listen," Noam says, holding up a hand, "you need to be quiet—"

"No, the two of you need to sit your asses back down!"

All eyes in the car have turned toward the front. They're watching Shira and Noam and the man. Shira looks back through the window. Nothing has happened yet. She thinks they're talking, but she can't hear anything from here.

"Sit down, now!" the man says. He's starting to stand. "Damn it, I'm not gonna get hurt on account of you two—"

Shira pulls the Glock. She points it in his direction. A gasp ripples through the car. The man finally falls silent. His eyes are wide. He swallows.

"Take your own advice," she says, "and shut up, and sit down."

He lowers himself back into his seat, hands raised. Shira turns back to the door. As quietly as she can, she opens it. Creeping through into the vestibule, Noam close behind, she can hear the voices now. A British accent. Charlie is talking. She catches the end of it.

"—we gonna do this?"

"Well," the man in the center says, "either you give yourself up, or we kill you."

Charlie whistles. "I don't like the sound of either those options."

"They're the only two you're gonna get."

Shira moves in. She presses the Glock to the back of the speaker's head. "No one move."

The three men freeze. Closer now, Shira can see Charlie. He's trying to see beyond the Nazis, to his unexpected allies.

"Who the hell are they?" The voice comes from the other end of the train. One of the men with blood on his face. "They've got guns? What the hell—you didn't check the passengers?"

"I didn't have time to check the passengers," says the man to Shira's left. It's a lie, though. He had plenty of time.

"Who are they?" says one of the men at the end. One of the armed men, no blood on his face.

The man on Shira's left tries to look back.

"Turn around," Shira says.

The man does, but he's already seen enough. He shakes his head. He laughs. "Oh, shit," he says.

"What's so funny?" says the man on the right.

"You're not gonna believe it."

"Who is it?" someone shouts from the other end.

"The fucking Jews," the man on the left says.

The man in the center, with Shira's gun to the back of his head, stiffens. "*What?*" he barks.

"You didn't check *that*, either?" says a bloodied man at the end. "The hell were you doing back there?"

"Shut your mouth, toilet boy," says the man on the right.

Shira sees Charlie looking between the two groups in bemusement. "The hell is going on here?" he says.

"They run a sloppy operation," Shira says.

The man in the center, however, remains rigid. "I'm not going out to no fucking Jew," he says, shaking his head. "Fuck this. I'd rather fucking die!"

He spins. He's raising his gun. There's no doubting his intentions.

Shira doesn't hesitate. She puts two bullets through his skull.

There's a moment of silence. Just one brief, passing moment, where time freezes. All eyes are wide. The realization of what has happened sinks in. It doesn't take long.

Chaos erupts.

39

Charlie sees blood squirt out the front and side of the Nazi's face as the woman shoots him through the skull. He was armed. She didn't have any choice. He would've done the same.

There's something familiar about her, but Charlie can't place it right now. There's too much happening. Too many bodies. Too much immediate danger for him to concentrate on why her voice rings bells in his mind.

If he survives this, he can work it out later.

One thing's for sure, though—whoever she is, she's clearly on his side. She and the guy behind her, presumably.

The other Nazis see their comrade go down. They're quick on the draw. Charlie is quicker. He fires upon the man nearest the woman, to her left. She keeps her own gun up. She turns it toward the man on her right. The man she fires at dives for cover behind the nearest chair. Charlie wings his target high in the shoulder, close to his neck. Blood sprays the wall. The man goes down. Charlie doesn't think he's dead. Still a danger.

The woman points her Glock at Charlie. "Get down!"

He throws himself to the floor. He hears the Nazis behind him open fire before the woman can. She falls into cover in the vestibule and shoots back. Charlie rolls to the left and crawls under the chairs toward the woman. The gunfire erupts loudly through the car, the sound of bullets pinging around the enclosed area. One of them hits the floor close to Charlie's head. Another tears through the chair above him. A window shatters, and the roaring sound of the wind fills the car. It's deafening.

Charlie pushes on. Ahead of him, the man who dived for cover is gone. Charlie doesn't search for him. The bullets are flying. He stays low.

He hears a gunshot close by. The bullet cuts across the front of his face and hits the wall beside him. He flinches and looks right. The man he wounded is attempting to crawl down on the opposite side of the train. He's trailing blood. He points his handgun at Charlie. His arm is shaking, but he's steadying it. Charlie finds himself looking down the barrel.

The man fires again. The bullet hits the chair above. Charlie fires back. He's unwounded, and his arm is steady. He fires twice. The first bullet catches the Nazi in the collarbone. The second gets him through the face, just under his left eye. He falls flat. Charlie hurries on. He's nearly at the end. It doesn't take him long to reach the woman.

The man with her is behind cover. He sees Charlie approaching and emerges long enough to grab him and pull him into the vestibule. The woman throws the door shut behind him. Bullets dent it and tear through from the other side. The glass shatters.

"We need to keep moving," the woman says. "Come on—up!"

Charlie scrambles after them as they race through the next door into the car beyond. It's empty.

"They must have run as soon as they heard the shooting," says the man.

The woman doesn't respond. She keeps moving and the two men follow her through to the next vestibule. Charlie can still hear gunfire behind. It's not as constant as it was. The Nazis have likely realized that their targets have moved on. They'll be regrouping, and then they'll continue coming after them. They'll be careful. They're two down now, and they have a better idea of what they're up against. The woman and the man Charlie has found himself with were likely just as unexpected for the Nazis, judging from what he heard them saying to each other before the shooting started.

In the next vestibule, they can see people panicking in the car beyond. They're running and screaming, crying out, trying to find shelter, trying to push through to the next car. There's only so far they can go.

The three pause together, looking back down the empty car they've just passed through. Charlie and the woman are calm, they're in control. Their breathing is level. The other man, however, is panting. He swallows. He runs a hand down his face.

"Have we met before?" Charlie says to the woman.

"Not quite," she says. She stays by the door, looking back. She tears her eyes away long enough not to look back at Charlie, but to peer around the vestibule. She looks at the door that leads to the outside. They can hear the wind whistling past. Finally, she looks at Charlie, but only briefly before she turns back to the window. "Underground, in DC."

Charlie remembers. "That's right," he says. "You turned up and saved our arses—a little like what you've done for me here." Charlie turns to the man. "Was that you in DC as well?"

The man shakes his head. He looks solemn doing so.

"That wasn't Noam," the woman says. "That was…someone else."

There is clearly a story behind her words. A sadness. Charlie can't ask further right now. It's not the time or the place. He doesn't press it. "Noam," he says, nodding at the man. "And you are?"

"Shira Mizrahi," the woman says. "You don't need to introduce yourself to us, Charlie Carter. We already know who you are."

"Well, if we get clear of here—*when* we get clear of here—I'm sure we can get better acquainted. Who are you, though? Where you from—Israel? Those names, your accent—"

"We're from Israel," Noam says.

"IDF?"

"Not for a long time," Shira says.

"Never," Noam says.

"I thought it was mandatory," Charlie says.

"I failed the physical," Noam says.

Charlie looks him over. Despite his breathlessness, Noam looks healthy enough to him. "You look fine."

"Not back then," Noam says. "I've lost a lot of weight."

"They're not coming yet," Shira says. "But it's not going to be long. There's nowhere for us to hide."

"We could fight them," Charlie says. "Right now, we're in a good position to open up on them when they come through."

"If this turns into a running gunfight, we put the other passengers at risk," Shira says. "We're outnumbered and outgunned. Noam is unarmed, and he's not trained with weaponry like we are. This five on three situation is effectively five on two."

She's right. They don't want to put the other passengers in danger. It's clear they're here looking for Charlie—and Shira and Noam, now that they're aware of their presence. If they can't find these three, will they leave the other passengers unharmed? They might rough them up a little, but they're unlikely to kill them. There's no need. It should be clear to the Nazis that the other passengers don't know the three. They have nothing to gain from trying to hide them or covering for them.

"We can't be far from DC now," Shira says. "And that shooting must have been heard through the whole train."

"But the train isn't slowing," Charlie says. "All that gunfire, you'd think we'd be stopping."

"They could be commandeering the train," Noam says. "That might be why they haven't come this way yet."

Noam pulls out his phone. Charlie watches him. "Shit," Noam says. He turns the phone around to show them. One of the Nazis has run through to the front of the train, to the driver. He's holding him at gunpoint. They can't hear what he's saying, but he's pointing at the controls and then at the window, down the tracks. The driver sits stiff, his eyes flickering from the window to the gun pressed to his temple.

"So what do we do?" Noam says. "Where do we go?"

Charlie and Shira both look at the door to the outside. They look at each other. Charlie is the first to say it. "We go out."

"Outside?" Noam says. He looks like he might be sick.

"We go outside, let the Nazis search the cars," Shira says. "Noam is into the onboard security system. We'll be able to see them. When they stop searching, we can get back inside. Catch them by surprise. Pick them off that way."

Noam stares at the door. He looks like he has his doubts.

"Just stick close to me," Shira says. "Same as always, right?"

Charlie can see how worried he is. "Don't worry, mate," he says, slapping him on the shoulder. "I won't let you fall."

"I appreciate that," Noam says.

"And if you do, I'll catch you," Charlie says. He tucks his gun away and goes to the door. "Come and give me a hand, mate. We'll get this door open while Shira keeps an eye out."

40

Since his meeting with Sarah, Zeke has felt a sense of euphoria come over him. A sense that finally, *finally*, he has some form of direction. That he's no longer struggling in the waves, trying to keep his head above the water. Sarah—and, by extension, Matt—have offered him a lifeline. He's clinging to it with both hands. For the first time in a while, he feels like he can breathe again. He has allies. Clear allies. He's not so alone anymore.

Sarah left a while ago, escorted away by Matt. Zeke is still awake, but he feels like he could sleep soon. He sits by the window and treats himself to a glass of scotch, taking his time with it, enjoying its warmth coursing through his system. He takes a deep breath and closes his eyes, savoring it. He's going to go to bed soon. He's going to enjoy this night of unbroken sleep.

There's a knock at his door.

Zeke feels a familiar chill run through him, supplanting the scotch's comfort. He grits his teeth. "Who is it?"

"It's me, Mr. President." Matt Bunker. "I'm sorry to disturb you again—"

"Come in, Matt."

Matt enters, closing the door behind him. "You're still awake?"

"Not for much longer. But I have a feeling that could be about to change."

"Just an update that wouldn't keep until morning. I've heard from Harlan."

Zeke straightens. "What's happened?"

"His men on the train have run into trouble. The Israeli woman is there, too, and she has help."

"Jesus Christ," Zeke says, pinching the bridge of his nose.

"Harlan's men have commandeered the train. They're keeping it rolling to DC. They'll be here soon. In the meantime, they're going to attempt to capture the three, but if they can't they'll at least keep them contained until they get here."

"The train is full of witnesses," Zeke says.

Matt nods. "They have a disruptor. No calls in or out. No emails, either. For now, *everyone* on that train is as contained as the three we want. I'm about to leave with a team to get to the station before they do."

"I assume a team of only people we can trust?"

"Of course. Order only. We'll clean this mess up, and by then, we should have Charlie Carter and the Israelis, too."

Zeke nods. He sees the sleep he was so looking forward to eluding him once again. "All right. You best go. Keep me updated. I'll be waiting."

41

The Nazis have taken control of the train.
The passengers have been driven to the front two cars like cattle. They're forced in, cramped on top of each other. Shira, Noam, and Charlie are outside of the train. They're on the roof. Atop the fourth car. They're stationary. Clinging on tight. Shira has Noam's phone, watching what's happening inside. Two of the Nazis are directly beneath them, patrolling. They're making their way down the train, through the cars, toward the back. The wind blasts Shira in the face. Her eyes water. She blinks the tears away. Glancing back, she sees how Noam keeps his head down, his face pressed to the roof, his eyes closed tight. Charlie is to his right, a hand on his back, holding Noam into place like he's at risk of slipping off.

They can't be far from DC now. Shira turns around, drawing Charlie's attention. She shows him two fingers, and then motions toward the back of the train. Charlie nods, then taps Noam and indicates that they're going to turn. Noam shakes his head. He's too scared to move. Charlie motions for Shira to get past. When she does, she pauses and looks back. Charlie moves around so he's face to face with Noam. He places a hand either side of his head and forces him to look up. Their faces are close. Charlie is talking to him, shouting into his face so he can be heard, but Shira can't make out any of it. Eventually, Noam nods. Charlie nods back. Noam starts to turn. Charlie bunches up a handful of his jacket in his fist, holding him flat to keep him from sliding off the edge.

It takes time, but Noam gets turned around. Charlie helps him along as they shimmy after Shira, following her toward the end of the car, to the vestibule and the door there that leads inside. Shira checks the phone again, checking the positioning of the five men inside. They're all armed now. Three of them have stayed at the front of the train—one of them with the driver, and the other two watching the passengers. The remaining two have performed regular sweeps through the train. Shira couldn't hear what they said whenever they spoke, but she saw how they conferred with each other while they searched, checking areas they may have missed in the past. It looked like they'd argued and bickered a few times, no doubt becoming frustrated with their inability to find the three.

The way inside is clear. The two men are nearly at the rear of the train. Shira forces the door open and falls inside. Her skin feels chilled now that she's in the warmth. The roaring in her ears continues. She turns and goes back to the open door and helps Noam inside. Charlie follows after them and then pushes the door closed.

Noam sits on the floor, his back against the closed bathroom door. His eyes are shut. Both hands are pressed flat to the ground. He's breathing hard.

Shira watches the phone. The two men on patrol. They haven't heard the opening of the door.

Now that they can hear each other, Shira quickly appraises Charlie of the situation. From her hand signals on the roof, he already knows that two of the men are toward the rear of the train.

"How are they keeping in touch?" Charlie says.

"Walkie-talkies," Shira says.

Charlie looks out the window at the scenery racing past. They're going too fast for anything to be in focus. "We must be close to DC."

Noam pushes himself up to his knees, finally settled after descending from the roof. He checks the time. "I'd guess at another twenty minutes," he says, sucking air. "Maybe thirty."

"We don't have long," Charlie says. "We need to get off this train before it pulls into DC. Either there'll be law enforcement waiting there, or more Nazis."

"What makes you think there could be law enforcement?" Shira says.

"The capture of my wife is a lure to draw me back. I'd be more shocked if there's *not* law enforcement waiting."

"Of course," Shira says.

"So what are our options?" Charlie says. "We deal with those two at the back and lay low another fifteen minutes or so until the train begins to slow, and then we hop off?"

"If the Nazis remain in control, they might not stop in DC," Noam says.

"The alternative is that we try to retake the train," Charlie says.

"Do you have a plan?" Noam says.

Charlie looks at him and grins. "Do you fancy going up top again?"

Noam blanches.

"No?" Charlie says. "Suppose that part will fall to me, then."

"What are you thinking?" Shira says.

Charlie lays out his plan. Shira keeps an eye on the security footage while he talks. The two Nazis are making their way back, but they're taking their time, and they remain a few cars back.

They appear flustered. They're growing stressed at their lack of success.

When Charlie is finished, Shira moves into position. She leaves the phone with Noam. They have to move fast. They don't have much time left. Noam stays behind in the vestibule. Shira pulls out her Glock and slides down behind a couple of chairs on the right side, lying flat. She waits for the two Nazis to reach her car. Noam is watching. Charlie is waiting by the door, ready to leave the train once again. Shira doesn't begrudge him for going back out there.

The door at the end of the car opens. The men don't hurry through. They're still searching. They're thorough. More thorough than they were earlier. Shira wonders if her calling them sloppy hurt their feelings. She squeezes the handle of the Glock.

Noam and Charlie are active now. They're forcing open the door. Shira hears the wind blowing in. Even from where she lies, halfway down the car, it's almost deafening.

The Nazis hear it, too. "The hell is that?"

The other doesn't answer. The speaker doesn't wait for a response. They're already moving, both of them, running down the train toward the sound. Shira sees their boots pass down the center aisle, one pair after the other as they race toward the sound.

Shira gets to her feet. She doesn't call after them. Doesn't try to stop them. She doesn't say anything at all. The only sound they hear is the noise of her gun. The man at the rear, her bullet catches him through the left side of the neck. He stumbles and falls, going down, sprawling across the back of a chair and then falling to the floor. The man at the front, leading the charge, she shoots through the back. He starts to turn. She shoots him twice more through the chest. Blood sprays, covering the ceiling and the chairs, and splashing upon the windows.

Shira goes to their fallen bodies. The man shot three times is dead. The other, the man shot through the neck, is still living.

He's bleeding heavily. A hand is clamped to his neck, attempting to stifle the flow. He'll die soon. Regardless, Shira puts a bullet through his head.

She returns to the vestibule. The door is closed now. Noam is looking at his phone.

"Did anyone hear?" Shira says.

Noam shakes his head. "They're all still at the front. Didn't register the door opening again, or the shots."

"And Charlie?"

Noam blows air. "He's back on the roof."

Shira looks at her watch. "Five minutes. We wait here, and then we move."

42

The wind pummels Charlie's face. Tears stream from his eyes. He pushes on, making his way down the top of the train, keeping his left hand on the edge as he drags himself along. He goes as fast as he can, battling against the force of the wind. He's freezing. Gritting his teeth, he ignores it. He's been colder. He's been in colder climates. He can block it out.

He checks his watch, but he doesn't slow. Keeps moving. Always moving. He told Shira and Noam to give him five minutes.

When he reaches the top of the vestibule at the back of the second car, he stops. He waits. He tries to look ahead, to get any kind of idea of how close they might be to DC, but it's hard to see through the moisture in his eyes. It's dark, too. Late. There are no lights, save for the glow that comes from the windows below him. He keeps his head down instead. From what he can see to his left and right, they're still out in the wild, surrounded by nature. It doesn't look like they're close to the city yet.

He presses an ear to the roof of the car. He can't hear anything beneath him, but when the shooting starts, he's confident it'll be loud enough. When it does, that's his signal to start moving again. To get to the front. To retake the train.

His right ear is pressed to the cold metal of the roof. He plugs his left. He needs to listen carefully. He's not expecting a full firefight to break out here. One or two shots, max. Shira and Noam are not planning to engage the armed men here. The plan is to draw them out. They can't hold a firefight with them in the same car where they're holding the rest of the passengers hostage.

Charlie keeps an eye on his watch, too. It's been five minutes. Two more, and he'll start moving again, whether he's heard anything or not.

As if on cue, a gunshot rings out. He hears what he thinks could be people screaming. They're likely scrambling for cover. There's another gunshot. Both come from directly below him—or at least it sounds that way. All going to plan, the Nazis are leaving the car. They're in pursuit of Shira and Noam, who will keep them preoccupied a car or two back.

Charlie gets moving. He pushes himself as fast as he can against the cold. When he reaches the end of the first car, he slides down the side, toward the door. He holds on tight. The fingertips of his left hand cling to the edge of the roof above him. With his right hand, he forces the door open. As soon as it's wide enough to fit through, he throws himself inside.

There are three people inside the vestibule. All women. They cling to each other and stare at Charlie with wide eyes. Charlie looks them over. He doesn't think they're with the Nazis, but he's not going to take any risks. They need checked over. They're unarmed. It's safe enough for him to turn his back on them momentarily and close the door. He looks left through the train, sees the people squeezed into the aisle of the sleeper car. Some of them are spilling out of the cabins. The passengers have been herded in like cattle.

Charlie turns back to the women. "Did they both go?" he says.

The women don't speak. They look shaken. One of them, the youngest of the three, has a little more color in her cheeks. Charlie focuses his attention on her. He clicks his fingers in front of her face. She blinks and looks at him.

"It's all right," Charlie says. "I'm not with the hostage takers. What happened? There were two of them here, right? At the front? Did they both go?"

"They were there," she says, raising a shaking hand to point toward the front of the train. Toward the driver's cabin. "And then —and then a man and a woman came here, they came to *here*, right in front of us, and the woman had a gun. The men at the front, as soon as they saw them, they started shooting—"

"I think they were shooting all the way down the train," says one of the other women, but there's still a vacant look in her eyes.

"They nearly hit us," the younger woman says. She points at bullet holes in the wall near to them.

"Two of them, right?" Charlie says. "Two of them went after the man and woman?"

The young woman blinks, thinking. "Y-yeah. Two. That's right. There were two of them."

The woman who hasn't spoken yet rouses suddenly. "Who are you?" she says, eyes narrowed at Charlie. "Why do you look familiar?"

Charlie turns away, toward the front of the train. "Stay low," he says. "This will all be over soon."

He leaves the vestibule and enters the front car. It's quieter here. He imagines the cabins have people inside, but they're not overfilled and spilling out into the aisle. The Nazis wouldn't have wanted too many people so close to the front. To the driver. Didn't want to risk them trying to rush the front and retake the train.

Charlie passes the cabin that was his home for a couple of days. He can hear movement inside. Other passengers have been moved in. He keeps going to the front. The remaining Nazi is nowhere to be seen. Charlie assumes he must be in with the driver. He quickens his pace. He reaches the door leading through to the driver. It's locked. Charlie wonders briefly how many drivers are on board—they've been on the move a long time. Too much travel for just one man or woman. They'd need to get their rest. He wonders where the other driver might be, and if the Nazis are aware of them.

Charlie braces, then pounds on the door with the side of his left fist. Putting on his American accent, he calls through, "We got 'em!"

After a moment, the door begins to slide open. Charlie keeps to the side, obscuring himself. He sees a shaved head begin to emerge. A tattoo on the side of the neck. "It's about damn time!" the man says, but then he frowns when he doesn't see anyone standing in front of him.

Charlie steps into view and slams the Glock across his face, grabbing him by the front of the shirt as he does so. The man is stunned, a deep cut across his left cheek and along his nose, but he's still fighting. He grabs at Charlie's hand holding onto his shirt, refusing to be thrown around, and he starts reaching behind himself. Grabbing at something there. Charlie assumes there's a gun. He shoves the man away, toward the nearby wall, though the man attempts to hold on. He's still reaching back. Charlie kicks him in the chest. He hits the wall. His arm comes out from behind. He doesn't have the gun. Charlie doesn't hesitate. He puts three bullets in his chest.

The car starts to come alive. People have heard the gunshots. Charlie hears them moving around in the cabins, but they don't come to the door and peer out. They know the shots were close. They aren't going to risk their lives just to take a glimpse and get caught in the middle of a crossfire. It's more likely they're all getting flat on the ground, keeping their heads covered.

Charlie looks in on the driver. There are two men inside, but only one of them sits at the controls. The other stands with his hands raised. The man driving is white. The man standing is Black. They've both been roughed up. The Black man has blood running down his face from his right temple, and his bottom lip is split deep.

"The two of you are the drivers, aye?" Charlie says.

The Black man nods. The driver doesn't respond. He concentrates on his job, turning only once, just briefly, to see who is at the door now. "Who are you?" the Black driver asks.

"I'm not one of *them*," Charlie says. He waves for the Black driver to put his hands down. "You're back in control of this train now, you got that? How far out from DC are we?"

The white driver speaks up. "Fifteen minutes."

"All right," Charlie says. "Just keep doing what you're doing."

"What about *them*?" the Black driver says.

"They're not going to come back," Charlie says. "Their threat has been neutralized. Just get us to DC."

He closes the door, checks the time, and turns. He sets off at a sprint down the train to catch up to Shira and Noam, and the two remaining Nazis. Shira knows how to handle herself. He has faith that she's kept both herself and Noam alive while he's retaken the train.

In the second car, the people are bunched together at the rear. They don't go any further, but it seems like they're trying to see through, to see what is happening, or else who will emerge victorious from the gunfight a couple of cars back. Charlie tries to push his way through, but the mass of bodies is unmovable. Charlie tries shouting for them to move, but nobody is listening.

Taking a step back, Charlie raises the gun and fires into the ceiling. They hear this. They scatter. "Everyone *move*! Get out the way and stay *down*!"

With an opening before him, Charlie pushes on. He hears gunfire up ahead—car four. He makes his way toward it. He doesn't slow. The gunshots cover any noise his boots might make.

At the end of car three, he spots a body. It lies crumpled on its side in a pool of blood. It's neither Shira or Noam. One of the Nazis, shot through the chest, cheek, and shoulder. He's still alive, but barely. He's shaking, like he's cold. Charlie shoots him in the side of the head, putting him out of his misery.

Up ahead, there's a pause in the gunfire. His shot has been heard. Charlie doesn't stay where he is. He moves on, staying low, in a crouch. The Glock is raised. He takes cover in the vestibule.

The Nazi realizes he's alone. "Motherfuckers! You motherfuckers!" he screams. He slams something into the wall. "God*damnit*! God fucking damn it! Show yourself, you kike bitch! I'm gonna fucking kill you! If it's the last thing I fucking do, I'm gonna fucking kill *you*!"

Via his voice, his rantings, Charlie is able to pinpoint him. He's to the left. The Nazi fires twice toward the back of the car, confirming what Charlie already knows. Silently, Charlie gets into position at the far right of the vestibule. He can see the Nazi through the window. He's taking cover behind the chairs. Looking down the car, there's no sign of Shira and Noam. Charlie guesses they're hiding out in the opposite vestibule.

Charlie raises the gun. He doesn't open the door. The Nazi will be expecting this. He'll spin on the sound. Instead, Charlie shoots through the window. He fires twice. The glass shatters. One of the bullets finds the Nazi. It hits him high in the right shoulder. He cries out and drops his gun. He falls back against the window. Charlie fires again, hitting him in the side of the neck. Blood squirts. He slides down the glass.

Charlie opens the door and moves through, keeping the Nazi covered. He takes the gun from him. He ejects the magazine and keeps it for himself, and discards the rest of the frame. He recognizes the man as one of the two he earlier bundled into the bathroom. The blood at the top of his forehead is very dry now. It's flaking off. The blood coming out of his neck, however, is very wet, and Charlie is careful not to slip.

Shira and Noam emerge from the far vestibule. "The train is ours?" Noam says.

"It's not theirs," Charlie says, nodding toward the dead Nazi at his feet.

Shira puts her gun away. "How close are we?"

Charlie checks the time. "We hit DC in just over ten minutes. We need to get off this train *now*."

43

It's getting late. The temperature has mercifully dropped. Keith has felt the sweat gradually freeze and dry upon his brow and his back, and all of his exposed flesh. They've been here for hours now, watching the cabin. It was already dark when they arrived. They approached with the lights off.

The closest town is fifteen miles away. It's a small, nowhere place—just a couple of blocks housing necessary businesses for the scant population. Nothing to see, and nothing to do. According to Winston, at least. Keith didn't drive anywhere near it. He stayed off-road, following Winston's directions. They didn't pass anything built up on the way to the cabin near the border.

The cabin of Derek Morrow. Kayla's father. Her fake father.

"We're coming in from the rear," Winston said as they drew closer. "We want to get close enough we can see, but not too close in case we need to escape."

"When I say, kill the engine," Ryan said. "We'll have to push it the rest of the way, to make sure he doesn't hear us. There are bushes. We can hide behind those."

Keith followed their instructions. They knew the area better than he did.

The closer they got, the quieter Kayla became. By the time Ryan pointed out a place for Keith to stop the car, she was staring straight ahead, her hands clasped together. Keith could hear her breathing. It was shallow and ragged. She barely blinked, but she wasn't seeing anything. Her eyes had a glazed, unfocussed quality.

Keith stopped the car and looked around. He couldn't see the cabin. "Where is it?"

"We push the car about half a kilometer that way," Winston said, pointing, "and then we should be able to see it."

The area was desolate. There wasn't much growing, save for a couple of scrubland bushes that wouldn't be enough to conceal both the car and them. As they got closer, Keith looked for the bushes Ryan had said would provide them cover. Eventually, they came into view. They looked healthier than the rest.

They stay behind the bushes and near to the car. As Winston promised, the cabin is in view. It's an old, rundown, ramshackle building that looks like it hasn't seen a coat of paint—or any other kind of maintenance—in at least a decade. The roof is at a slant, and likely offers little protection against the weather. Of course, out here where it's dry and arid, a leaky roof probably isn't a great concern. Down the side of the cabin, on the side closest to them, is a jeep, though it doesn't look like it's been driven in a long time. It looks as rundown as the cabin. The windscreen is covered in an inch of sand, and there's more on the roof. There's a light on inside, but they don't see any movement.

As they wait and watch, Kayla stays close to Keith. She drinks water, but she won't eat anything he offers.

"You okay?" Keith says.

Kayla doesn't answer. She stares straight ahead. Her eyes are seeing, now. They see everything. Intensely focused, and unwilling to look away from the cabin housing her fake father.

"You were in the military, right?" Ryan says to Keith from his other side.

"Navy Seals," Keith says.

"Okay," Ryan says. "Did you spend a lot of time on watch like this?"

"Not often," Keith says. "There were scouts. That was their job. I was usually part of the smash and grabs—or sometimes just smash."

Winston clears his throat to draw their attention. "It's quiet right now," he says, looking at Keith, "but we can't guarantee it'll stay this way."

"I'm aware," Keith says.

"What I'm trying to ask is, how is your PTSD?"

Keith grits his teeth.

Ryan frowns. "PTSD? You have PTSD?" He turns to his father. "You didn't think it was worth mentioning that to me?"

Winston ignores his son. He stares at Keith, awaiting a response.

"It's under control," Keith says, staring back.

"You're sure of that?"

"For now," Keith says. He can't lie about it. His breathing has been fine, and his hands haven't shaken, but at the same time, it's been a while since someone has last shot at them or directly pursued them.

A small gasp comes from Kayla, drawing everyone's attention. Keith sees her still staring straight ahead, through the bush and toward the cabin.

There is movement. A man has stepped out onto the porch. He stands with his arms dangling down at his sides, his posture slumped. He stares through the dark toward the Mexico border. He stares for a long time, unmoving.

"Is that him?" Ryan says, keeping his voice low, though it's unlikely they'll be heard at this distance.

Kayla is shaking. Her jaw is clenched tight and her hands have balled into fists, curling into the base of the bush and squeezing the mix of sand and dirt there. After a moment, Keith realizes she isn't breathing.

The man comes down off the porch. He isn't in any kind of rush. He goes to the side, in front of the cabin, and gets down on his knees.

"What's he doing?" Ryan says.

"Kayla," Keith says, nudging her lightly. He keeps his voice soft. "Kayla, you need to breathe."

She gives no indication that she's heard him, except for her flaring nostrils. A slow breath in and a slow breath out. Gradually, her shaking slows. She remains frozen, though. Staring straight ahead. Watching the man.

"He's tending something," Winston says. "A flower bed, or a vegetable patch, something like that."

"Out here?" Ryan says.

"It wouldn't be impossible," Winston says. "It would just take a lot of regular care."

"At this time of night?"

"Look around. What else does he have to do?"

The man digs at the ground for a short while, and then goes back into the cabin. He returns a moment later with a watering can. He sprinkles the ground, then stands and watches it. Then, turning and wiping dirt from his hands, he goes back inside.

"I can hear the song again," Kayla says. "As soon as I saw him, I heard it—this piece of music. Like someone humming it. It got stronger, but I still don't know what they're saying—"

"That's okay," Keith says. He pats her back and can feel her heart hammering. "Just take some deep breaths, okay? Try to calm yourself down."

She forces herself to turn away from the cabin. She lowers her face and massages the corners of her jaw where she aches from clenching so tight.

"I don't know what happened," she says, looking up, looking at Keith. "As soon as he appeared, I just...I just *froze*." She's still breathing hard. She rubs her chest.

"Are you okay?" Keith says. "Do you feel ill? Do you need a drink? We can walk away for a bit if you want. We can wait until you feel better."

"See, this is why I was asking if you were ready," Ryan says.

Keith ignores him. "You can sit in the car, get your head straight."

"I'm not going anywhere," Kayla says, swallowing. "I'm staying right here. I'm fine."

"What about that song?" Ryan says. "Any clearer yet?"

Kayla shakes her head.

"That's a shame," Ryan says. "I'm invested now. It's like I've got an earworm of my own, but I don't have a clue what it sounds like."

She shoots him a sour look. "If it comes to me, you'll be the first to know."

They resume their watch of the cabin. They watch the surrounding area, too. No one approaches. There are no roads close by, and an approach would be easy to spot.

The man—Derek Morrow—leaves the house a couple more times. Both times he tends to the garden or vegetable patch. They're too far away to be sure what it is. He doesn't go any further. He never goes to the jeep. Never gives any sign of going further afield. Not once does he look toward the bush where they hide. No one comes to see him, either, though it's late and it would be concerning if someone did. It could mean The Order knows they're here.

Inside the cabin, they've seen Derek move around a couple of times, his head bobbing near the window on the side of the house closest to them, just above the jeep. They assume this is where the kitchen area is. For more than an hour now, there has been no sign of him.

The group is cold. "What now?" Ryan says, shivering. "Do we sit here and wait to freeze, or do we go and knock on his door and ask to talk?"

Keith glances at Kayla. Her teeth chatter, but she can't tear herself away from the cabin. She's been better the other times Derek has come outside. She didn't freeze, and she didn't forget to breathe, but her jaw and her fists still clenched.

Keith looks into the darkness surrounding the cabin. It's a clear night. The stars are shining. There's a half-moon. It provides light, but not as much as he'd like. There are still too many dark edges in the distance. Too much that he can't see.

"We're not going over there tonight," Keith says. "We go in the morning. First light, catch him while he's still sleeping."

"Why not tonight?" Ryan says.

"Because I want to be able to see if anyone is coming when we go over there," Keith says. "Because I want to know that there isn't anyone else watching him, waiting for us to make a move. This guy is a part of The Order and we're expected to believe they're *not* keeping some kind of watch on him?"

"It's likely," Winston says.

"First light, I secure the perimeter," Keith says. "Check for concealed security cameras, or anyone that might be lying in wait, waiting to creep up, just like we are. Then, if it's clear, we move in."

"What about the rest of tonight?" Ryan says. "If we stay out here, we're going to freeze to death."

"We sleep in shifts," Keith says. "Someone always needs to have eyes on the cabin. I'll take first shift. You three sleep in the car—backseat, all three of you. You're going to have to huddle together for warmth. We can't run the engine."

Ryan is already moving. "Fine by me, I'll see you in a couple of hours."

Winston and Kayla are slower to follow. Kayla is reluctant to go.

"It'll still be there in the morning," Keith says. "And if anything happens, I'll wake you first."

She sighs and tears herself away. "How are you going to stay warm?"

"I'm okay," Keith says. "I have my jacket." He grins at her. He also has his training. Breathing exercises. So long as he has the cabin to focus on, to distract himself with, he'll be okay.

44

As the train begins to slow, Shira, Noam, and Charlie prepare to get off.

They're in the vestibule, five cars back. They didn't want to go all the way to the rear. They need to use the train for cover. At the back, people on the platform would be able to see them as they try to slip away.

"Can you get into the cameras in the station?" Shira says.

"We never dealt with the disruptors," Noam says.

"Then we're just going to have to play it by eye," Charlie says. "It's fine. We've just got to be careful."

"And *quick*," Shira says.

"How's that sound to you, mate?" Charlie says to Noam, slapping him on the arm with the back of his hand. "You ready to go quick?"

"As fast as we need," Noam says.

"Then maybe we can get ourselves somewhere quiet and actually get to know each other," Charlie says, "and find out how we've all got tangled together."

"We'll tell you everything about ourselves," Shira says. "It's only fair, considering we already know everything we need to about you."

The passengers have not redistributed themselves to the rest of the train. They've remained in the front two cars, sticking together, waiting to reach the station and finally get off.

The train is slowing. The platform is to their left. Shira looks to the right. The platform there is empty. "We go that direction and find a way outside," she says.

"I don't suppose you have a vehicle waiting?" Charlie says.

"We don't, but we'll find one. Let's open the door."

Charlie prizes the door on the right side of the train wide. The three of them are keeping low. Shira looks left, to the platform. As they prepare to dismount, she sees bodies standing guard. They're armed.

Charlie and Noam are off the train. Shira is about to follow. The train is almost at a stop. Charlie and Noam are keeping pace beside it. Something—some*one*—catches Shira's eye. A familiar body shape. A familiar way of moving.

A familiar face.

Matt.

It's Matt Bunker.

Shira doesn't freeze, but she feels her blood chill. Matt hasn't seen her. He isn't looking her way. He's looking toward the front of the train, and motioning toward the armed men near him. The men are special ops. They wear body armor and balaclavas. They carry automatic rifles. Matt is the only man on the platform not masked. He wears a suit, with a black overcoat. His hands are in his pockets. Shira looks beyond the men. To the rest of the platform, and toward the station. There's no one else around, no one who works here or future passengers waiting to get on the train.

"*Shira!*" Noam hisses. The train has stopped. He's leaning in at the open door. "What are you doing?"

Shira gets off the train. Charlie pushes the door closed. "What's happening?" he asks. "What did you see?"

Shira looks at Noam when she answers. "It's Matt."

Noam's face drops. "He's here?"

"Who's Matt?" Charlie says. "And look, it doesn't matter—you can tell me later. We need to go—I saw those blokes on the platform and they were packing serious weaponry. Our Glocks aren't going up against those."

Shira doesn't hear all of what he says. "He killed James," she says. She bites her bottom lip.

"The train doors have opened," Noam says.

Shira can hear chatter from the other side of the train, at the platform. She hears a voice rise above the others, barking commands. She knows the voice. Of course she does. She's heard it so many times. She's held so many conversations with it.

"Everyone please get off the train," he calls. "Line up in an orderly manner on the platform. Don't worry about your luggage right now, you can collect that later. Come on, come on, everyone out, form a line. That's good. Sir—*sir*, I said leave your bags. You don't need them yet."

Shira can't tear herself away. Her blood is no longer chilled. It's boiling. The sound of his voice stabs through her like a knife. She moves toward the sound, staying behind the train and out of view, stepping as lightly as she can on the stones around the train tracks, though it's unlikely with all the motion and shouting on the other side that she will be heard. She ducks low so she can see through the tracks and between the cars. She can see the platform, and all the passengers lined up. The drivers and the other workers from the train are lined up with them. Some of the armed men stand guard, but a lot of the others have gone onboard to search the train.

Noam and Charlie are close to her, watching too. "We can't hang around here much longer, pet," Charlie says. "We've already let our perfect opportunity to get away slip by. When we bolt now, they're probably going to see us through the window."

Shira doesn't listen. She watches. She wants to see Matt again. She holds the handle of her gun.

"What are you thinking, Shira?" Noam says. "You can't shoot him. They'll kill us."

Shira swallows. She knows he's right. She removes her hand from the gun. "Okay," she says, nodding. "You're right. You both are. We need to go."

Before they can move, she hears Matt's voice again. "Anything on the train?"

"Nothing obvious," someone answers. This voice is strangely familiar to Shira, too. She doesn't know who it belongs to, but she recognizes it from the sewers, shortly before Matt killed James. "If they're still onboard, they're hidden." She looks at Charlie. He's frowning. He recognizes the voice, too.

Shira can see Matt's face through a gap between cars.

He strokes his chin. "All right," he says. He's stepped closer to the man. He's lowered his voice, but Shira can hear. "Last we heard from the Nazis, they were still onboard." Matt sighs and pulls out his phone. "All right. Have your men kill the passengers, then tear this fucking train apart. I'm going to get the cops to enforce their cordon."

"What did he just say?" Charlie says.

Before Shira can respond, the man gives a signal to the others. They open fire on the passengers and the staff. Matt is already walking away. He's on his phone.

Shira feels her legs go weak. She sees blood spray. Sees the bodies fall. Out the corner of her eye, she sees that Noam has his phone out. He's filming the massacre.

Charlie grabs them both. "We need to fucking *go*—right now. Those people are fucking dead and there's nothing we can do for them."

Shira's breath catches in her throat. She swallows it, staring at the dead bodies bleeding out. Men, women, and children. She turns to Noam. He's already put his phone away. "Did you get that?"

Noam nods solemnly.

She turns to Charlie. He's right. There's nothing they can do here. These people are already dead. There's nothing they could have done to prevent this, without getting killed themselves. Now all they can do is claim vengeance for the dead.

They cross the tracks and slip out of the station, sticking to what darkness is available all the way. They need to get out of the area, before the cordon can be fully enforced.

"The sewers," Charlie says.

Shira nods. It's fitting. The place they first met, though Charlie had not known it at the time. And the sewers were where they'd been last time shortly before Shira witnessed Matt Bunker commit another shocking murder. As much as she misses him, James was one man. Those people from the train, they were dozens. And then of course the explosion—she can't forget about that. The explosion that set all of this in motion, destroying the hospital and killing the Vice-President. She wonders, as they make their escape, just how much blood is on Matt Bunker's hands.

She grits her teeth. There is a lot of blood that Matt Bunker needs to pay for.

45

Niamh stares at the ceiling, and the fluorescent light there that burns into her eyes. She lies upon the thin mattress. She might as well be lying on the floor.

She's tried to stay strong. She meditated. Worked out. Paced the floors. Kept her mind and her body preoccupied. So much time has passed. She has no idea how much time. It's been so long since she last saw daylight. So long since she felt natural light upon her skin, or a cold breeze that would raise the hairs on the back of her neck. So long since she breathed fresh air.

Down here, in this cell, everything is stale. The air. The temperature. The smells—the *food*. Despite her exercises and her stretches, she feels boxed in. Like her muscles are shrinking and her limbs are contracting.

Does anyone know she's here?

Has the outside world remembered her?

Does the outside world know she's gone?

As she suspected since she got here, she's now certain that something sinister is happening. She's not being held legally. If she were, someone would have spoken to her by now, at the very least. Instead, they continue trying to break her.

They're succeeding.

Whatever it is they're trying to break her for, she's about ready to tell them anything and everything just to get out of this damn room. Every insignificant little thing they want to know. Her mother's maiden name—Charlie's mother's maiden name—where they do their shopping—what kind of car they drive—what her first car was—her first pet's name—her first boyfriend—her first crush—the first boy she kissed. *Anything.*

She closes her eyes tight and feels tears squeeze out and roll down the sides of her face.

There's a noise and the hatch in the door is opened. A tray is pushed through. The hatch closes. Niamh looks at the tray, but she doesn't move toward it. She can't move at all. She raises an arm and it flops lifelessly back to the cold, dusty ground. She's never felt so weak. It's mental, though. She knows this. There's nothing wrong with her, physically. They've worn her down. The bastards have locked her up and thrown away the key, and it's drained her. There's nothing left to give. She's waited for so long for something to happen, and nothing has.

There's no rush for the food. It's not hot. It's not even warm. A sandwich with something grey and wet that might be ham. A soft, bruised apple. A green jello cup, though no spoon to eat it with. A bottle of water.

She closes her eyes again. Keeps them closed. Her breathing is hard, heavier than it should be. Strained, like she's out of shape. She's not out of shape. She's never been out of shape. She takes care of herself.

This room has defeated her. This isolation. This illegal fucking lock-up.

Not everyone has forgot about her. That's the room talking. The imprisonment. The lack of human contact.

Charlie is coming.

He's coming for *her*.

No matter where he is, or what he's up against—no matter where they've hidden her from the world, he will find out, and he will come. Nothing will stand in his way. Nothing will stop him. She doesn't know when, and she doesn't know how, but he *will* get here.

And when he does, she needs to be ready. She can't be lying on the floor, feeling sorry for herself. This accomplishes nothing.

Niamh forces her eyes open. Wipes the tears from her face. She slows her breathing, gets it under control. She forces herself up. She turns. She starts doing push-ups. She does them until her arms and shoulders and chest are all screaming. Even then, she doesn't stop. Doesn't give up. She gets up and squats. She keeps moving. She won't stop. She stays sharp.

Charlie will come, and when he gets here, she'll be ready.

This capture is temporary. They won't break her. She's stronger than they think she is. They will not break her.

46

It's morning. The sun is coming up. The temperature is rising. Kayla woke early. She's already out of the car, lying next to the bush with Ryan, watching the cabin. Ryan was on watch when she woke. She left Keith and Winston sleeping in the back of the car.

Ryan looks toward the horizon. "It's coming up quick," he says. He licks beads of sweat already forming on his top lip. "Do you think he's awake already?"

"Who?"

"Your dad," Ryan says. "Sorry, your not-dad."

"I don't know," Kayla says. "I'm going to wake Keith and *your* dad. Keith will decide when we're going up to the cabin, and how to do it."

Keith wakes with ease. "How long have you been up?" he says, leaning out the open back door. He looks toward Ryan, making sure he's still keeping watch on the cabin.

"How could I sleep in?" Kayla says. "How'd you sleep?"

"Fine," Keith says. "How're you doing? How you feeling?"

"I'm okay. I want to get going. I need to do this."

"It's like a band-aid," Keith says. "Just need to rip it off and get it over with. How's the music in your head?"

"Same as ever, and just as indecipherable." Kayla looks toward the cabin, chewing her bottom lip.

"You wake Winston," Keith says, getting out of the car and stretching out. "I'm going to recon the area, and then we go and talk to the man in the cabin."

Kayla appreciates that she does not refer to the man as her father, or non-father. Keith disappears for a while and Kayla, Winston, and Ryan watch the cabin while they wait for his return. Kayla doesn't keep track of the time. She concentrates on staying calm, knowing what is soon to happen, and who she will be face-to-face with. When the moment comes, she does not want to be afraid. She does not want to shake, or to break.

Keith returns to them. "It's clear," he says. "No cameras, no one else nearby. The guy inside is awake, though. He's moving around."

"Did he see you?" Winston says.

"Would I sound so calm right now if he had?"

"What's the plan?" Ryan says.

Keith outlines what they're going to do. He tells Ryan to get his rifle, and Keith pulls out his own Glock. Kayla and Winston are going to remain behind, at the bush, hidden. Keith and Ryan are going in to secure the man. Kayla doesn't want to stay behind, but she doesn't complain. Winston doesn't say anything either way. Once the man in the cabin is captive, the two of them will be signaled.

Kayla watches as Keith and Ryan make their way toward the cabin. Keith takes the lead. Ryan follows close behind. They run, bent-double. They head for the rear. They duck down by the dirty jeep. Ryan stays there, then Keith heads around the other side of the cabin via the rear. Ryan lowers himself to a knee, his rifle resting across his front. He doesn't move. He's waiting for something to happen.

After a couple of minutes, Ryan starts moving. He must have heard something inside, something that Kayla and Winston can't. Ryan stays low but makes his way to the front of the cabin. After a moment, the sound of breaking glass reaches Kayla's ears. Ryan mounts the porch, and stands to the side of the front door. He doesn't go straight in. He's listening. Then he turns, rifle raised, and kicks open the door. He goes inside.

Kayla and Winston wait. Kayla realizes she's holding her breath. Winston is doing the same. The minutes tick by.

Ryan emerges on the porch. He waves to them.

"Are you ready for this?" Winston says.

Kayla nods, then gets to her feet and makes her way over. Winston walks beside her. They don't run. They move at a brisk pace, yet Kayla feels a dragging at her feet. It feels like the longest walk she's ever taken.

She doesn't see the man straight away. She sees the cabin first. The inside is as rundown as the outside. There's a sunken sofa, a spring having burst through one of the seat cushions. There are a couple of wooden chairs strewn randomly, one of them by a window, but their varnish has worn away. The rug in the center of the floor is tattered and threadbare. The floorboards are dusty, and scarred where things have been dropped on them. These, too, look in need of a varnish.

To her left, she sees shards of glass on the floor. Keith broke the window to draw the man's attention, whereupon Ryan broke into the cabin and held him at gunpoint. That was the plan. Keith would keep the window covered to make sure he didn't try to escape through it.

Battling through her reluctance, Kayla sees him now. The man. Derek Morrow. Father. He's bound to a wooden chair with rope, close to the smashed window. He's not struggling. There are no bruises or cuts upon him, either, indicating that he has not put up any kind of battle. He's looking back at Kayla. He looks different from how she remembers—though these memories could be lies. This could be how he has always looked. Thinner. Bearded. His hair unkempt. She has no way of knowing.

He swallows as she looks upon him. "Kayla," he says, and his voice almost breaks.

Kayla takes a step back as if his voice were a slap.

"Keep your mouth shut for now," Keith says. "Speak when spoken to."

Winston looks around the room. "Was there much struggle?"

"None at all," Ryan says. "Soon as I came in, he dropped to his knees with his hands in the air."

"Have you checked the rest of the cabin?" Winston says, though there's not much to search. It's all in this one room, save for a small area at the back, near the kitchen, that could be the bathroom. There's a cot in the far corner, which comprises the entirety of the bedroom.

"It's clear," Keith says. "No weapons, no alarms, nothing. There's barely anything electrical in here, just what runs the lights and the oven and a small refrigerator. A cell phone, too, but it's dead."

Derek's eyes have not left Kayla. He looks like he wants to speak, like he has so much to say, but he's aware of the weapons in Keith and Ryan's hands.

Everyone stands in silence, staring at the captured man. Keith is first to speak. "Shall we get down to it?"

Winston and Ryan nod and step back, closer to Kayla. Ryan sweeps some of the broken glass aside with his boot. "Ryan," Keith says, "go outside, keep an eye out. Shout if you see anything."

Ryan doesn't protest. He does as he's told.

Keith steps in front of Derek, crunching glass, blocking the man's view of Kayla. Kayla understands why he's done it, but she wants to see. She wants to see his face as he speaks. She moves around to where she has a better view. Derek doesn't look at her now. He's craning his neck to look up at Keith.

"First thing's first," Keith says. "What's your name? Your real name."

The man swallows. "It's Darrin. With an 'i.' Darrin Rankine."

Kayla feels nothing at this. She was prepared for it. She already knew the names she thought her parents went by were fake. This is no great revelation. It will be easy for her to think of him as Darrin as opposed to Derek. As opposed to *father*.

There is a numbness coursing through her. She balls her fists down by her side, digging her fingernails into her palms.

"Where's your wife, Darrin?" Keith says.

"I'm unmarried," Darrin says.

"You know who I'm talking about."

Darrin takes a deep breath. He sighs. "I don't know where she is."

"Keep in touch?"

"We haven't spoken in a long time. Not since..." He falls silent, then looks at Kayla. There is a sadness in his face. Kayla ignores it. She won't be fooled by it. She knows Keith won't, either.

"That why you're all the way out here?" Keith says. "Lying low, hiding out?"

"Something like that," Darrin says.

"Never mind *something*," Keith says. "Tell me *everything*. You've been compliant so far, Darrin, but you're being vague. I don't like vague. You know what I'm asking, and you know the kinds of answers I'm expecting."

Darrin nods. "After—after what happened in DC—we were told to go into hiding. Our objective was complete. The mission was over. Kayla... Kayla was supposed to be dead. We needed to lie low and wait for our new assignments. Except Kayla wasn't dead, as you know. We were told to stay in hiding. I...I came here. I didn't think anyone would find me. I didn't...I don't want a new assignment. I don't want any more assignments. I don't want anything to do with The Order, or the plans. I'm done. I'm through."

"You thought you were just going to wait it out here?" Winston says. "You thought The Order would just forget you, let you go on your own way?"

Darrin looks at Winston, and it's clear he doesn't know who he is. Kayla wonders if he would recognize his name, and what he did for The Order. "Of course I didn't," Darrin says. "But I had to try. Let me tell you this, and it's a warning. I hope you heed it. I thought no one would be able to find me here, but you have. If *you've* found me, you have to know that The Order must know where I am, too."

"We expect they do," Winston says. "But we got here first."

"This isn't good enough," Keith says. "We need answers from you, Darrin. So far, we've been fighting with shadows. We need something more substantial. We need names, and we need locations."

"What do you think I know?" Darrin says. He nods toward Winston. "I don't even know who he is, or the guy outside."

"This is Dr Winston Fallon," Keith says, then watches to see if this elicits a reaction.

Darrin's jaw goes slack, and Kayla sees she assumed right. He is familiar with the name.

"I thought you were dead," Darrin says.

"Not dead," Winston says. "Just a ghost."

"So you know some names," Keith says. "We want to know them. Whether you think they're important or not, whether you think they're *living* or not. You're going to tell us everything you know about The Order."

"Okay," Darrin says. He sighs. "I'm not being difficult, am I? I'm behaving. I'll tell you whatever you ask. But first, can I...can I speak to Kayla?"

Kayla stiffens.

Keith doesn't turn away from Darrin. He doesn't look at Kayla before he responds. "No," he says. "There's nothing you need to say to her."

"There's a *lot* I need to say to her," Darrin says. "I need to tell her I'm sorry, for a start—"

"Do you think that could ever be enough?" Keith says. Kayla can hear an edge in his voice. He's angry. "You molded this girl to be a weapon. You made her a robot. You took away her autonomy and used it in service to people you don't even know."

"I used her for a *cause*," Darrin says. "A cause is more important than whether I know who the people running it are or not. But that doesn't matter—it was nonsense anyway. The cause...I didn't believe in the cause the way I used to. Not when I saw what it was doing. How many people it was hurting. I knew there would be death, I *knew* that, but I wasn't prepared for how much..."

Kayla feels ill. They're talking about her like she's not even here. She feels herself trembling with incandescent rage that she can barely give word to. She can't contain it. She clears her throat. "I'm right here," she says. "I'm right *here*, damn it."

Darrin lowers his eyes. They don't stay down for long. "Kayla," he says. "Honey, I—"

"I don't wanna hear it," she says, snapping. "Don't *honey* me."

Darrin looks at her. "Okay," he says. "I won't call you any kind of pet name, but I *am* going to talk to you. I *need* to talk to you."

"Kayla," Keith says. She understands the look he gives her. A silent question. He's asking her if this is all right. Asking if she *wants* Darrin Rankine to talk to her.

She nods. Keith doesn't like it, but he steps back.

Darrin picks up on this. He looks between them both. He wets his lips. His expression remains morose. "Kayla... Listen, I know it doesn't matter what I'm going to say. You're not going to believe me. I'm going to say it anyway." He takes a deep breath. He steels himself. "I know I'm not your father, but I *did* raise you. You were so small when we got you. A toddler. When I think of you—and I think of you often, I *do*—I think of you as my daughter."

"What's my real name?" Kayla says. She stares at him, her face hard.

Darrin says nothing.

"Who were my real parents?" Kayla says. "Where am I from? Where was I taken from?"

Darrin shakes his head. "I don't know any of that. I was never told. If I'm honest, it was better for me not to know. If I'd known that, you'd stop being Kayla. You'd stop being...mine."

"I'm not yours. I never was."

"I know, I know, I understand. I just want *you* to understand where I'm coming from. You *were* my daughter. I raised you. I took care of you."

"We saw the house in the basement," Keith says. "I saw what your idea of raising her was."

"What do you mean?" Kayla says.

"You don't understand," Darrin says. "That's how it had to be. That was for...for the programming. If he is really who you say he is,"—he nods toward Winston—"then he knows. He set it up, the programming chambers. I just tried to make her comfortable. It wasn't perfect, but I did what I could. I made it so it could be a space of her own, so it could be like a real bedroom for her."

"Is someone going to tell me what you're talking about?" Kayla says. "What the hell is the programming chamber?"

"It's where they kept you," Winston says. "You would have been kept captive, chained to a bed probably, while a television played images and sounds designed to keep you docile, and to keep your mind malleable to the needs of The Order. The set-up likely changed from household to household, sleeper to sleeper. Keeper to keeper."

"You saw that?" Kayla says to Keith. "Why didn't you tell me?"

Keith doesn't respond. He shakes his head.

"Keith," she says.

"Because we didn't understand it," Keith says.

"You and Charlie?"

He nods. "We didn't understand it, and it scared us. We chose not to tell you, because what *could* we tell you? You'd already been through so much."

"You said you thought of Kayla as your daughter," Winston says, directing attention back to Darrin. "You said you cared for her. What about the woman? The mother?"

Darrin shakes his head. "She wasn't a mother," he says. "She was a professional."

"Where's she now?" Keith says.

"I don't know."

"Does she know where you are?"

"Probably. It wouldn't surprise me."

"When did you last speak to her?"

"After the DC bombing," Darrin says, his eyes flickering toward Kayla. "After it became known that…that Kayla was still alive."

"Do you still have her number?"

Darrin shakes her head. "Like I said, she's a professional. She won't still have it. She's probably run through three or four

251

phones since then." He looks at Kayla. There's clearly still much he wants to say to her. Kayla stares back. Keeps her face hard. She does not falter.

Darrin surprises her by turning away, looking toward Winston. "Have you wondered how she survived the explosion?" he says.

"It's crossed my mind," Winston says. "She was obviously supposed to die. All trace of her, and what she'd done, was supposed to be evaporated. I know in the past, the programming started to lose hold as they got older. That's what happened to the first sleeper. But my understanding was that it didn't falter like that anymore, not since the introduction of the programming chambers. Of course, anything is possible and nothing lasts forever. I assumed her programming had faltered at the explosion. The lizard brain had reasserted itself, the will to live pushing through. It got her to walk away from the worst of it. To seek shelter somewhere safe."

"In the house," Darrin says, "the programming was left to me. It had always been that way, ever since you were small. Elizabeth —that was Heather Morrow's real name—she didn't have any maternal instincts. She never wanted anything to do with you, not really. Her duty was the more physical side of things. Keeping on top of your fight training. Escorting you to missions. She was the handler, I was the carer. Our paths did not intersect as much as you might think they did, considering how long we lived together as husband and wife. We each left the other to their duties. Elizabeth wasn't down in the basement with me. She wasn't there to care for Kayla, and she wasn't there for the programming, either."

"What are you saying?" Winston says.

Darrin takes a deep breath. "I'm saying that as the time came, and it was clear that Kayla was becoming too old to remain the Prime, too old to remain useful… I knew they'd send her on one last mission. When we started to hear that the machine was finally moving, and the shift was beginning, I knew it wouldn't be long. So I...I was slipping with the programming. I wasn't sticking to it the way I was supposed to. I don't know what I expected to happen... I didn't know that she would walk away, that she would survive. I just—I couldn't send her to her death like that. Subconsciously, I wanted her to get away. I wanted her to escape and to live and to make her own life, away from all of this shit, away from The Order. Away from everything she was put through and forced to do. I couldn't just send her to her death."

"So, what?" Keith says. "Do you think that's enough? Do you think I'm going to untie you now?"

"I just want you to *understand*," Darrin says. He's looking at Kayla.

Something he said stuck with her. She hasn't heard it before. "You said I was the Prime," she says. "What *is* the Prime?"

"It means you excelled," Winston says, his lips pinched. "It means you were the number one sleeper. You were the Kayla Morrow."

"There's a lot you still haven't told us," Keith says, looking at Winston with hard eyes. "We've had the time. All those long drives, you could have explained this to us before then."

"I've told you everything that came to mind," Winston says. "We've been running and hiding for our lives, Keith. Some things are going to slip through."

The two men are staring at each other. Keith does not look happy. Winston is apologetic, but he's not backing down. He shrugs and holds out his hands.

Kayla feels Darrin's eyes. They glisten with tears. He's smiling at her. "I'm very glad you survived," he says. "I'm sorry for everything I did to you."

She stares at him. The music is loud in her head. It rises. Almost deafening. A tear rolls down Darrin's cheek. Kayla starts to hum the music.

The room is silent. Everyone looks at her. Darrin sits up straight. He blinks. He smiles. He's crying.

"You remember?" he says.

Kayla stops humming. "No," she says. "What does it mean?"

Tears fall from Darrin's face, landing in his lap, small dark blotches on his already dirty jeans. "You wouldn't stop crying," he says. "When you first came to us, you were always in either two states—programming, or tears. Elizabeth said to just leave the programming running, but I didn't want to do that. We weren't supposed to do that. It could turn you into a vegetable. She hated the tears, though. I felt so bad for you. I just wanted you to stop crying. I'd lie with you through the night, and eventually, I started singing to you." He starts humming the tune now. It's clearer than when Kayla does it. More focused.

Keith cocks his head. "I recognize it," he says.

"What is it?" Kayla says.

"It's Carole King," Darrin says. "Child Of Mine. My mother used to sing it to me when I was young. She would sing it at night, when I was trying to get to sleep. She'd sing it if I was scared, or if I was sick. So I sang it for you. And it worked." He's smiling. He's *beaming*. "It would send you to sleep. When you were small, you would hold my finger in your little hand. You'd hold it so *tight* that when I'd leave, I was so scared it would wake you up when I took my finger back."

Kayla has a name for the song. A mystery concluded. And yet still, she does not feel anything. Still, she feels numb. Darrin looks at her almost with love in his eyes, but she does not feel the same. She doesn't feel hate, either, not anymore. Not like she thought she might. She feels nothing.

The front door bursts open, breaking the silence that has fallen between the four in the cabin. Ryan's eyes are bugging, wide. "Someone's coming," he says, and he's breathless despite only having come in from the porch.

"How many?" Keith says.

"Two vehicles," Ryan says. "There's a van, coming from the east—but that's not the big problem. It's further out."

"What's the big problem?" Keith says.

Ryan holds up a finger. "You're about to hear it."

Kayla doesn't need to hear it. She steps to the right and looks out of the broken window. She can *see* it.

A helicopter.

47

Gunfire erupts from the helicopter. It thuds into the cabin, blows out the windows that aren't already smashed.

Keith throws himself to the ground. He looks around, searching for Kayla. She's on the floor, crawling under the sofa. Winston is near her, lying flat on his front, covering his head with his hands. Darrin remains bound to the chair. He tries to make himself as small as he can while bound as the high-caliber rounds punch through the wood, piercing the air around him, thudding into the floorboards. Keith rolls over and kicks at the chair, knocking it onto its side. Darrin remains contained, but he's lower at least.

Ryan is not on the floor like the rest of them. He shelters in the doorframe, on his knees, rifle raised. He flinches as chunks of wood spray around him.

Keith crawls toward him. "Ryan! *Ryan!*"

Ryan can't hear him. The air has erupted around them. The gunfire is tearing the cabin apart around them. They're lucky none of them have been hit yet. Their luck in that regard will not last forever.

Keith hurries. Ryan sees him coming. He throws himself to the ground and crawls toward him.

"Give me the rifle!" Keith says.

Ryan shoves it forward. Keith takes it and crawls toward the door. He only caught a glimpse of the helicopter before it opened fire, but it did not look military-grade. The gunfire is not coming from a mounted rifle. If it were, the cabin would already be in pieces. Instead, it sounds like an automatic rifle to Keith. He assumes the shooter is hanging out the side, firing upon them while the helicopter hovers.

Keith gets to the door and pauses before going out onto the porch. Most of the gunfire is concentrated toward the center of the cabin. He looks back toward Kayla. She's still under the sofa. She doesn't look wounded. None of them do. Keith can't see any blood.

There's a pause in the shooting. Either they think they've done enough damage, or the magazine is empty. Keith steps out onto the porch. He presses the stock of the rifle into his shoulder, raising it. He sights along the scope. As he suspected, the shooter is hanging out of the open door, a leash on their back keeping them from falling all the way out. The shooter is reloading.

Keith doesn't aim for the preoccupied shooter. He moves the rifle to the right. He aims for the pilot. He fires off a tight grouping, six rounds, hoping they'll break through the glass. At least one of them does. The inside of the glass splatters with blood. The helicopter goes into a tailspin. The shooter starts to panic. He drops his rifle. He grabs at the cable on his back, trying to get himself loose, but it's already too late.

The helicopter crashes. It explodes. Keith ducks back inside the cabin. Parts of the helicopter thud across the ceiling and into the side, nearly breaking through the already weakened wood.

"Everyone up!" Keith says. "Come on, we need to go!"

It's too late. The van has reached them from the opposite side. Four men, all dressed in black, wearing balaclavas despite the rising heat, have leapt out. They're armed with AR15s, pointing them toward the cabin. They look like black ops or mercenaries. A woman is with them. She's dressed all in black, too, but different to the men. She's in trousers and a blouse buttoned all the way up. There's no weapon in her hand, but Keith can see she has a handgun on her waist.

"Drop the weapon," she says, calling to be heard over the noise from the burning helicopter. "And any others you have. Throw them out here."

Keith doesn't release the rifle straight away. He sees the automatic rifles all trained on him. His tongue flickers out, wetting his lips. He tastes sweat. He doesn't see any alternative.

"Shit," he says and throws the rifle down.

"And anything else," the woman says.

He takes out his Glock, then motions for the others to throw out anything they're carrying.

Kayla has come out from under the sofa. She stands in the center of the cabin. Her head is cocked. She's listening. She's frozen the same way she froze when she first saw Darrin.

"What is it?" Keith says.

"Back up," the woman says. She and her armed men are advancing. One of them remains outside on lookout. "Into the cabin."

Keith raises his hands and does as he's told. He stands next to Kayla. The woman looks at her. She smiles. She claps her hands together. "Ah, there she is," she says. "My beautiful, bouncing baby girl."

Keith understands why Kayla froze. She recognizes the voice and the face. This woman is Heather Morrow. Darrin referred to her as Elizabeth.

For a long time, this woman was Kayla's mother.

Elizabeth looks around the room. Her eyes settle on Winston.

He quickly raises his hands in surrender. She didn't see what he was doing before he raised his hands. Keith did. His left was in his pocket. It was fiddling with something. Keith doesn't know what is in his pocket, but he doesn't stare, not wanting to draw attention to whatever Winston might have done. Elizabeth looks the doctor over.

"I know who you are," she says. "I've seen your picture. You look older, Winston. These last few years, hiding out from The Order, they haven't been kind to you." She smirks and turns away from him, sees Darrin on the floor. "A family reunion. How sweet." She's smiling, but it looks more like a sneer. She nods at one of her men. "Is he hurt?"

The man goes to Darrin. He hauls the chair upright, but does not untie him. "Still alive," the man says.

The tendons in Darrin's jaw and cheeks dance under the skin, showing through the twitching of his beard. He looks back at Elizabeth. He doesn't seem pleased to see her.

"Don't you have a smile for your wife, dear?" Elizabeth says. Her tone is mocking. It's a show, for everyone gathered. "Did you really think we didn't know where you were?"

"I knew," Darrin says. "I just thought they'd get away before you turned up."

Elizabeth shakes her head. "You know your problem, Darrin? You're weak. It's always been your problem. That's why we've been watching you. That's why we couldn't just leave you alone. Sooner or later, you'd start talking. And if anyone came to find you, we knew you'd tell them everything you know." She turns on Keith and Kayla suddenly, her eyes burning into Kayla. "And he has, hasn't he? He's told you everything."

Kayla can't answer.

"Not enough," Keith says.

"I wasn't talking to you," Elizabeth says, barely deigning to

259

spare him a glance. "I was trying to have a moment with my daughter."

"You're not my mother," Kayla says, finding her voice. She straightens. She returns the woman's sneer. Kayla is defiant.

Elizabeth laughs at this. "Did he tell you how he used to mother you? Did he tell you about how he used to sing to you? He's such a godawful singer." She laughs again. She pulls her handgun. It's a Sig Sauer. She doesn't point it at Keith and Kayla. She turns on Darrin. She shoots him through the chest. He rattles in the chair with the impact of the bullets, and then he slumps forward.

"No!" Kayla says.

Elizabeth chuckles. "Were you getting attached?" She motions to her men. "Bind them and get them to the van. Let's go."

48

Anthony Tomasson wears a grin that makes Zeke's blood boil.

Zeke is in the Oval Office. He's not alone. Sarah is with him. Zeke keeps Sarah by his side as much as he can. He's noticed how others have eyed up their sudden closeness, her constant being near him despite her recent appearance on the scene, but Zeke doesn't care. What they think doesn't matter.

Anthony helps himself to a seat. He crosses a leg and watches Zeke and Sarah. They stare back at him. "What do you want?" Zeke says.

"To talk," Anthony says. "It's a pressing matter. Perhaps you should get your girl to go someplace else." He waves a dismissive hand.

"She's not going anywhere," Zeke says.

Anthony cocks an eyebrow.

"Anything you have to say to me, you can say in front of her."

Anthony's eyes narrow. Sarah does not back down to him. He already knows she's part of The Order. He knows he can speak in front of her. He's being purposefully difficult. He's being disrespectful.

"All right," Anthony says. He shifts his weight in the seat. Despite professing to the importance of his message, he doesn't appear in any real rush to share it. "I've been contacted by the Quinquevirate."

Zeke tilts his head. This has his attention. He keeps his eyes focused on Anthony, though he wants to exchange glances with Sarah. "Oh?" he says.

"*Oh*," Anthony mimics. "They know you have people after the girl and her associates. They're closing in, correct?" He doesn't wait for a response. "The Quinquevirate want you to pull your people back."

Zeke frowns. "Why?"

"Because they said so." Anthony looks pleased.

Zeke grits his teeth. "*Why?*"

Anthony shrugs. "What does it matter? They're dealing with it themselves. Personally."

"Personally? All of them?"

"How should I know?"

"Well who called you?"

"You think a member of the Quinquevirate called me directly?" He laughs. "They've passed on their message. The rest of us need to listen."

Zeke does not let his frustration show. "All right," he says. "Is there anything else, Tomasson?"

Anthony shakes his head, still grinning. He makes no effort to leave.

"Then get out," Zeke says. "I have work to do."

Zeke does not say another word until Anthony is gone. "*Shit*," he says as soon as the door is closed. "Where's Matt?"

"He's still at the train station," Sarah says. "He's feeding lines, dealing with the fallout."

"Fuck." Zeke looks off to the distance, his right knee jostling under the table as he thinks. "I need to call Harlan. I need to call him myself, tell him to pull his men back."

"I can call Harlan." Sarah waits a beat, then adds, "But are you sure it's such a wise idea to pull them back completely?"

Zeke's leg stops bouncing. Sarah is standing. He looks up at her. "What are you thinking?"

"Tell Harlan to stay on it," she says, stepping away from him and pacing. A finger curls around her chin while she thinks. "Tell him to keep his distance, but to observe. To report back to you regularly. Let you know what's happening. Let you know which members of the Quinquevirate are there."

"He won't know who they are."

"No, but he can provide a description, and *you* will know."

Zeke considers this. "To what end?"

"Leverage. If you know which members are there, you can find out *why*. What is so important that they would go out there *personally*? That's important. That's something you're going to want to know."

Zeke doesn't commit. Not yet. He sits back, thinking over what she has said.

"The clock is ticking, Mr. President," Sarah says. "I know you'd probably like to run this by Matt, but he isn't here. I am. And this is exactly why you have me. This is my job."

"But then what?" Zeke says.

"Information is power," Sarah says. "The more we know, the better prepared we are should we need to make a move."

"A move?" Zeke stands. "What are you thinking? I make a move against the Quinquevirate?"

Sarah has stopped pacing. She doesn't falter. She's ice cold. "Give the word," she says. "Tell Harlan and his men to keep their distance, but to follow. To remain abreast of the situation. To keep us informed."

Zeke bites his lip. "Make the call."

There's a faint flicker of a smile at the corner of Sarah's mouth. "Right away," she says.

She's already pulling out a phone, heading for the door. She pauses before she leaves.

"When I get back," she says, "I think it would be important that you bring me fully up to date on any and all operations The Order and the Quinquevirate have been running."

"I thought you were up to date?" Zeke says.

"Not everything. The army base bombings. The ARO. I need to know everything. And perhaps you should give me the names of the Quinquevirate, too."

Zeke's mouth dries out. What she's asking is taboo.

"I know you're not supposed to tell," Sarah says, and there's a gleam in her eye. That gleam first drew Zeke to her, when Matt introduced them. It makes him weak. "But it can be our little secret. We're in this together, Mr. President—*Zeke*. I told you that. I am hitched to your wagon, and if anything happens to you, well, it happens to me, too. That loyalty needs to extend both ways."

She doesn't leave. She's waiting for affirmation. Zeke nods. "Okay," he says. "When you get back, I'll tell you everything."

49

Georgia and Jack see the helicopter. They see the armed man hanging out the side of it. They hold back.

They're still a few miles out from the cabin. From Kayla Morrow, Winston Fallon, and the rest. They haven't gone off-road, yet. To the helicopter, there's nothing about them to raise suspicion. "That didn't look like border patrol," Jack says.

"No, it did not," Georgia says.

Jack puts his foot down, speeding up. The helicopter is far ahead of them. "We get closer and then we leave the truck," he says. "This area's looking wide open. If there's a problem, we don't want them to see us coming."

Georgia starts gathering their weapons. They go another mile. The road is beginning to curve, away from where the helicopter was going. Jack pulls off road, into a dip. "No time to hide it," he says. "We're just going to have to leave it here."

"Can you do two miles?" Georgia says.

"Shut your mouth," Jack says. "Maybe not as fast as you, but I can keep up. I haven't been sitting on my ass all those years out in the woods."

Georgia passes him his Springfield rifle. She carries the M16. She slings it over her shoulder. Jack does the same.

They set off. In the distance, they can hear gunfire.

"Jesus Christ," Jack says, breathing hard as they run. "We could be running into a massacre."

Georgia doesn't say anything. If they're all dead, Georgia and Jack are back to square one. All alone. They've lost their potential allies. She tries not to think about them being dead, though she knows the likes of them surviving an attack from a helicopter are slim.

Soon after, though, there is an explosion. They're close enough to see. They witness the helicopter go into a tailspin, and hit the ground. They see it erupt.

But they also see the van that approaches from the opposite side.

"This way," Jack says. "Stay low. Out of view. We'll go around the back."

Georgia and Jack no longer carry their weapons on their backs. They sling them round the front, carrying them in their hands. Prepared. On the plus side, their potential allies look to still be living—some of them, at least.

Jack stops. He drops to a knee.

"What is it?" Georgia says. She drops beside him, wondering what he's seen.

He hasn't seen anything. He pulls out his ringing phone.

"What are you doing?" Georgia says.

Jack holds up a hand, silencing her. He answers, but does not speak. He listens. He mouths to her, *It's Winston*. Then he waves and gets back up, keeping the phone to his ear, *Let's keep moving*.

He's still on the phone as they draw parallel with the cabin, still maintaining their distance. Georgia hears gunshots. Jack flinches, pulling the phone from his ear. "Keep going," he says. "It was the fake dad. The Order were done with him."

"Jesus," Georgia says. "What about the others? Are they still alive?"

"It sounds like it." He ends the call and slips the phone back into his pocket. "They're restraining them now and they're going to bring them out. We head for the van, get in the back of it, surprise them there. But listen, there's a guard out on the porch. Keep your eyes wide, and be careful of those windows, too."

They're turning toward the van. Georgia glances at the cabin. She can't see the porch yet. "Crawl," she says, dropping down to her stomach.

Jack does the same. Georgia leads the way. She slows as the front of the porch comes into view. She looks toward the window on the side of the building, too. She can see movement inside, but it's mostly shadows. Dark silhouettes. No one is at the window looking out.

At the porch, however, she sees the man standing guard. He's not looking their way. He's not looking out. He's looking back—into the cabin.

Jack sees him, too. "They're coming out," he says. He still has the phone pressed to his ear while he crawls. "We need to *go*, while he's not looking."

Georgia stays low, but she's not crawling anymore. She rises, staying bent double, and she runs toward the van. The rear doors are open. She glances toward the porch. The man on guard is still looking back. He's holding open the door. Georgia can see other bodies coming out. Armed men, and prisoners.

And then she's in the back of the van. She steps in lightly, to prevent it from moving too much and giving away that she has just climbed into the back. Jack is careful, too. They get into position at either wall of the van. Jack raises his rifle. Georgia raises the M16.

"No hesitation," Jack says. He's ended the call and slid the phone into his pocket to keep both of his hands free for the rifle.

"They've already come for us once. They realize who we are, they're not going to give it a second thought."

"I'm ready," Georgia says.

They wait. Georgia grits her teeth. The rear of the van is pointing away from the cabin. She listens. It doesn't take long before she hears people approaching. Bodies moving and being dragged down the side of the van. The front doors open. Jack turns. Georgia remains facing the rear.

The driver and the front passenger climb inside. Out the corner of her eye, Georgia looks toward Jack. He waits. He doesn't want to alert the people outside. The two in the front haven't noticed them inside the van yet. It's just a matter of time before they turn. Georgia adjusts her body so she can see them in her peripheral. She can still see the open rear doors of the van. She's still got them covered. The approaching sounds are getting closer and closer.

The driver starts the van. The front passenger begins to turn.

The group appears at the back door. The prisoners are pushed ahead. Two men and a woman, all in black, are behind them. Georgia stands.

Jack opens fire. He shoots the two men in the front. Two shots each, through both of their heads.

Georgia fires. She keeps her bursts short and controlled. Looses a tight volley into the chest of the man on the left, and then swings to do the same to the man on the right. They both go down. She trains the M16 on the woman. The woman is armed, but she doesn't reach for the gun on her waist. She raises both hands.

"Don't shoot her!" the oldest captive says. Georgia thinks this is the man who has stayed in contact with Jack. The man who called him as they were taken captive. Dr Winston Fallon. "Keep her alive! We can question her."

Georgia keeps the rifle trained on the woman, but she doesn't shoot. "Take out your handgun and throw it away," she says. "Nice and slow."

Jack slides out of the van. He points his own rifle at the woman and backs her up to create some space away from her former prisoners.

Georgia gets out of the van and inspects how the prisoners are bound. Plastic ties. She takes a finger hole knife from one of the dead men and uses it to cut the prisoners free. She notices how the Black man and the girl stay close together. The man looks toward Winston.

"You know these people?" the man says.

Winston nods. "They're allies."

"Did you know they were near?"

"I knew they were coming. We're lucky they were so close."

"We can discuss this later," Jack says. "Right now, all you need to know is, I'm Jack, and this is Georgia." He points at each of them in turn, looking at Georgia. "This is Winston and his son, Ryan. This is Keith. This is Kayla—but you already worked that out." He turns back to the others. "We need to clear this area. You, big guy—Keith—get a tie on this woman. Everyone else, in the back of the van. Georgia, clear the bodies from the front."

Georgia does so, dragging the bodies out and dumping them on the ground. She pulls the balaclava from one and uses it to wipe the blood from the inside of the windshield on the driver's side. She gets behind the wheel. Everyone else is in the back.

"We need the truck," Jack says, leaning over. Keith has closed the rear doors. The woman is sitting cross-legged in the center of the floor. Ryan covers her with an AR15 taken from one of the dead men. "We can't drive around in this vehicle."

"We won't all fit in the truck," Georgia says.

Jack lowers his voice. "We won't all be in it for long. Get the truck."

50

Harlan has seen it all.
He and his men, all thirteen of them (fourteen including him) across their two vans, reached the area early this morning, but they were told to stop. They were told to go no further.

"Who is this?" Harlan didn't recognize who the voice belonged to. He didn't recognize the number, either. "And how the hell do you have my information?"

"My name is Anthony Tomasson," the voice said. "And I am the current vice-president, and future president. You'll do well to remember that."

They were still moving at the time of the call. Harlan motioned to Earl to pull over while he dealt with it. The van behind would follow. "All right," Harlan said. "You're the vice-president, and it sounds like you've got lofty ambitions. Should I be impressed?"

"Maybe not now, but you will," Anthony said. "Listen to me—I know what you're doing. You're on the trail of the girl and her friends, and you're more than likely closing in by this point.

You need to stop where you are, immediately. Do *not* get involved."

"We don't answer to you," Harlan said.

"No, you answer to the President or one of his lackeys—but this message is coming from above. This comes from who the President answers to. Stay exactly where you are. You'll soon receive a call either from the President himself or one of his aides confirming what I've told you. I'm going to hang up now. You'll be updated soon."

The call ended and Harlan sat and sucked his teeth.

"What was it?" Earl said.

Harlan didn't answer. He waited. Ten minutes passed, then twenty. Sure enough, half-an-hour later, Harlan received another phone call, this time from Sarah Cuthbert. They'd never spoken before. Harlan told her he'd already heard from Anthony Tomasson. Sarah grunted, then she introduced herself. Said she was the President's new aide. Said that going forward, Harlan and the Vanguard Whites would be talking to her.

"With that said," she said, "disregard what the Vice-President has told you. Continue your approach, but do so with caution. Do not engage. We want you to watch. Stay in touch with me—tell me what you see. We'll guide you from there."

Harlan grinned as he slid the phone back in his pocket.

"Are you going to tell me what's happening?" Earl said.

Harlan looked at him, still smiling. "It sounds like we're in the middle of a power struggle." He told Earl everything that had been said to him, by Anthony and then by Sarah.

"So what do we do?" Earl said when he was finished. "Who do we stand with?"

"For now, we stand with the man who hired us," Harlan said. "And we see how things play out."

It feels strange to Harlan to have so much to do with the government. He's spent nearly his entire life being chased by its representatives, as well as fighting against them, and now he's taking calls from Secret Service agents, presidential aides, and vice-presidents. Part of him wonders sometimes if he has lost his mind down in solitary. If this is all some fantasy—recruited into a shadowy organization that appears aligned with his ideals and has recruited him and the rest of the Vanguard Whites and funded them into a veritable army? It must be a dream.

But then he feels the fresh air on his face, and filling his lungs. He looks to Earl, and the other men with them, and he knows it's real.

They've kept their distance from the action. It's been hard, in such a wide-open area. They had to stay back a few miles, concealing their vans in trees. They went closer on foot. Harlan told the drivers and a couple of others to stay behind with the vehicles, in case they needed to move fast.

Harlan and Earl have watched through binoculars. They've seen everything at the cabin—they saw the helicopter get shot down, and then the girl and her friends taken captive. They saw the new man and woman arrive, and sneak to the back of the van. They saw the brief firefight.

Harlan shakes his head. "Should've let us take point on this," he says to Earl. "How many of them did you count—five, six? Plus whoever was in the helicopter? We've got fourteen. If they'd sent us in, this would be over by now."

Harlan has kept in touch with Sarah Cuthbert. Initially, he was sending her message updates. After the firefight, and the capture of the van by the girl and her friends—including her new friends—Harlan placed a call to give her a running appraisal.

"They've killed them all?" Sarah says. She doesn't try to keep her voice down, and Harlan assumes she's found somewhere private in the White House to conduct their conversation.

"Save for the woman," Harlan says, "whoever she is. They've got her captive, and it looks like they're taking her with them."

"They're on the move?"

"Just started rolling."

"Are you able to follow?"

"We can catch them up, no problem. How quiet it is out here, be wise to give them a bit of a head start. We don't want to spook them—unless, of course, that's what you want us to do."

There's a moment of silence while Sarah considers this. "Follow, but don't engage," she says finally. "Keep me updated. I want to know where they go. I want to know if they have friends there. If we have a chance to capture them and others we're unaware of in one fell swoop, we want to be ready to take it."

"Capture or eliminate?" Harlan asks. He probes at an eye tooth with the tip of his tongue.

"Capture the girl," Sarah says. "And possibly the newer woman on the scene. The rest I leave to your discretion."

"We're on it," Harlan says, still watching the van as it drives away from the cabin, getting clear of the area. He waves to Earl to get his attention. "You hear that? Good. Call the vans, bring them up. We follow."

51

After they got clear of the train station, Charlie and his new friends needed to find a place to lay low. They spent a long time in the sewers getting away. They knew the people after them would have cast a wide net.

Staying on the move didn't give them much of a chance to become acquainted. They had more pressing concerns. Staying alive and evading capture being chief among them.

They've got a chance to catch their breath now, though. They got clear of the cordon—Noam was able to get into some CCTV and see if their way out of the sewers was unmarred. They've since found a hotel to check into. A seedy little place, rundown and cash-only. They can hear people having sex in the other rooms, and in the ones that are silent, they're likely shooting up.

Shira stays by the window. Charlie likes this. If she wasn't there, he'd be there himself. Noam crouches in the corner, his laptop balanced on his knees and plugged into a power outlet. They're all staying away from the furniture, of which there isn't much. A small sofa and a bed. Both are likely covered in fluids none of them want any part of, and the bedsheets are probably crawling with bedbugs. It's a small room, the three of them all squeezed into it, but Charlie doesn't want to be here for long and he doubts they do, either. They just need a place they can lay their head down for a little while and plan their next course of action.

"See anything out there?" he says to Shira.

"Nothing that concerns us," she says without turning.

Noam clears his throat. "You can leave the window," he says. "I've gotten into every camera in a five-block radius and set up an alert."

"An alert for what, exactly?" Shira says. She still doesn't turn away from the glass.

"Any form of law enforcement," Noam says. "And anyone with a questionable tattoo. I ran the whole database through it."

"Mate," Charlie says, "in an area like this, with criteria like that, your alerts are gonna be going off constantly."

"And I'll check them constantly," Noam says. "I'd rather be safe than sorry. Always."

Shira doesn't leave the window. Charlie watches her. She stands stoic, slightly to the side to make herself harder to see. She's drawn the curtains but has left a wide enough gap for her to see out of. Charlie says her name. "Maybe we should let Noam's software do its thing for a while," he says. "Give us a chance to actually talk now that the bullets aren't flying."

Shira doesn't move at first, but he can tell she's heard him. A moment later, she turns, nodding. "Okay," she says, stepping away. "I suppose I need to bring you up to date."

"The two of you know a lot more about me than I know about either of you," Charlie says.

Shira clears her throat. "A couple of years ago, I was brought to America to go deep cover. My government had heard and seen some things that concerned them."

"What kind of things?" Charlie says.

"I wasn't privy to *all* of that information, but I can tell you what I do know. Our analysts were picking up on coded messages that concerned them pertaining to a seismic shift soon to come to American politics. It didn't seem like much, but the verbiage used must have raised some eyebrows. Similar messages were intercepted. The encryptions used could not always be broken. My government decided to take a more proactive approach. We were able to discern who some of the message recipients were, and Mossad agents were dispatched to investigate them. Nothing major, not at first. Observe and report. I'm sure you understand.

"These agents were posted for less than six months, and then they turned up dead. Their bodies were found in ditches, states apart, bullets through their heads. Execution style. We don't know what exactly happened, but it was clear they had been found out."

"So then you were sent in?" Charlie says. "That seems risky."

"It was too late to hide the fact that I had been Mossad, but we were able to change the dates of my service. To make it look as if I had left a long time ago, and that there was nothing political related to my moving to America. A backstory was built that I won't bore you with now.

"To cut a long story short, I came to America and was instructed to spend my first year with my head down. To *not* investigate. I was told that they—whoever *they* were—would be watching me, and I was not to elicit any suspicion. So, I did as I was told. I got a job. I built a life as if America was my new home. I…I met someone. I fell in love." She grits her teeth. Charlie sees a flash of pain on her face. "I'm not going to get into it, but *they* killed him. I saw it happen. It was a man he trusted. Matt Bunker. A Secret Service agent. These people—you called them The Order?—they're everywhere. They could be anyone. People we know and trust." She shrugs. "That trust cost James his life."

"I'm sorry to hear that."

Shira sets her jaw. "I'm going to repay it."

"I'm sure you will. Why were your government monitoring

the chatter in the first place? America and Israel are supposed to be allies."

"Do you think your government *isn't*? All governments watch each other, especially the ones who are aligned. And when the chatter we hear is concerning, then we need to act. We have to, because if we don't, who else will?" She takes a deep breath. "My government—my *people*—we remember what happened the last time someone tried to implement a new world order. It did not go well for us. We will never forget, and we cannot stand by and allow it to happen again, to us or to anyone else."

Before Charlie can say anything, Noam speaks up.

"You need to look at this," he says while typing.

"What is it?" Shira asks.

"I've just read that news has broken of the massacre at the train station. It's still breaking. I'm bringing up footage." He turns the laptop so they can see.

The camera is outside of the train station. It's live. As if the massacre has only just occurred. Bodies are being wheeled out, covered by blankets. There are ambulances nearby, waiting to take them away, but none of them have their lights on. There are police cars, and a cordon. A crowd of people have to be forced back.

The reporter looks into the camera with a solemn expression. She details the attack—how the train was overthrown, and all of its passengers and crew were executed. Upon arrival into the station, the perpetrators fled, leaving the bodies behind. The motive is unknown, but responsibility has been claimed.

The ARO.

"They've always got their fall guys," Charlie says.

"We have the footage," Noam says. "We can prove what really happened."

No one speaks for a while. They're thinking about the footage. Considering it.

"We could upload it online," Shira says, "but then what? Can it accomplish anything? They could maybe erase it before it has a chance to go wide."

Charlie nods along. He thinks she's right. "Maybe we should keep it close to our chest for now. Use it when we need it, to our benefit. Somewhere down the line, we could go public with it, but right now might not be the time."

"Then what *is* now the time for?" Noam says.

"We sit tight," Shira says. "Things are hot right now. We hide out, and the second they cool, we move on. We have a lot to do. We're going to make these sons of bitches pay."

Charlie nods. "We're going to see them *burn*."

52

Jack jumps out of the van and hurries to the stashed truck. He climbs inside but he doesn't get behind the steering wheel or start the engine. Instead, he re-emerges with two AR-15s. He comes to the back of the van and hands one to Keith, and the other he tries to give to Winston. Winston holds up his hands and waves it toward Ryan. Ryan takes it instead.

"Stay close to me," Keith says to Kayla, whispering. His eyes glance from Jack to Georgia. Georgia is getting out of the van and going to the truck. "They seem like they're on our side, sure, but the only people we can really trust are each other."

Kayla stares at Elizabeth. At her fake-mother. Elizabeth stares back. There's a gag in her mouth. Winston insisted upon it. Despite this, she wears a smug smile, like she knows something the rest of them don't.

"Kayla?" Keith says.

"I heard you, Keith," Kayla says, her eyes never leaving Elizabeth.

Jack ushers everyone out of the van. "Come on, let's go. We can't hang around here."

Keith and Ryan each take one of Elizabeth's arms and lift her down from the back of the van.

"You're going to have to ride on the bed," Jack says, pointing into the back of his truck. "Get on and hold tight."

"It's gonna look suspicious with her all bound like this," Ryan says, nodding at Elizabeth.

"Uh-huh," Jack says, his tone frustrated, showing that he's not an idiot and he wasn't finished talking yet. "There's a tarp back there, right behind the cab. Drape it over her, keep her hidden."

Jack and Winston get into the front of the truck. Jack is driving. He starts the engine. The rest of them climb onto the bed of the truck. Georgia rides with them, sitting close to Keith and Kayla. Ryan is opposite. Elizabeth lies flat beside him, the tarp covering her. Georgia keeps her M16 low, out of view of anyone they might pass on the road, but she doesn't let go of it. Keith and Ryan do the same.

Jack pulls back onto the road. They lurch with his speed. Kayla falls into Keith and uses him to steady herself. She turns to Georgia. Looks between her and the back of Jack's head.

Keith finds himself doing the same. He wonders about these people who Winston clearly knows. Or, at least, he knows the man.

He finds his eyes drawn most to the woman, however. She's tall, athletic. Her hair is tied back, and her features are strikingly attractive. He tries not to stare. Things have been so crazy for what feels like such a long time now, he can't remember the last time he was able to admire the way a woman looks. She feels his eyes and looks back, but Keith doesn't hold her gaze. He gets such thoughts out of his head, and turns to Ryan. "Did you know these two were on their way?"

Ryan raises an eyebrow, unimpressed. "What do *you* think? He tells me about as much as he's told you."

"You knew about them, though?" The wind whips by, and Keith raises his voice to be heard.

"I knew he was in touch with people,"—Ryan shrugs—"People who were in The Order. People who are fighting against them now."

Keith looks around. The road is quiet. They speed down it, in the direction of the cabin, though they run parallel to it. They don't leave the road. From here, the cabin can't be seen.

He turns to Georgia. "Where are we going?"

"We're getting clear," she says. "Beyond that, I don't know. We'll find somewhere quiet where we can talk to this one." She nods toward Elizabeth under the tarp. "We're all looking for answers. We're all trying to figure out where to go next, what our next move will be. That's why The Order keep everything so vague, even amongst themselves. To make it difficult for their enemies to strike at them."

Kayla speaks up. "Were you part of The Order?" Keith can see a defiance on her face, and a narrowing in her eyes. She wants to know what Georgia's part in this is. She wants to know what role she played—if she was a 'mother.' If she was just like Elizabeth.

"Not quite," Georgia says. She smiles, sadly. There's an understanding in it. "I was like you," she says, then she grits her teeth. "I *was* you. I was Kayla Morrow. I was a sleeper. I was the first sleeper."

Ryan's eyes widen at this. "The *first?*" he says, leaning forward.

"The first who was field-ready, at least," Georgia says.

Kayla stares at her. She blinks. There are tears in her eyes. "Then—then you *know*, right? You know what it's like."

Georgia places a hand upon her shoulder. "It *will* get better. I promise. You just need the right kind of people around you." She glances at Keith. He can see her wondering if he's the right kind of person.

The truck speeds on. The road does not remain empty. They pass other vehicles, all of them going the other way. They catch up to another in their lane. Jack motions for the people on the bed to brace themselves, then he overtakes. He leaves the car behind.

It's cold on the back of the truck. Keith keeps an arm around Kayla, both to brace her and to warm her. She stares at Georgia. It's clear there's a lot she wants to ask. A lot she wants to say, and to know. Georgia can feel her eyes. She understands. She leans in close. Keith can hear. "We'll talk," she says. "As soon as we can. I don't have all the answers, but I'm a good listener."

Kayla nods gratefully.

The truck drives on.

53

They spend a couple of hours on the road, heading east, keeping the Mexico border on their right. The desert begins to fade. There is more greenery, gradually at first, and then a lot. The road twists and turns and takes them further from the border.

Georgia's muscles ache from holding on, and the cold chills her to the core. She keeps her head on a swivel, though. Checking the other vehicles that appear, and looking down the road behind them to make sure no one is following.

The road is not busy. They've seen other vehicles, but mostly they come in concentrated clumps. Most of the time, they have the two lanes to themselves.

Jack pulls over suddenly. He climbs out of the truck so he can talk to the back, sharing something he's obviously already discussed with Winston. "Apparently there's a hunting cabin near here," he says. "I'm going to head to it. We can ask our questions there." He doesn't hang around but gets back into the truck and resumes driving.

It takes another half-hour to get to the cabin. This one isn't so close to the border. It's further north. Concealed in woodland, hidden among the trees. It's private, so long as no hunters come along. Georgia doesn't think that should be a problem. She doesn't keep up, but she doesn't think it's hunting season in Texas.

Jack stops the truck in front of the cabin. Georgia gets to her feet. She motions to Keith. "Help me check the area, big guy." They get down off the truck bed and go in separate directions, circling around the cabin to make sure it's clear. When they get back around the front, Jack and Ryan have removed the tarp from Elizabeth and they're leading her inside.

Keith hangs around for Kayla. Georgia leaves them and goes inside. The cabin is one room. There's a woodburning stove in the far-right corner, and off to the left is an area that looks like it could be used for sleeping. There's a circle of four wooden chairs in the center. Jack moves three of them away, and motions to Ryan to sit Elizabeth down. Once she's sat, she takes a deep breath in through her nose, then looks around at them all. She smirks.

"What's so funny?" Jack asks.

Elizabeth is still gagged. She shrugs one shoulder.

Georgia slings the M16 over her shoulder. She stands near the stove, away from the windows. She has a clear view of the room. Jack, Winston, and Ryan stay close to Elizabeth. Keith and Kayla are close to the door. Keith has shouldered his AR15, but Ryan still holds his in both hands. The end is pointed toward the ground at Elizabeth's feet.

"I'm going to ungag you," Jack says. "The only reason I'm taking it off is for you to answer what we ask. That clear?"

Elizabeth makes no kind of response. She ignores Jack. She turns toward Kayla and she winks. Georgia sees how Kayla recoils, stepping closer to Keith.

Jack takes off the gag.

Elizabeth smiles. She looks at Kayla again. "West," she says. "Clementine. Buds—"

"No, no—shut her up!" Winston says, his eyes bugging, looking toward Kayla like he expects her to explode.

Jack hurries forward and clamps a hand over Elizabeth's mouth.

"You should go outside," Winston says to Kayla. "Get out of earshot while we talk to her."

Kayla is shaken. Keith places an arm around her shoulders and guides her out. Georgia watches them go.

Jack waits until they're gone, and then he uncovers Elizabeth's mouth. She chuckles. She looks at Georgia. "What about you?" she says. "How deep does your programming run?"

Georgia stands her ground. She doesn't know if the words still work or not. The men who came after her in Alaska tried them. She didn't want to run the risk then, and she doesn't want to run the risk now, but she won't back down to Elizabeth. She calls her bluff. "It's been a long time," Georgia says. "Try me. Maybe you'll get what you want. Or maybe you'll get the barrel of this gun in your mouth, because frankly, there are very few answers that I want from you. I'd rather see the inside of your skull."

Elizabeth is smirking still, but she doesn't speak. She doesn't attempt the words.

"Keep smiling at me like that," Georgia says. "What do you think it's gonna accomplish? Try me, bitch."

The smile falters, though does not leave completely. Slowly, she tears her eyes away from Georgia. She looks at Jack. She looks at Winston and Ryan. She does not attempt the words again.

"We want names," Jack says, "and we want addresses. We can do this the easy way, or otherwise. We have no qualms with doing whatever it takes to make you talk."

"Cool," Elizabeth says. "Go fuck yourselves."

Jack stares at her.

Elizabeth chuckles. "You were wise to send the girl outside. Out of earshot. She's the Prime, after all. I'm sure you've worked that out by now. If I'd triggered her, she could kill everyone in this room, and then what would become of your stupid little *rebellion*?" She sneers at the word. Her focus zeroes in on Winston. She shakes her head. "I would have enjoyed seeing her gouge your eyes out and snap your neck. Perhaps I'll get the opportunity myself? I know many who would envy the honor." Her eyes flicker toward Jack. "Same goes for you."

Jack ignores her. "Give us names. Give us addresses. Everyone and everything you know about The Order."

"Come on, Jack," Elizabeth says. She speaks his name like they're old friends. Georgia doesn't know if they've ever met before, or if she picked up on his name during their hurried introductions. "You know how it's run. How much do you think I really know?"

"More than the man who was pretending to be your husband," Jack says. "That much is evident."

Elizabeth doesn't have a response to this.

Georgia steps closer. "This isn't getting us anywhere. It's time to start hurting her."

"Go for it, sweetheart," Elizabeth says, showing her teeth. She's defiant. "You can't hurt me. None of you can. Not enough to make me talk. Do you know why? Because I'm not weak like the rest of you. I have a belief system. I have an ideal. I'm working toward a better world. The rest of you have turned your back on that. You *can't* hurt me."

"Wanna bet?" Georgia says. The two women stare at each other.

Slowly, Elizabeth looks at each of the people gathered around her. She looks at their weapons. She checks the rest of the cabin, considering the damage that could be done to her with the items available.

"Broken bones," she says finally, looking back up at Georgia. "That's not enough. Nowhere near."

"We'll see."

Elizabeth grunts. It sounds like a laugh. "Do you think you have enough time?"

54

Keith doesn't try to comfort Kayla. Not straight away. He gets her clear, and then he leaves her alone.

He watches as she goes to the nearest tree and strikes it with her fists, bloodying her knuckles. Her face is red. Tears stream down her cheeks. She spits angrily to the side, then presses her forehead to the rough bark. She cries. Keith lets her. It's hard not to go to her, but she needs her space.

She sniffs hard, catching her breath. The red is draining from her face. She presses her back to the tree and breathes. She stares off into the distance, composing herself. She frowns.

When she's calm, Keith goes to her. "I'm sorry, Kayla."

She doesn't respond. Gives no indication that she has heard. She wipes the tears from her face. Dries her eyes. With the crying over, her expression is blank.

Keith glances back at the cabin. He can't hear anything inside. They're out of earshot of it. If Elizabeth chose to shout the trigger words, they didn't want to be able to hear her.

Kayla speaks. It's almost a whisper. Keith turns back to her. "What was that?"

She's not looking at him. "It was all a lie," she says. "Everything was a lie. Not a single thing was true. Just…just the song." She looks like she might cry again.

"I'm sorry," Keith says. He feels like he's repeating himself, but he doesn't know what else he can say.

Kayla takes a deep breath and pushes herself off the tree. She taps the side of her head. "Everything in here is fake. Even the little things—like her kindness. That's what I remember most— what I've been *programmed* to remember. That she's kind. Sweet. *Nice*. Always smiling—just the most wonderful mother." Her voice is bitter. She points at the cabin. "The woman in *there* is not the woman in *here*." She taps her head again. "How long is it going to be like this, Keith? When will I find something that's— that's just *real*?"

"Everything's been real since DC," Keith says. "I'm real. Charlie's real. Those are memories you can trust."

She's crying. This time, Keith goes to her. He wraps his arms around her. She buries her hot face in his chest. Keith holds her. Her body trembles against him. He strokes her back and her hair.

Keith has never had children. He's never thought of himself as having much paternal instinct. But holding Kayla, feeling the wet of her eyes soak through his shirt, feeling how she shakes, feeling her pain—he feels it in turn. He feels everything she does. It almost brings tears to his own eyes. He grits his teeth and swallows. It's hard to see her suffering. It's almost impossible to see her like this, and to doubt if his comfort is enough. He has nothing else to offer. He wonders if this is what it's like to be a parent, and to see your child hurting. If it's not, he's not sure he could bear the intensity of fatherhood.

They hold each other in silence, neither saying a word.

And then Keith hears something coming.

He raises his head at the sound, turning a little. An engine. Multiple engines. Getting closer.

"Wait here," he says, then moves through the trees, closer to the road.

Kayla hears it, too. "Someone's coming?"

Keith can see the small convoy. Three vans with blacked-out windows. "A lot of someone's," he says, feeling his throat tighten. He turns and grabs Kayla by the arm and runs back toward the cabin, bursting through the door. "People are coming," he says, "three vans."

"Cover her mouth," Georgia says, pointing at Elizabeth when she sees Kayla following Keith in. "Gag her with something."

Elizabeth is laughing before they can silence her. "You thought they wouldn't come for me?" she says. "You thought they didn't know where I was this whole time?"

Keith sees how Jack's face hardens with realization. He glares at Elizabeth. "There's a tracker on you," he says. It's not a question.

"Never leave home without it," Elizabeth says, and then Ryan hooks a rag he has found into her mouth from behind and ties it at the back. She can't speak, but they can hear her still laughing at them.

Georgia speaks to Keith and Kayla. "She hasn't told us anything," she says. She looks toward the door, and the road behind it, her jaw set. "She's been killing time. She's been waiting for them to come."

55

Sarah hurries Zeke to his office. "We need privacy," she says to him, whispering to him while glancing around to make sure no one is close enough to hear. "They're making a move on the group. We need to be reachable in real time."

She locks the door behind them. Zeke doesn't take a seat. He remains standing. "Bring me up to speed."

"Harlan says that people are moving in," Sarah says. "Three vans. He can't tell how many men yet."

"It could be any number," Zeke says, "with more in reserve. Douglas Morrow has an army behind him, I saw them—if every member of the Quinquevirate is the same…"

"Listen to me, Zeke," Sarah says, holding his eyes with a hard and cold stare.

She doesn't blink. Zeke can't recall if he's ever seen her blink when they've spoke. That's foolish, he knows. She must have. But the intensity of her in this moment gives him doubt.

"I'm listening," he says.

"As far as the Quinquevirate are aware, the Vanguard Whites could be operating of their own accord. If they were to involve themselves in what's happening down there, you have plausible deniability."

Zeke blinks. "What are you saying?"

"You know exactly what I'm saying, Zeke. Don't play dense. We don't have time. Give them the order to engage—but if you do, you need to be prepared to follow through. You know what that means, Zeke. This could mean war with the Quinquevirate."

Zeke swallows.

"But you need to be aware of *this*, too—either way, your head is on the chopping board. You're in a corner. They put you there, Zeke. Through no fault of your own, that's where *they* put you. There's only one way out of it. You need to make a choice on whether you're prepared to fight your way out, or let them keep backing you up."

Zeke stares at her.

Sarah stares back.

Zeke moistens his lips. "But then what? What comes next? Without the Quinquevirate—"

"Without the Quinquevirate, you're still president. Don't forget that. Without the Quinquevirate, you still have the people. You can win them over."

Zeke stares at the phone in her hand. "How?" he says. His voice is almost a whisper. He clears his throat.

"We don't have time," Sarah says.

Zeke looks at her. His voice is firmer this time. "*How?*"

"I asked you about the ARO. I asked you why The Order had 'them' bombing army bases—to create a villain. A fake villain to take the blame for the bombing of DC. A fake villain for The Order to stand against. A villain for a hero to vanquish. *You* will be that hero. *You* will vanquish the ARO—you'll destroy them. And then the people will support you. They'll see you as their protector. They'll love you. *That's* what's next."

Their eyes are locked. A moment passes.

SLEEPER RUN

"Is Harlan on the phone?" Zeke says.

"No," Sarah says. She raises the phone and presses a button. She holds it out to him. She holds it up before he can grasp it. "Remember—the girl seems important to the Quinquevirate. We don't know why, but we can use her as leverage."

Zeke takes the phone. Harlan answers.

"Yeah?" he says. "You want something done, you better make your mind up quick."

"Move in," Zeke says. "I want the girl. The rest of them—" He pauses. He breathes deeply. "I don't care what happens to them. Kill them all if you have to."

56

There's no time to get to the truck and attempt an escape. Jack and Georgia smash out windows and open fire on the three vans as they approach. They're able to shatter the windscreen of the lead van, and burst its front tires. It veers to the side and hits a tree.

Keith stands back with Kayla, but he has the AR15 shouldered. He can see past Georgia's shoulder, can see what is happening outside. While they battle, he concentrates on his breathing. He keeps it calm and steady. Deep in, long out. He can feel the distant edge of a panic attack, but it's creeping up from afar. It's not close, nowhere near. His breathing, for now, is regular and calm. There is no tightness in his chest or throat. He swallows, and it doesn't feel like he's choking. He needs it to stay this way. He needs to remain in control.

To their right, Elizabeth is gagged in the chair. She doesn't struggle. It's hard for her to smile with the gag in her mouth, but her eyes gleam. Her shoulders rise and fall exaggeratedly. She's laughing at them, and she wants them to know it.

Winston and Ryan are behind them, covering the rear door.

Ryan has the other AR15. Winston is unarmed. He's down on one knee, flinching at the sound of every gunshot.

Jack and Georgia fire upon the second van. The third van stops advancing. Almost frantic, it slams into reverse and backs up, away from the worst of the shooting. From the rear of the first van, men clad all in black and armed with automatic rifles jump out and scramble for cover, opening fire upon the cabin. Jack and Georgia have to duck behind cover. They move between windows so as not to present a static target. Bullets smash out what remains of the glass. They thud into the side of the building, splintering the wood, and some burst through, embedding themselves in the floorboards and the ceiling.

Keith breathes. Deep in, and long out.

The men in the second van are more freely able to get out and fire upon the cabin. Keith counts ten men still standing—there are more, but they lie dying or injured on the ground, courtesy of Georgia and Jack.

The third van does not advance. It stays back, away from the fighting. Some men get out, though Keith doubts it's all of them. One of the men is not like the others. He's dressed the same, all black, but he's not wearing a mask, and he's older than Keith would expect.

Jack has seen him, too. He curses and takes cover. When he speaks, it's loud enough for everyone to hear. "That man—he's Douglas Morrow."

Keith notices the surname—the same as Kayla. "Who's he?"

"He's one of the heads of The Order," Jack says. "Perhaps the most powerful."

Georgia is looking back over her shoulder. She's heard what Jack has said. Behind her, Keith spots one of the men in front of the cabin pulling something from his belt. It fits in his fist.

Keith quickly realizes what it is. "Grenade!"

He steps forward, closer to a smashed-out window. The man

pulls the pin. Keith opens fire on him, a tight burst that slams into the center of the man's chest. His body shudders and he falls. The grenade rolls under the first van. Some of the other men have seen. They dive for cover.

The grenade explodes. It touches off the van's gas. It fireballs.

Keith dives back from the window. The cabin shakes with the explosion. It shakes so hard it seems like it might collapse around them. Georgia and Jack either throw themselves to the ground or they're knocked off their feet—Keith can't tell. He can't hear, either. He finds himself momentarily deafened. Up ahead of him, Elizabeth's chair is knocked down, landing on its side. She has no choice but to go with it. Kayla is already on the ground, hands over her head. She saw the explosion begin, and she braced herself. Keith crawls to her. He pinches his nose and blows, trying to bring his hearing back. He stretches his jaw, feeling pops.

As his ears clear, he can hear men screaming outside. He can hear burning, too. Glancing back, he sees some trees blazing.

He reaches Kayla as the front door bursts open. A burning man runs in. His screams are bloodcurdling. Keith can see how the skin on his face and hands blisters. The man is looking for water.

Ryan guns him down. It was a mercy more than anything else. "Come on!" Ryan shouts. "Out the back while they're stunned!"

There's a moment of panic on Ryan's face, and he starts to raise the rifle. A splash of blood hits the wall behind him. Keith sees it all. He blinks, not understanding, then realizes there is a hole in the center of Ryan's forehead. Realizes that the most recent gunshot sounds closer than all the others.

Ryan's eyes flutter. He stumbles on his feet. His father screams his name, and the sound is as chilling as the cries of the burning man.

Ryan drops. His eyes remain open. Blood pours from the back of his skull. He's dead.

Keith turns. The man in the doorway is not dressed like the others. He's not head-to-toe in black. His shaved head is uncovered. He wears sunglasses. He wears a T-shirt that shows off the tattoos on his arms. Nazi tattoos. He grins. He sees Keith looking and turns the gun toward him.

Keith tries to raise the AR15, but he can't move fast enough. He feels the tightness, now. He pictures the blood spraying out the back of Ryan's head. It plays on a loop behind his eyes. How he didn't fall straight away. How he's lying dead now, with his father screaming like an animal beside him. Keith can't breathe.

Gunshots come from Keith's left, from the Nazi's right. Georgia is dazed, but she's firing. The shots go wide, but they're enough to back the Nazi up, to make him dive for cover out of the cabin.

Keith doesn't know where the Nazis have come from. They aren't the men who came out of the vans. He can't think about it, though. Not now. He needs to keep moving. Needs to get Kayla clear.

Georgia gets up to a knee, shaking her head. She drags herself to the doorway and positions herself with the rifle pointing out. She waves at Keith. "Go—*go*! I'll hold them!"

Jack is stirring nearby. "Get clear—we'll catch you up!"

There are so many people present, coming after them—and if there are more Nazis out there, Keith's not sure how many people they're up against now—he's not sure if they'll be able to catch up.

If they'll be able to get clear.

If they'll survive.

He hesitates. Georgia and Jack fire out of the cabin. Keith looks at Kayla. She clings to his arm. He looks at Ryan lying on the ground, and the blood that spreads from his skull.

The edges of the panic attack have gone. Keith feels calm. He breathes deep. "Stay low," he tells Kayla.

They stop by Winston on the way. Keith tries to drag him from his dead son. Winston won't let go. He won't be moved. Tears roll down Kayla's cheeks at the sight. Keith shakes his head. Winston isn't coming with them.

Keith kicks open the back door. There are three men, clad all in black. Attempting to sneak around the back. The flung open door has surprised them. Keith does not hesitate. He spreads a wide field of bullets, mowing them down.

Keith and Kayla run. Behind, he can hear the pitched fighting at the front of the cabin. It sounds fierce. Keith holds the AR15 in both hands, but Kayla stays close. They run for the trees. Beyond that, Keith has no idea what they'll do, or where they'll go. He prays that Georgia and Jack stay alive, and that they're quick to follow.

Bullets tear into the ground around them and slam into the trees. Kayla stumbles. Keith rolls and comes up on a knee, raising the rifle. The people coming for them now are not the men in black—they're Nazis. Six of them. Dressed the same as the man inside the cabin, a uniform of jeans and plain T-shirts, and all of them with shaved heads and tattoos. Keith opens fire. They back up and dive for cover. He hits one of them, strafing him across the chest.

The AR15 clicks empty.

Keith doesn't drop it. He doesn't want the Nazis to know he's unarmed. He keeps hold of it and grabs for Kayla. They run deeper into the trees.

The Nazis pursue. Keith can hear them. Holding Kayla's arm, he runs to where the brush is thickest, and they hide behind a tree, ducking low.

He hears a radio crackle. *"Earl, what's it looking like back there?"* It's close. If Keith had bullets, he could kill them now. As it is, he stays very still and holds his breath.

"We've seen them, Harlan," Earl responds. "Hunting them

now. They ain't gonna get far."

"*They're back there? Shit's getting heavy here—get the girl and come back to us, we ain't gonna be able to make it to you.*"

The Nazis are closing in. They're armed. Keith is not. He looks left and right. It's going to be hard for him and Kayla to slip away—impossible. The Nazis are surrounding the tree. They're coming from both sides. Keith can hear their cautious footsteps crunching through the dirt and twigs.

Keith grasps the empty AR15 by the barrel. Squeezes it with both hands. He braces himself. Waits. Angles himself toward the left. The man coming is almost on top of them.

Keith steps out and swings the AR15 like it's a baseball bat. The stock slams into the Nazi's face. It crushes his nose. It knocks his jaw loose. Teeth fly. The stock cracks. The Nazi crumples. He's carrying an AR15 of his own. Keith grabs for it.

"You best leave that where it is, boy."

The voice is familiar. It's the man who was talking into the radio. Earl. He points a Sig Sauer P220 at Keith's face. There's less than six feet between the two men.

Keith sees it—sees the gun, and the distance. He does not freeze. Does not pause. Does not panic—he can't. He won't let the panic in. Instead, he moves. He ducks low, he darts left, then right, and he charges. As he makes impact with Earl's midsection, the Sig Sauer goes off, twice. The bullets are too high. Keith is too close. He lifts Earl and slams him down. Stays on him. Grabs at his wrist, forcing it back. The gun fires once more. Keith slams it down, then punches Earl across the face. He drops the gun.

Kayla screams.

Keith spins to the sound. Two of the Nazis have grabbed her. They've dragged her out from behind the tree. She calls Keith's name. He sees another of the Nazis running towards them. Keith reaches for the AR15 of the Nazi he dropped.

From behind, Earl wraps his arms around Keith's legs and

trips him. Keith rolls onto his back. Earl scrambles over him, and punches him twice in the side of the face and head. Keith is dazed. He feels his throat begin to tighten. His chest begins to compress, as if an anvil is being slowly lowered onto it. He gasps. And then Earl has his hands around his throat. He's looming over Keith, pinning his arms and showing his teeth. He's laughing.

Through the laughter, Keith hears Kayla. She's screaming his name. Three of the Nazis have her. They're dragging her away. She struggles and fights against them. Claws at them, bites at them. It's not enough. They're too strong. They're too many.

Earl's grip is strong. Keith's lungs burn. His vision darkens at the edges.

Kayla screams his name. It breaks through the fog. It's all he can hear.

He bucks his hips and gets his arms free. He slams his fists down into Earl's elbows and breaks the grip. He gasps for breath, slipping his fingers between Earl's hands and his neck. Earl is still trying to squeeze. Keith keeps the space. Sucks breath. He rolls his eyes. He can see Kayla. She's still struggling. They're marching her past. She's not far. If Keith calls, she'll be able to hear.

Keith closes his eyes, and he remembers.

"West," he says as loud as he can. As quick and as clear as he can. "Clementine, buds, harvest, red, run, ghost!"

Kayla stiffens. Her face goes blank. The change is so sudden, so abrupt, that the Nazis register it, too. It stalls them. She stares straight ahead. It's unnerving.

She's blank. Empty. Awaiting instruction. Keith has activated her. Keith needs to tell her what to do next.

"Fight!"

It all happens fast. Kayla catches the men holding her by surprise. Her movements are a blur. She strikes at pressure points.

She follows through with blows to throats and eyes. She flings elbows and strikes at crotches.

Earl's grip loosens, distracted by what is happening. His eyes narrow, struggling to believe what he is seeing. Keith takes advantage. He grabs Earl's thumbs and wrenches them back, snapping them both. Earl screams. His weight rises. Keith shoves him off. He pounces. He grabs at Earl's head. There's a rock close to where he's landed. Keith raises his head and slams the back of his skull down on it. There's a deep thud. Earl goes limp. Keith lifts him again and slams him back down. Keith feels the skull crack. Blood sprays out the back. Earl's eyes flutter. He goes into a seizure. Keith slams him down again, and finally, he's still. His eyes are closed.

Keith falls back. He looks toward Kayla. The three men who held her are on the ground, broken and pained. Kayla is standing. She's still. She stares straight ahead. Slowly, her head turns. She looks at Keith. There's nothing in her eyes.

She awaits instruction.

57

Georgia does not understand what is happening outside. Earlier, as if from nowhere, two more vans had arrived. She spotted them after she'd chased off the man who killed Ryan, and after she'd ushered Keith and Kayla out of the back door. Georgia counted over a dozen men who had come from the new vans, all of them armed. They weren't dressed like the others already besieging the cabin. They wore casual clothes, though they'd made a uniform of them—jeans and T-shirts, sometimes a jacket, mostly all with shaved heads and all with tattoos upon their arms, some on their necks, a couple on their faces.

What has thrown Georgia, though, is that they're not solely attacking the cabin. These new arrivals—these Nazis—are attacking the other men, too. A pitched battle rages outside, men falling on both sides, their bodies torn apart by automatic fire, their faces wiped off their skulls. The bullets that impact the cabin, that threaten to tear it apart, are not coming so thick.

Georgia and Jack have ducked low and fired back. Whatever the two factions' reasons for fighting, neither of them are allies of Georgia and the others.

Neither side appears to have an advantage, but they're

distracted with each other. Jack gets close to Georgia. "Out the back," he says. "Follow Keith and Kayla. We need to get out of here now—this is our best chance."

Georgia looks at Winston. He's not screaming now, but he's on his knees still. He's holding Ryan and rocking back and forth, tears streaming down his pained face. Blood coats him, none of it his own. "What about him?"

"Either we can drag him out, or he's gone," Jack says. "We can't hang around."

A sound cuts through the fighting and the shouting. A van. Georgia peers around a window frame. The third van, the one that has held back from the fighting, is moving. It stays clear of the gunfight, but it's not leaving. It's going wide, heading around the back of the cabin.

"We need to go," Jack says.

They run, bent double, toward the rear of the cabin. They leave Elizabeth where she lies, still bound to the chair. They try to grab Winston, but he shrugs them off. He won't move. His shoulders sag. He doesn't want to keep going. He's given up.

Georgia hears footsteps behind them. She doesn't look back. She dives clear. Jack follows. Gunfire erupts, and bullets fill the space where they previously stood. They tear up the doorframe, and fly through the empty air. Georgia and Jack scramble for cover, heading toward the trees. They dive behind a fallen tree and peer out.

No one appears at the back of the cabin. They see the van, though. It's parked close to the trees. Armed men are getting out the side of it. The older man is in the middle of them. Douglas Morrow.

"His last name," Georgia says.

Jack doesn't answer. He looks into the trees, through them, searching for Keith and Kayla.

Georgia listens. It's getting quieter at the front of the cabin.

"There's not as much shooting going on," she says. This concerns her. If they're not still fighting, that means one side has won. They've either eradicated the opposition, or the opposition has fled. Either way, Georgia and the others are back to being on their own.

Jack pushes himself up. "Come on—they're going for Keith and Kayla. We need to get to them before they do."

They run through the woods. They're careful where they step, and cautious not to run into anyone who'll try to shoot them. Georgia wishes she could call out. Shout their names and run toward the response.

They don't hear voices. Instead, they hear gunfire.

They both drop to a knee, raising their rifles. The shots are distant. They're not directed at them. They keep moving, heading toward the sound.

They find bodies. Six dead Nazis, all of them shot up. Georgia spins. Keith and Kayla are not present. She can hear the van. Its engine roars. It speeds away.

Footsteps behind them. They both wheel on the sound. Keith emerges, pointing a Sig Sauer. Both sides lower their weapons when they realize who the other is. "They got Kayla," Keith says, breathless. "I had to—I had to use the words—they were going to take her, he was going to kill me—I didn't have any choice—" He's stammering.

Georgia goes to him. She places a hand on his shoulder. "Keith—*Keith*. Take a breath. What happened? Who took her?"

"Her father," Jack says.

Georgia and Keith look at him. "*What?*" Georgia says.

"Well," Jack says, "not exactly. He's your father, too, Georgia. The father of the Sleeper program. Douglas Morrow. One of the five who run The Order. The Quinquevirate. The most powerful of them all. The one true head of the hydra."

"We need to go after them," Keith says.

"They're already gone," Jack says.

"We still need to follow," Georgia says.

"And we will," Jack says, "but right now, right here, this is over. They won't stay in the van for long. They'll get to a helicopter or head to an airstrip. They'll be in the air before we can catch them up." He turns to Keith. "What happened? How did he take Kayla? You said you'd activated her."

Keith doesn't speak for a moment. He stares off through the trees, the way Kayla was taken. He snaps back to attention. "I had to," he says. "I couldn't get free. I didn't know what else to do. But then that man appeared—Douglas—and she just...as soon as she saw him, she just *froze*. She went blank."

"There's a dead-switch in her programming," Jack says. "She can't attack him. If he's in sight, she can't do anything without his say-so. What happened?"

"He held out his hand, and she went to him. The men with him fired at me. They killed these men here—they weren't already dead. Kayla had just hurt them, put them down. I had to run. I had to take cover."

Georgia hears movement in the trees. "We need to go," she says, lowering her voice. "People are coming."

"We need to go after Kayla," Keith says. "I don't care what you say. We need to get her back."

"Keith," Georgia says, getting his attention. "We *will*. But we can't save her if we're dead. We need to go now. We need to find a vehicle. *Then* we can look for her."

Keith grits his teeth. He's torn. Georgia can hear the rushing footsteps coming through the woods, getting closer. Jack takes a defensive position, looking back toward the sound.

Georgia puts a hand on Keith's arm. She looks in his eyes. "We *will* get her back. But now we need to go."

Keith knows she's right. He nods. They tap Jack, and then they run.

58

Noam is busy on his laptop. He's never been off it. He blinks and rubs at his eyes, but he persists.

"You're gonna give yourself a migraine, mate," Charlie says. "You need to be careful, staring at the screen like that."

Noam grunts but doesn't look up. "I'm trying to find your wife," he says.

Charlie doesn't respond. He clenches his jaw.

Shira sits by the window. She runs a hand down her face. They've barely slept, all of them. Charlie stands close to Shira, peering past her shoulder and out of the window. "How you holding up?" he says.

"I'm fine," Shira says. She doesn't turn.

"Don't have to act tough for me, pet," Charlie says. "I've already seen how tough you are. It's all right to admit if you're tired."

"Of course I'm tired." She turns. The skin under her eyes is dark and puffy. Charlie hasn't looked in a mirror, but he reckons he's probably the same. "But I'm angry, too. That's all I need. It's enough. That can sustain me."

Before Charlie can respond, Noam clears his throat. He speaks up. "Shira. Charlie."

They turn to him.

"I might have something."

"What is it?" Shira says.

"Mossad have gotten in touch."

Charlie looks between them both. He sees Shira narrow her eyes. "They're not supposed to contact us," she says. "Complete radio silence."

"Yes, I know—but they *have*. The message has been heavily encrypted—it's taken me a long time to get into it."

Charlie steps closer. "What are they saying?"

"They're monitoring the situation," Noam says. "And they've found someone who could potentially help us."

Shira steps up next to Charlie. "Who?"

"They're NSA," Noam says. "Maybe they could help us find Charlie's wife, too."

"Who is it?" Charlie says.

"His name's Ben Clark," Noam says, closing the laptop and getting to his feet. "They know where he is. They've sent his address."

The three look at each other.

"Then we go now," Charlie says. "We go meet this Ben Clark."

"But we're careful about it," Shira says. "Mossad have looked into him, but we need to look into him for ourselves. We can't just walk in there full of trust."

"Goes without saying," Charlie says.

59

Matt Bunker has returned. Zeke is pleased to see him, but he's not as comforted by his presence as he once would have been. Now, instead, he finds more comfort from Sarah. He turns to her. She has the answers he needs. Matt is no longer the right-hand Zeke envisioned he could have been. He's support, and valuable, but he has usurped his own position by bringing in Sarah.

Of course, Zeke does not make this apparent. "Things are under control at the train station?"

"It's a media circus," Matt says. "But we don't need to be concerned about it any longer."

Zeke nods. It's the three of them in the office. The doors are locked. They sit close and keep their voices low. They're waiting to hear back from Harlan. Sarah's phone sits in the center of the desk. They stare at it, willing it to ring.

Zeke understands what he has done, and what this means. If the Quinquevirate realizes what he has permitted, he's a marked man. His days are numbered. Inside, his mind races. A silent scream fills his skull. Outward, he thinks he appears calm. He needs to present a sturdy, strong façade. He needs to be their leader.

Matt has been told what they've done. He sat in silence, considering this action, and all of its implications. Now, completely, Zeke would know where he stood.

When Matt finally spoke, he said, "We need to be prepared for what comes next. Whether the Vanguard Whites failed, or they were successful, the Quinquevirate are going to have questions. *Hard* questions. We need to be ready."

Zeke nodded, satisfied at this response.

The phone rings. Sarah answers. She does not put it on speaker. They don't want anyone else to hear. Zeke and Matt lean in closer.

"Well?" Sarah says.

"They got the girl." Harlan's voice is trembling. He sounds angry. He snorts and spits. His breathing is harsh and ragged through the phone. "They got the girl—they got the fucking girl—and it looks like some of her friends got away. Not all of them. I saw the boys in black take at least one of them."

"Who?" Sarah says. "I need details, Harlan. Tell me everything."

"The older guy—the doctor."

"Winston Fallon?"

"Yeah. They took him out the cabin, got him in one of their vans. The woman that Kayla and her buddies were questioning, too—they took her."

"Elizabeth," Sarah says.

"Uh-huh. I've lost nine men here. I've lost *Earl*, goddamnit. Bashed his fucking skull in—I reckon it could've been the girl's friends did that. The boys in black, they were shooters. I dunno, something about it—" It sounds like Harlan is pacing. He's snorting, like a bull. "We got them, though. We got them good. I count twelve of them. Not all from us, sure. The guys in the cabin took some of them out. But we gave as good as we fucking got. Mother*fuckers*."

"I'm very sorry about your friend, Harlan," Sarah says. "But I need you to try and calm down."

"I'm gonna go after them."

"No—*no*. That's not what you're going to do. Not right now. You're going to go home, Harlan. You're going to call everyone in—are you listening? Do you hear me?"

He's stopped pacing. "I hear you."

"Every member of the Vanguard Whites, you're going to call them in. And then you're all going to come *here*."

"DC?"

"DC."

There's silence on the phone. "Why?"

"I'll explain that when you get here."

Zeke and Sarah have already discussed what they're going to do next. Matt glances between them both before looking back at the phone.

"All right," Harlan says.

"We need you here ASAP," Sarah says.

"And you'll get me, but I want revenge for what's happened here—for what's happened to Earl. That clear?"

"You'll get it, Harlan. You'll get that, and then some."

Sarah hangs up and nods to Zeke.

Zeke turns to Matt. "Adam Neville," he says.

Matt sits back. He frowns. "What about him?"

"Where do his loyalties lie?"

"His loyalties?" Matt snorts derisively. "He's a mercenary. His loyalties lie in *money*."

"Good," Zeke says. "Is he still at the train station?"

"No. He and his men left before we allowed the media through."

"Call him. Bring him in. I want he and his group on side."

"On side for what?"

Zeke sets his jaw. "For the war that's coming."

Matt falters a moment. He looks between Zeke and Sarah. He takes a deep breath. A resignation crosses his face and fills his body. He knew this was coming. It's time to prepare, like he said earlier. He's realizing now that Zeke and Sarah were already prepared. "I'll call him," he says. He doesn't leave straight away. "Adam Neville and his group, and the Vanguard Whites. It sounds like you're building an army."

Zeke doesn't answer. Matt understands. Zeke told him what he saw out in Bethesda, at Douglas Morrow's house. He saw an army there. He needs one of his own in turn. Matt knows this.

He stands. "I'll make the call."

60

Ben Clark lives in a modest house on the outskirts of DC. Shira, Charlie, and Noam have stolen a car. An old, rusted Ford they didn't think anyone was likely to miss. They've switched the plates. Charlie drove. Shira sits up front with him. Now, they sit down the road from Ben Clark's home, watching. They've been watching for a few hours.

Noam is in the back. He leans between them. His laptop is not open, but the alerts on it are still running active.

"You take the front," Charlie says. "I'll go around the back."

Shira nods. "Noam," she says, "wait here until we signal you."

Shira and Charlie get out of the car. They start walking, hands in pockets, clutching their handguns.

"Just keep him busy," Charlie says. "It won't take me long to get inside."

Charlie peels off as they get close, heading down the block to circle back and get to the rear of the house. Shira slows. She takes her time crossing the road, and heading up the path leading to Ben Clark's front door. She waits a beat, takes a deep breath, then rings the bell.

It doesn't take long for Ben Clark to answer. Shira keeps her hands in her pockets. Keeps hold of the gun.

"Ben Clark?" she says, tilting her head, though she already knows it's him.

Noam found a picture, and they've all committed his face to memory. He's forty-two, which Shira knows from what Noam found online, but he looks mid-thirties. His blond hair is cut short. He keeps himself in shape. His face, which was clean-shaven in the picture they saw, is stubbled. He hasn't shaved in a few days.

"Yes?" he says, eyes narrowing. "Can I help you?"

"My name's Shira," she says, trying not to look beyond him into the house, to see if Charlie is sneaking up from behind. "I was told you might be worth talking to."

Ben frowns. "About what?"

Charlie presses the Glock to the back of his head. "Don't panic," he says, his voice soft. "There's no reason for there to be any trouble."

Ben stiffens. "What do you want?"

"Step back into the house. That's it, nice and easy."

Shira turns and waves to Noam. He gets out of the car. Shira follows Charlie inside. He's taken Ben through to his living room.

The curtains are drawn. The only light comes from the laptop set up on the coffee table in the center of the room. There are newspapers spread out beside it, and clippings from past papers arranged on a corkboard nearby. Text is highlighted on some of them. There are takeout boxes on the ground beside the sofa.

Noam enters the house and closes the door. Shira turns on a light. Ben squints against it, covering his eyes.

"Check the sofa," Charlie says to Shira.

She pats it down, checking for any concealed weapons. There aren't any. She checks under the coffee table, too. It's clear.

"All right, mate," Charlie says, "take a seat."

Ben does as he's told.

"Listen," Charlie says, "we're not here looking for trouble. We don't want to hurt you. I don't want to keep this gun pointed at you. We just need you to sit tight while we talk to you."

"I know who you are," Ben says, looking at Charlie.

"That's what we need to talk about," Charlie says. "Things aren't what they seem, mate, and we think you might know that."

Ben looks doubtful.

"You knew Lloyd Nivens," Shira says.

"I knew him," Ben says.

"And after he died, you started asking questions. You wondered what he was doing where he was killed, and who he was with. But you weren't getting answers."

"You were getting shut down," Noam says. "Which created more questions."

Shira nods at the open laptop and the newspapers. "So you tried to find your own answers."

Ben stares at them.

"We'll get on the level with you," Charlie says. "These two, they're Mossad. And Mossad is aware of what you've been doing, and they've singled you out as someone we might be able to trust. Someone who can help us."

Ben frowns. "Why would I do that?"

"Because we have the answers you're looking for," Charlie says. "Not all of them, maybe, but enough."

"Whatever you're selling, I'm not sure I'm interested in buying."

Shira turns to Noam. She tilts her head. Noam pulls out his phone and steps forward.

"The recent massacre at the train station," Shira says. "I'm sure you've heard about it."

"Of course," Ben says. "How could I not?"

"The ARO strikes again, right?"

"They claimed responsibility."

"It wasn't the ARO," Shira says. "The ARO doesn't exist."

Ben tilts his head. He looks doubtful.

Noam plays the video. Ben watches in silence. He blanches. A hand covers his mouth.

When the video ends, they give him a moment. He swallows. "What...what is this? What's happening?"

Shira takes a seat. "We have a lot to tell you."

THANK YOU FOR READING SLEEPER CELL!

We hope you enjoyed it as much as we enjoyed bringing it to you. We just wanted to take a moment to encourage you to review the book. Follow this link: **Sleeper Cell** to be directed to the book's Amazon product page to leave your review.

Every review helps further the author's reach and, ultimately, helps them continue writing fantastic books for us all to enjoy.

You can also join our non-spam mailing list by visiting www.subscribepage.com/AethonReadersGroup and never miss out on future releases. You'll also receive three full books completely Free as our thanks to you.

Facebook | Instagram | Twitter | Website

Also in series:

THE FIRST SLEEPER

Sleeper Cell
Sleeper Run

Check out the entire series here! (Tap or scan)

Looking for more great Thrillers?

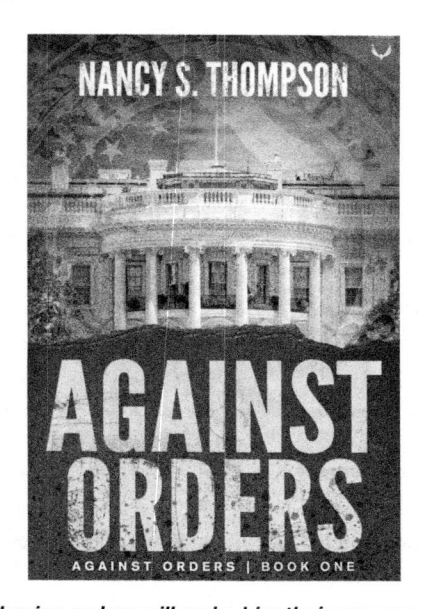

Obeying orders will make him their scapegoat. Defying them will make him their enemy. Captain Kynan Esprit served six years in the Marines, then four more in the Secret Service. Both ended in disgrace. Jobless, his former commander recommends him to weapons manufacturer Whit Lasette, who doesn't care if Kynan's moral compass sometimes conflicts with orders from above. Whit admires the captain's uncompromising valor and hires Ky to protect his adult daughter, Reina, while he campaigns for the US presidency. Determined not to torpedo another opportunity, Kynan vows to never again disobey orders or get personally involved, but he forsakes both after a kidnapping attempt forces him to hide Reina at her father's Mediterranean compound. But the danger has only just begun. After unearthing documents about a global conspiracy designed to fatten the wallets of certain power players by sabotaging peace overseas, they find themselves on the run, hunted from every angle. With millions of lives in the balance, they must find a way to expose the truth…if they can survive against all odds. **AGAINST ORDERS is an exciting geopolitical conspiracy thriller, a fusion of Matthew Quirk's *Hour of the Assassin* and *The 500*, and Simon Gervais' *The Last Protector*, and a reckoning of our recent political climate.**

SLEEPER RUN

Get Against Orders Now!

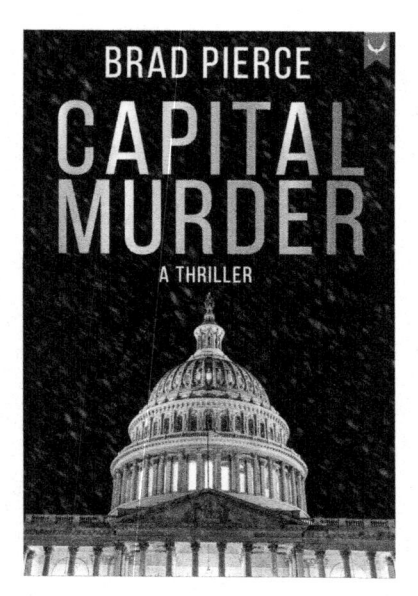

A traitor in the Government. A Senator savagely murdered. A conspiracy years in the making. As a massive snow storm paralyzes the US Capital, a secret congressional committee is handed evidence of the unthinkable. A high-level traitor in the U.S. Government selling secrets to China. Before they can act, one of their own is murdered. Enter Colin Frost, an ex-special forces operator. He and his highly-classified black-ops team have been hunting a dangerous serial killer across Afghanistan who is destabilizing the entire region. When they get the call to find the Senator's killer, they are startled to see the similarities between the murders in Afghanistan and the Senator at home. They instantly know the two are related and must get to the bottom of the conspiracy before more Senators are killed and the United States is irrevocably harmed.

But Colin has a secret... His sister was murdered seventeen years ago, and the unsolved crimes of the past are too similar to the present conspiracy to ignore.

This snow-filled political conspiracy thriller by debut author Brad Pierce takes the reader through a dark mystery, decades-long conspiracy, and a personal journey of revenge and justice against a literal angel of death. *Will Colin Frost succeed, or will he lose himself along the way?*

Get Capital Murder Now!

SLEEPER RUN

In a daring act of piracy, Yemeni terrorists have not only seized a special oil tanker but they've also captured a high-value asset. With President Lewis desperate to save his biggest donor's assets and protect his deepest secret, he orders Director of National Intelligence Camille Banks to deploy her secret team to recover the asset. Garrett Knox, along with his hand-picked team members of elite operatives, must attempt the impossible: infiltrate the treacherous Yemeni mountains and bring the asset home alive. Battling hostile terrain and relentless attacks, Knox and company close in on their target only to have the tables flipped on them as a far deadlier plot emerges. The terrorists offer a chilling ultimatum—the asset in exchange for a notorious bombmaker in U.S. custody. With time running out and the world watching, Knox and his team embark on a pulse-pounding mission to retrieve the bombmaker. But when a shocking betrayal threatens everything, Knox must make an unthinkable choice to save Rico and save the president. **From the Oval Office to the explosive climax, Terminal Threat is a non-stop thrill ride packed with jaw-dropping twists. As a sinister conspiracy tightens its grip, will Knox's team prevail, or will the President's dark secrets destroy them all? The clock is ticking in this electrifying novel by R.J. Patterson.** *This action thriller is perfect for fans of Tom Clancy's* **Jack Ryan**, *Vince Flynn's* **Mitch Rapp**, *Robert Ludlum's* **Jason Bourne** *or Stephen Hunter's* **Bob Lee Swagger**!

Get Terminal Threat now!

For all our Thrillers, visit our website.

ABOUT THE AUTHOR

Paul Heatley is the bestselling author of the Tom Rollins thriller series, as well as numerous standalone crime novels and novellas. He lives in the north east of England.

Printed in Great Britain
by Amazon